THAT KIND *of* MOTHER

ALSO BY RUMAAN ALAM

RICH and PRETTY

THAT KIND
of MOTHER

RUMAAN
ALAM

An Imprint of HarperCollins*Publishers*

THAT KIND OF MOTHER. Copyright © 2018 by Rumaan Alam. All rights reserved. Printed in the United States of America. No part of this book may be used or reproduced in any manner whatsoever without written permission except in the case of brief quotations embodied in critical articles and reviews. For information address HarperCollins Publishers, 195 Broadway, New York, NY 10007.

HarperCollins books may be purchased for educational, business, or sales promotional use. For information please e-mail the Special Markets Department at SPsales@harpercollins.com.

FIRST EDITION

Designed by Renata De Oliveira

Library of Congress Cataloging-in-Publication Data

Names: Alam, Rumaan, author.
Title: That kind of mother : a novel / Rumaan Alam.
Description: First edition. | New York : Ecco, [2018]
Identifiers: LCCN 2018000165 (print) | LCCN 2018002136 (ebook) | ISBN 9780062667625 () | ISBN 9780062667601 (hardcover) | ISBN 9780062864383 (softcover) | ISBN 9780062667618
Subjects: LCSH: Race relations—Fiction. | Motherhood—Fiction. | Nannies—Fiction. | Domestic fiction. | BISAC: FICTION / Literary. | FICTION / Contemporary Women. | FICTION / Family Life.
Classification: LCC PS3601.L3257 (ebook) | LCC PS3601.L3257 T48 2018 (print) | DDC 813/.6—dc23
LC record available at https://lccn.loc.gov/2018000165

18 19 20 21 22 LSC 10 9 8 7 6 5 4 3 2 1

FOR A. AND FOR V.,
who made us a family

You give love a little shove and it becomes terror.

—JOANNA NEWSOM

PART ONE

1

THE BOOK LIED. BOOKS LIED; SHE KNEW THAT. *WALK*, IT SAID. HOW? Rebecca felt anchored, or not quite: like she was immersed in honey or quicksand, something thick and sticky. Books were bullshit. What could a book tell you? Her knees ached and there was—well, effluvia was the word for it, a word so lovely it disguised its meaning. What if she *leaked* onto the linoleum? How humiliating, but the book said *Walk* and the doctor said *Walk* and the nurse said *Walk* so Rebecca, obedient student, walked.

"You're all right, darling?" Christopher was English; he could use a noun like *darling* without sounding patronizing.

"Fine." Small talk seemed silly when giving birth. She was holding on to her husband's arm, despite feeling herself the sort of woman who did not need to hold on to a man's arm. They'd been married in front of a judge, for God's sake. "Fine," she said again.

Christopher was eager. "You'll tell me. If you need to sit."

"Doctor Brownmiller said to walk." Rebecca was more curt than she meant to be. It was embarrassing to conform to type. To snap at her husband while ceding to labor was predictable if less shameful than discovering she'd defecated in her polyester maternity pants that morning. That was hours ago. It had been a long day, it would be her child's birthday. "He said it's good for bringing on the labor."

"Do you want a Popsicle?" Christopher's Etonian vowels rendered the childish word something funny but of course it was still pathetic, like Rebecca was a toddler who needed placating instead of a patient giving birth.

Rebecca released Christopher's arm. *You're free,* she thought. *Go away.* She rounded a corner, leaving him behind, telling herself to hurry, colliding with a woman who was stapling something to a corkboard. "Oh." This was the beginning of an apology that dissolved into pain. Rebecca was too distracted to be polite.

"I'm sorry, Mom." The woman smiled at Rebecca.

Mom? Rebecca looked at the corkboard: a pamphlet, folded in thirds but splayed open, amateurish line drawings of a placid mother and her indistinct newborn. *Mom,* then, soon enough, and forever. Rebecca was still standing too close, so the other woman, black, solid, but somehow vague, stepped back. "My fault." Rebecca breathed as they had practiced in the childbirth class her sister Judith had recommended she take. Judith was an obstetrician, a mother herself, but most important, she was the oldest child and used to having her instructions followed. "I wasn't"—Rebecca breathed in again—"watching."

"No problem at all." The woman put a hand on Rebecca's arm. "No problem."

Someone, maybe this same woman, had stapled up a magazine clipping showing the princess of Wales, on the steps of St. Mary's, resplendent in red with a demure bow at the neck, her hair in two perfect waves. You couldn't see the infant (the spare) in her arms, but weren't they just the Madonna and child? Behind them stood the prince in his double-breasted jacket, about as interested in the baby as God is in the rest of us. Rebecca didn't know what the coming hours would hold but knew she wouldn't come out looking like Diana.

She continued on her pathetic walk. Time passed. Discharge emerged. Her body thrummed. It seemed to have nothing to do with her. Their birthing class rehearsals hadn't approximated this. Pain! Christopher hovered in Rebecca's line of sight and implored her to breathe. His approach was more martial than she'd have liked. She was annoyed by his imprecations, puzzled by Christopher's very presence. It was like having him by her side when she was going to the bathroom. Two or three times she forgot altogether what they were doing in that room, sorry, they called it a *birthing suite,* with its rose-beige wall covering and forlorn fake flowers.

"Breathe, breathe, that's it." Christopher sounded like he was urging the horse on whom he'd bet his paycheck to cross the finish line.

Rebecca felt like her spine was on fire, but why her spine? There were three or four or eight or eleven people in the room. The cotton gown did not cover her, an idea more than a garment. For some reason Rebecca was more conscious of the bareness of her breasts than the desire on the part of the assembled party to see her body fold out like an O'Keeffe. They attended to their business, its ceremony a mystery, like the College of Cardinals just before a new pope. What went on in there, anyway?

Her sister had warned her of *fire,* and Rebecca had planned for this by thinking of devout Buddhists protesting the war by placidly immolating. She didn't have what it took to scream. Bugs, mice, the things she didn't like; her response was always to shudder, think, *Oh this, I don't like this,* as though the mind could do anything about it.

She knew it was happening, the moment Judith called *fire:*

the baby was passing over her bones, her pelvis just a speed bump before he made his exit. Rebecca had assumed hyperbole but *fire* was right. Everything seemed white, which was said to be the color of heat at its hottest. Rebecca knew that someday she'd be fine, be delivered of this pain, be mended like that Japanese porcelain with a gilded crack, more beautiful once broken. But still, pain like she would faint, or maybe like she would die? Good thing she was already in a hospital! The baby slipped through her and the fire dimmed, the white dissipated, and eventually she heard it cry; her baby cried. It didn't even sound that loud. No one was paying any attention to her.

Look at me, she wanted to say, but she couldn't say anything. She wasn't sure whom she meant, but anyway, no one looked. One of the nurses had Rebecca's hand in hers, and Rebecca pulled away. She wanted the attention of Christopher, the doctor, the men. The baby was placed on top of her, and it tickled, and he moved slightly, and the doctor was doing something, and Rebecca was looking down at the child. Then someone covered him with a cloth and pushed the baby up her body.

At this moment (life's first!) we all look red, wet, furious, like a small bird or rodent, a fearful and fragile thing. Longed for, long imagined, and now she couldn't see, not actually. It wasn't sight, it was some chemical reaction: a general sense of light and beauty, warmth and perfection. Her blood percussive in her ears, her eyes damp and unable to focus. Rebecca felt someone lift the baby off her. Dr. Brownmiller was saying something.

"I'm thirsty," Rebecca said.

Christopher shouted something at her. Her body was not finished with its work. Rebecca breathed—that's what he was saying, Christopher—*breathe.* Now it was almost impossible to remember how to do this thing her body had always done without her active involvement. The pain was different because she thought she'd been done with it. She'd seen the baby! Rebecca looked down at her chest, and there, at her feet, were the doctor and a hundred, a thousand, other people, staring up into her body. The tableau struck her as hilarious. She heard music. Where was the music coming from?

Christopher told her to breathe. She wanted to defend herself. *I'm trying.* It was lost in the music. Was it—Tchaikovsky? Was music what elevated a room into a *birthing suite*?

The stirrups against which her feet were braced seemed to be hands pulling her body apart like a Thanksgiving wishbone. Some unseen person was counting, and Rebecca wondered where the baby was. She opened her eyes, which she had not realized were closed. There was the plash of something wet against something dry. Her knees shook. Rebecca heard a piano, tentative, tinkling, climbing. She wanted to ask about the music but couldn't think whom to ask.

Christopher pressed his dry lips against Rebecca's forehead.

She willed her eyes to focus. Where was the baby? She had seen the white, the void, and she had survived, and now she was impatient, and why wouldn't she be? The fire had forged her into something else entirely (a superhero) and she didn't have time to waste.

"He's perfect." Christopher had a postcoital blush after all that yelling.

Rebecca felt no lighter. There still seemed to be so many people, a dozen maybe, and she was wet with something, absurdly thirsty. She saw the tape deck across the room and knew she had not imagined the music. She saw the baby in someone's hands and knew that she had not imagined the baby. She did not see Dr. Brownmiller. She was alone with these dozen strange women.

One of the nurses approached with the baby. Rebecca reached for him as though she knew how to hold a baby. She did not. She pulled his small body toward hers, which felt larger, now, than it had when he was inside of it. Grotesque, a marvel: like Everest, the Grand Canyon, the sheer majesty of the ocean. *I could do it again. I could do anything.* The baby wore a hat, which seemed hilarious, and was wrapped tight. His eyes flickered, then settled shut. She wanted to kiss him. She wanted to lick him. She wanted him to always be right there in front of her. Her knees hurt like she'd been pedaling a bicycle.

"What a beauty." Christopher patted her arm. "I should get your mom. Your sisters. They're dying to see you."

Rebecca nodded or said nothing, it did not matter. The nurse touched her and the touch felt like a violation. The baby's skin on hers was euphoria, religion, blunt feeling. Anything else was intrusion. The nurse said *rest* or *consult* or something but nothing made any sense, and Rebecca stared at the wall or the ceiling, she couldn't tell which, or she fell asleep. It wasn't clear.

At some point, she was awake, and they were there, her sisters, her mother; it was women, at times like these, wasn't it? Where were Christopher, her father, her sisters' husbands? It didn't matter! None of the women cared in the slightest.

"You did great." Judith was holding her nephew, and of course Judith would say something like that. "Christopher told me everything. I guess you read *What to Expect,* after all."

Rebecca remembered it, guiltily, that fat book, untouched and intimidating at her bedside as sacred texts always were. "Thanks." Why fight?

"I remember how nervous I was with Jennifer! And babies are my *job*." Judith laughed and passed the baby on to her younger sister.

"Can I tell you—it's crazy, but this makes me want to have

another baby. Like, immediately." Christine had a flair for the dramatic, curly hair unruly, eyes slightly manic, her words mostly ignored, poor middle child. But come what may, Christine was in touch with her own feelings. She kissed the child's head.

"He's just perfect, Rebecca." Technically, a compliment for the baby, but Rebecca remembered: Lorraine (gently, but quite clearly) on Rebecca's gait ("Don't stomp"), her ambition ("You could get A's in algebra if you *wanted to* get A's in algebra"), her circumspection ("Look at your sisters—so many friends!"). Recalled, this maternal scolding sounded meaner than it was. Whether Lorraine loved her was not fair to debate but still it seemed possible that Lorraine didn't altogether *like* her.

Christine screwed her eyes up in an ecstasy that was not mockery. "They smell so wonderful, when they're new."

Rebecca itched to have the child in her hands. She wanted that smell back, the promise of it enough to make her forget the lumbar throb, the embers of pain, from her navel to her knees.

"One more grandchild to spoil." Lorraine relieved her middle child of the baby. He didn't stir. With her hair, quite black still, her full eyebrows, her smart plaid sweater, she didn't look much like a grandmother.

Rebecca didn't know if that would come to pass, sleepovers and presents from Grandma. It didn't matter. For now, theirs was a happy little conclave, Rebecca welcomed into a circle she'd been unaware existed, the sisterhood of motherhood, or maybe it was the medication.

"Oh, careful. Watch his head." Lorraine relinquished the baby to his mother.

Rebecca barely heard this, barely registered it. Some kind of magic! Let her mother disapprove. Let Judith enjoy the sororal advantage of always getting there first. Let Christine panic, vacillate between sisters, trying to decide which to side with, or how to assert that she, too, existed. None of this seemed to matter, suddenly. They were her family, but also, not really: her family was Christopher, her family was Jacob, this thing she had made by the magic of her body.

The next day, a nurse appeared in her room. "Your consult is in half an hour." The woman was drying her hands on a paper towel. "I'll bring him right back."

"What is my consult?"

The woman left the room with the baby. Then she returned and put the baby in Rebecca's arms. "Here you go." Rebecca stared at the baby. He mostly slept.

"OK, Mom. She'll be in shortly." The nurse left. They called Rebecca *Mom*. Maybe to habituate her to a lifetime of being thus reduced, maybe mere efficiency, one syllable instead of three. Perhaps it was rejoinder from women not called *Doctor*, women known by their names like servants in an Edwardian household. It was not unkind and was truly most likely because Rebecca was but another of the women who came and went in this never-ending business of being born. It was easier than to try to commit her name to memory. *Who's Mom? Whose mom?*

"Ms. Stone." The woman entered the room with an air of confidence, of efficiency, as befitted someone whose trade entailed entering hospital rooms but also with a smile not quite on her face but certainly in her *Stone*. It was not a question, the way she said it, but an assertion. Of course, to enter a hospital room was often to change a life, wasn't it?

The *Ms.* was a surprise. Rebecca was used to the *Mrs.* "Yes. That's me." Rebecca felt silly to be in bed. Dr. Brownmiller didn't want her to take anything to mitigate the pain. *A bit of ache is only natural,* he'd said. Rebecca had tried to evaluate how much ache she was feeling. There were pictograms, in hospital rooms, to help you identify the level of your pain, but what use were doodles? She thought a bad car crash might feel better, but what did she know?

"Of course it is." The woman deposited a package of papers on a chair. "I'm Ms. Johnson. I'm the hospital La Leche liaison. I coordinate between the obstetrics nurses and our volunteer lactation consultants. Of which I happen to be one. And you've been scheduled for a consult by—Emily."

Emily had been the woman who had pulled at Rebecca's breast the day before—that was only yesterday!—and finally pushed the thing aside with disdain. She had threatened a *consult,* landing hard on that first syllable: a con, that's how it sounded. Rebecca wanted the baby to eat. She wanted to be good at motherhood.

"La Leche." Rebecca felt her capacity for discourse had been reduced to reiteration. She couldn't manage *nipple + mouth;* she couldn't manage anything.

"La Leche." Ms. Johnson had the faintest whisper of an accent, or it was the foreignness of the words themselves. "I saw you yesterday, you remember? The doctor had you out walking."

When they first moved in together, she and Christopher lived in his old apartment in Dupont Circle, and there were mice. Rebecca had set out waxy paper traps thick with glue, and one mouse had been stuck, horribly, in the morass. That's how she'd felt, yesterday: trying to move her legs like a doomed rodent. "Yesterday."

"You don't remember." Ms. Johnson laughed. "Almost ran me down in the corridor. You were determined. You must have been the perfect patient, following doctor's orders."

"Oh—Princess Diana." She remembered. "You were near that picture of Princess Diana."

"I pinned that up." She sounded pleased. "Modern motherhood. But maybe she makes it look too easy. Our moms don't get their hair and makeup done before checking out. But I think she's a nice reminder, that you'll still be yourself, beautiful, normal, after you become a mother. Maybe even a better you than before. You're pretty enough to be on the cover of *People* magazine yourself!"

Rebecca had no idea how she looked. She'd gotten so used to her stomach stretching toward every table, and now that stomach was empty.

"Let's meet Jacob, shall we? Oh goodness." The woman stared into the bassinet, which reminded Rebecca of the cart a stewardess pushed. "Well, he's beautiful. Mom, I'm going to pick him up, OK?"

I'm not your mom, she wanted to say. "OK."

"So, we're going to work on latching. The nurse said it wasn't working, but that's completely normal." She dropped her voice. "Those nurses, they have no patience. I can say that because my daughter is a nurse. They've got no time. But we have plenty."

Rebecca remembered one of the nurses wielding her breast like a weapon, dragging the nipple across the baby's chin. *Wake up wake up,* the woman had said and Rebecca had said, *I'm awake,* and the nurse had frowned because she'd been talking to the baby. "I guess." Latching seemed not her responsibility but Jacob's, if someone so small could be said to have responsibilities.

"Just because something is natural doesn't mean it's easy."

Rebecca nodded.

"Think about menstruation. There's a lot you need to know that your mother or your big sister or your cousin or whoever shows you. This is the same thing. I'm here to show you, Mom."

Christine, fourteen, had explained maxi pads to her. "Please. Call me Rebecca."

"I'm Priscilla. OK, Rebecca. Jacob." She included the baby in her direct address, but smiled as though she knew it was funny to do so. "Let's start by getting you comfortable. Sit up, like you're eating breakfast in bed. Which one of you is! Put a pillow in front, like it's the tray, and put Jacob right on top of it."

Priscilla set the baby on the white pillow, sacrificial lamb. He had been inside of her and now he was not. If Priscilla had set her liver or pancreas on the pillow before her, would Rebecca have recognized it as part of her own body?

"OK, I'm going to stop you here." With a firm hand, Priscilla divided the baby from Rebecca. "You need to be comfortable. Mentally, but also physically. This is *work*, Rebecca. So make it easier. Relax your shoulders."

"Telling someone to relax is not very relaxing."

Priscilla laughed. "I have to remember that. But pretend until it feels true. Take your breast in your hand. Like it's not attached to your body. I think that helps, to treat it like a tool. Rub your nipple right up against his mouth and his chin. He'll fuss, and then he'll latch."

Rebecca traced the baby's chin with the distended tip of her breast.

"Wake up, my love. Wake up, now." Priscilla bent her head and blew gently onto the baby's ear. Her Afro brushed against Rebecca's skin.

Priscilla put a hand on Rebecca's. "I know I'm making you tense. Pretend we've known each other for years. I'm an old friend of the family. I've come for a visit. Move your finger away from the areola. So you don't slow the flow."

The baby's eyes were shut, his mouth on her breast.

"Is he there? He's not there." Priscilla put her finger between the baby's wet mouth and Rebecca's rigid nipple. "It's coming, is the good thing."

"The milk?" This woman had her finger on Rebecca's breast and in that moment she was indeed an old friend of the family. It was as before, with her sisters and her mother, a private but powerful conference. There was magic between them, or it was the baby.

"It's colostrum. It's like cream on top of the old-fashioned bottle, from the farm. The good stuff. That's what he needs now."

"He's not there?" Rebecca didn't know who *he* was or where *there* was but she was trying.

"You'll know when he's there."

"How will I know?" This was baffling.

"You'll know." Priscilla's confidence was reassuring. "Take Jacob's head in your right hand and lift it up and turn him onto your breast. He won't like it. Cup him gently, but firmly. He's your baby. You're not going to break him."

"Has he eaten?" Rebecca looked at the baby, gasping and fussing in her hands, eyes closed like he couldn't bear to see her, to be seen. "Is he starving?"

"Nature is smarter than us. Don't worry. You just need to learn how to work together. So put him right onto your nipple. Then what should happen is he should take hold and your nipple will be right up at the top of his mouth, deep in there."

He had already been inside her. Deeper seemed impossible.

"But we need to wake our friend up." Priscilla had the child's small ear between her fingertips. She kneaded it, like she was forming pasta. Once again, she leaned forward, breathing on the baby. Once again, her soft hair brushed against Rebecca's chest. That big room and the three of them huddled together like the survivors on Géricault's raft.

The baby had his arms clenched close to his face, his knees curled up to his chest, like a folded piece of paper that's accustomed to its envelope. This time, her nipple slipped past his gums and into him. The pressure, pull, pinch were a surprise. It hurt. By some magic, she knew her nipple was at the back of his throat; it was as though there was something pressing against the back of her own throat. "Is it working? How can I tell?"

Priscilla laughed. "If you listen very closely, you can hear it. Two sucks. One gulp. It takes two sucks to coax the milk out, one swallow." She was intent for a moment. She smiled. "I can hear it. Soon you'll be able to tell. And there are other ways. The breast he's not on might leak, which may be a sign that the one he's on is also working."

"So that's it then?" Rebecca felt a rush, hormonal, physical, like when you've had too much to drink and stand up suddenly.

"That's it. For now."

The baby suckled. Rebecca worried the spell would break if Priscilla Johnson left the room. "I didn't tell you," she said. "About Princess Diana."

"What's that?"

"My husband met her. At a party."

"Go on!"

The books said *bonding* was important. But this woman, this Priscilla, didn't seem to be interfering with that. Rebecca stroked his barely there dark brown hair and Jacob's skull vibrated beneath her fingertips, delicate as a summer fruit. "It just happened! He works for the embassy, my husband. He's English." There was a note of apology that she didn't intend. "She was at the White House. He was there, too."

"That's something!"

It *was* something. Rebecca pretended to find it less impressive when discussing it with Christopher. It was too embarrassing to explain, that she had a special feeling about a *princess*. Rebecca was high-minded; Rebecca was a poet, at least that was the intention, now that she'd left Woodley Park Montessori. That had been a stopgap. It was Lorraine who had found Rebecca the job, as a teacher's assistant and not, important to note, an *assistant teacher*. Rebecca poured cups of juice and played the cassette of the *Brandenburg Concertos* to rouse the napping pupils. The children were sweet but had damp noses and coughs like a dog's bark: you needed a passion for such work. She'd quit after marrying Christopher. "I was so jealous! But I was so pregnant. I couldn't have gone, even if I had been invited. What on earth would I have worn?"

"I do wonder what she looks like in person. I've seen the pictures, but you can just tell that she looks different in person."

Rebecca had never admitted that she'd bought a purple cashmere sweater vest like the one she'd seen Diana in, as she shepherded those pallid kindergartners. She couldn't point out that she herself had been a school helper, had married a taller, older Englishman. The coincidence was delicious but secret, tinged with shame but also pride, like the orgasm you only ever achieve alone. "Even my husband said she looked lovely, and he never notices that kind of thing."

"He was at the White House!"

Rebecca relished the transitive glamour of Christopher's work. So much easier to comprehend than her own work. People always wanted to know what you did. She was a poet but what had she done, the past two years? She'd bought a sofa, Italian, leather, the gray of an elephant, an ingenious glass coffee table, floor lamps that cast halos onto the ceiling, an espresso maker, All-Clad pans, and bamboo baskets that hung from the ceiling, which she filled with bananas, apples, tangerines. She'd been to parties as host (unwrap cheeses from wax paper and sweep Carr's crackers in tidy arcs, light votives in the powder room) and guest (spritz on Opium, make never-to-be-realized plans for ski vacations). She'd honeymooned in London, she'd bought a Volvo, she'd found the house on Wisconsin Drive. It all looked like subjugation, but it didn't feel that way. Poetry was a thing that she could never finish, therefore poetry could wait.

"Did you see the pictures, from that night?" There was the pain at the nipple, but there was also the slow creep of satisfaction. It spread from somewhere near her breast—her heart— and down her arms, to the tips of her fingers, even through her hair, passion but more placid.

"I must have." Priscilla clutched the manila folder of papers to her breast.

"She wore blue. Midnight blue, velvet."

"A sapphire choker. Set in pearls. I remember. I saw the pictures. Those gloves to the elbow."

"She danced—"

"—in the arms of that movie star!" Priscilla chuckled. "Too perfect, if you ask me."

"That's what I said!" That *was* what she'd said, the morning after, going back over the night with Christopher. He told her what details he remembered, though he couldn't think of the movie star's name. Rebecca had listened and said it was *too perfect*. Diana did everything right, somehow.

"Well, I feel special now. Just one step removed from Lady Di. Think of that!" Priscilla smiled down at them. "He'll fall asleep, you'll see. It's fine, just keep him close for now, learn to listen for when he's hungry. I'll come back later."

"There's more?" Rebecca had it under control! She gripped the baby with one hand, that was how small he was. She wondered, idly, where Christopher was.

Priscilla wore a black cardigan that looked very soft. She smoothed it out. "We can review how to pump, if you're going to be working, or away from the baby, or just want to have a bottle on hand. We can talk about some of the effects—you may have some contractions as your milk begins flowing."

"Contractions?" These were present only in the vaguest way, the memory of a meal. Rebecca knew that contractions had meant fire, light in her peripheral vision, a dulling of her sense of hearing. She could now barely conjure how it had felt.

"Not like labor. But they can be bad." Priscilla nodded. "I'll check on you tomorrow. It looks like you've got his needs covered, but we should go over yours. There might be pain, discomfort. It's all the usual stuff. Nothing you can't survive."

"Survival seems like a pretty low metric for success."

Priscilla laughed, a proper laugh. "There's no truer measure, if you ask me. But you're funny, Rebecca. I'll be back tomorrow."

2

THE BABY—JACOB, HIS NAME WAS JACOB, BUT IT WAS EASIER AND more honest to think of him as *the baby,* a specter, a force, not an actual person—made everything seem different. The house was unrecognizable, but not for the ministrations of Joyce Cohen, the interior designer, a blur in a bouclé skirt forever talking about *occasional tables* and *finishes.* Dangers loomed. The hard tile underfoot: Jacob's skull was so soft, Rebecca's grip on him so unpracticed. The books on the shelf: What was stopping a poltergeist or seismic event from sending the whole thing down upon them as upon poor Leonard Bast? The baby made life seem both triumphant/powerful/enduring and horribly fragile. What on earth was she doing?

Everything was, in fact, the same. Christopher woke, dressed, smoked a Silk Cut on the back steps (it's bad for the baby, she said), kissed her, and drove off into the District. The Maryland streets bled into Washington, reality bled into motherhood, and Rebecca slipped across that unmarked border.

Rebecca lay in bed, cold—the house was old—but unable to bear the pressure of the down comforter on her body. Her right breast was ossified, diamond hard, hot to the touch though Rebecca shivered. The baby was noisily dozing in the bassinet beneath the window. Mysteriously, it didn't seem to bother Christopher, not the heavy nasal wheeze of the infant or the slow build of his imprecations, stir whimper lick lips cry wail. Absent actual sleep, the restorative sort, that deep oblivion, Rebecca began to feel mad. She thought of her sisters. Judith had Jennifer, Christine had Michelle, and both had said they were *tired* but no one had said anything about *going crazy*. It had only been a few days, the baby so new his life span could be measured in those units. Rebecca tried to imagine her own mother, and herself, curled up as small as Jacob. She couldn't.

Jacob began the first in his steps toward fussing. It had been almost two hours that he'd slept. Not so bad. Four thirty was near enough morning. She took him downstairs, switched on the electric kettle, but he was ready to nurse, so the thing clicked off and the water cooled once more while Rebecca sat with the baby, massaging her rock-hard right tit with her left hand. This required dexterity. She folded her knees up and rested the boy on them, but the nipple slipped from his mouth and his brow furrowed, and he began to cry, silently at first, then quite loudly, uncannily, like an animal in the abattoir.

She'd always been competent. Rebecca never got lost driving, even to unfamiliar places. It took her one phone call to coordinate even a complex plan. If she was curious about something, she'd note that curiosity and look it up in a book when convenient. She was unfazed in the face of emergency. Once when she was in college, a man on the T had a cardiac event. Rebecca took the man by the arm, led him off the train at Boylston. She wasn't even late to class. There was nothing for her in *What to Expect*, just some silly illustrations. But if your heart races all the time, you're having a cardiac event yourself.

Rebecca wished there was some other person in the room who could prepare her a cup of tea. Hard to imagine that she'd once spent so much time in these rooms with Joyce Cohen, the interior designer. People appeared and then they disappeared and that was life. She looked back at the baby. Someday, he'd go off to college. The crying wasn't so loud, wasn't so disruptive, but it had some other sort of effect on her, something chemical, or akin to those whistles that only dogs can hear. His crying affected her uniquely among all living people because he had issued from her body; it was her own cells calling back to her, saying, *You feel hungry and you don't even know it*. She tugged at her right nipple and no milk came out, just a vague oily secretion that seemed like, but was not, blood. Her baby needed something and she didn't understand why she was unable to provide it.

The baby back at her breast, Rebecca turned on the radio, filling the silence with warm voices discussing Reagan's meeting with Gorbachev. She turned the kettle back on. Her breast throbbed and then, as had been happening for a couple of days now, her uterus kicked, seemed to flip inside her much as Jacob once had, when he'd been just a preening, anxious fish. The pain made her woozy. Rebecca touched her breast again. She'd been reading Ovid, only weeks ago, and here she was, Galatea in reverse, the tissue hard as marble, the nipple a faceted jewel.

Christopher came into the kitchen: pinstripe pajama pants, morning squint. "Morning then."

"We didn't wake you?" She found herself speaking of herself and the baby as one, with the same interest, Siamese beings.

Christopher filled a mug, steam rising to fog his glasses. He was still slender, Christopher, so little give on his body it was like his very torso was tucked into the elastic waistband of his pants. The flat plane of his chest, punctuated by those pointless pink nipples. Women's bodies had these useful appendages but no one ever spoke of men envying them. "No, no. It's time I was up." Christopher inhaled deeply, like a con-noisseur with a wine. "What's today, then?"

He liked an accounting of the day to come, and at night, in bed, an accounting of the day just passed. He liked to hear what Rebecca had read, what Rebecca had bought, what Re-becca was thinking about making for dinner the next day. Where once she'd have considered hours spent exploring the etymology of a given word or puzzling over another writer's choice of line break or planning a party time well spent, where once the day reliably included some acquisition (shoes, a new dress, a library book, a pork loin), now Rebecca found herself drawn to a smaller, more concise existence. She hadn't read anything more than a page or two of Anne Tyler in weeks. "Today is the same." Rebecca tried not to commit. She had the strangest sense that Christopher meant to make a point. "We're seeing Doctor Anderssen at ten." You had to go to the doctor all the time, when they were little.

"Good then." A touch of the philosophical, maybe. Morn-ings made him melancholy. Christopher sipped the tea. He would not ask how she was. He might have wanted to know it—how she was faring, whether that was sadness in her eyes or simply sleeplessness. He did love her, of course. But babies were a matter for mothers. It was Christopher's duty to make silly faces at the boy. He went outside to smoke while Rebecca made him an egg, runny yolk and a square of brioche, then he showered, dressed, disappeared into the day. There was noth-ing deeper in this, and Rebecca didn't feel abandoned: the way of the world.

Blood out of a stone, somehow Jacob was sated or simply gave up. The baby dozed and Rebecca showered, the spray electric on her chest, impossible on her vulva. Even the towel was painful. She gave the baby her left breast once more, then dressed, then dressed him. It felt that this had been the way she'd whiled away all her days, weeks, years. Sleep wake sleep wake, the house cold and smelly, the baby an utter mystery. He dozed as she drove the station wagon downtown.

Rebecca couldn't find change so she didn't feed the meter. She lifted the heavy plastic car seat out of the backseat and hurried into the building. The receptionist frowned because they were late. The nurse frowned because the baby was dressed but needed to be nude to be weighed, though Rebecca couldn't see how the tiny cotton undergarment could throw the scale off by even an ounce. Doctor Anderssen frowned because that was his way, at least with adults. He chuckled and clowned for the children, but seemed not to understand what Rebecca was saying.

"Is he gaining enough?" Thriving. They called this thriving.

"He seems good to me." As though he didn't have the data at his disposal; as though he were making a guess.

"I just can't tell." Rebecca held the nude baby close, daring him to urinate on her Ralph Lauren sweater. Let him piss on her. Perhaps it would be a salve, as when a jellyfish stings. "He takes the breast. I hear the sucking. Then he falls asleep. I can't tell. The diapers are supposed to be wet. They don't seem wet. I don't understand."

"Just get some Similac, Rebecca. Make it easy on yourself. Enjoy being a mom. Go for a walk. Watch *Days of Our Lives*. Get your hair done. Take him to the zoo." Doctor Anderssen closed the manila folder in his hands and winked at the baby. "He's a lady-killer. Job well done."

There was a ticket from the Montgomery County police, as she knew there would be. It was only money. Rebecca buckled the belt over the seat, pulling and tugging to be sure it was firmly in place. Jacob looked at her like he'd never seen her before, like she was no one to him. She sat in the front seat, started the car, turned on the radio. Dionne Warwick was singing, that song about friendship that was also, somehow, about AIDS. Rebecca felt like she had a fever and she certainly had the chills. She began to cry.

She forgot to remove the ticket from beneath the wiper blade, and drove to the hospital, and parked in a lot because she still couldn't find a quarter. She took the elevator to the fourth floor, and eyes still a little teary, approached the woman at the desk—maybe she was a nurse, maybe she'd peered into Rebecca's vulva and watched a baby emerge into life. "Do you know Priscilla?"

Priscilla: (1) smiled in recognition, (2) recoiled in surprise, (3) procured an ice pack and secured it beneath the strap of the nursing bra, (4) pulled at Rebecca's distended nipple and filled her own palm with Rebecca's milk, (5) smoothed Rebecca's bangs, brought her some ibuprofen and a plastic cup of cold water, (6) held the baby until he slept. The woman smiled so much that Rebecca cried, then, remembering Dionne Warwick and her song about AIDS, cried harder. *Get your hair done?* Did her hair not look nice, on top of everything else?

"All those men in New York are dying," Rebecca said, nonsensically. Imagine if your own blood was the thing making you sick.

"The baby is fine," Priscilla replied, equally cryptically.

"I'm not a very good mother." Rebecca prodded at the swell in her breast, cold to the touch from the ice.

3

IT WAS THE TWENTY-SEVENTH BUT TECHNICALLY CHRISTMAS WAS A
season. It wasn't too late! It was the thought that counted! Re-
becca made a mandala of frosted cookies, wrapped the plate
in plastic, taped beneath that an envelope; a gift certificate,
which didn't make any assumptions. As it was, Rebecca felt
uncertain. What was the line between generosity and pom-
posity?

"It's my favorite visitors!" Priscilla stood as they entered
the by now familiar room. "How are we today?"

"This is a social call, for a change." Rebecca felt suddenly
embarrassed. "Jacob and I wanted to come. To give you this."
She thrust the plate at the woman, unable to summon the grace
required of the gesture because there was another agenda, as
was so often the case.

"Well, my goodness. That was unnecessary. Thank you
so much."

"There's this, as well." It was awkward to indicate the en-
velope taped to the plate. "Just something." She sat on the roll-
ing stool by the counter.

"My goodness. Thank you." Priscilla put the plate on the metal desk. "That's very kind."

"I just . . ." Rebecca still felt too near tears too much of the time. This had never been her way before having Jacob. "I truly appreciate what you've done for me."

"That's what La Leche does, dear." Priscilla unwrapped the plate. "These are almost too pretty to eat."

"Not La Leche. You, Priscilla." It was hard to tell it. "I've felt—"

"A lot of women feel alone after having a baby. I know I did. It's very common. It doesn't make any sense, because you're not alone. You never are again, not really. My baby is all grown up and I still don't ever feel like I'm alone."

"It's been . . ." Rebecca was at a loss. In the carrier against her chest, Jacob sighed. "You've been very kind."

"It's my job, Rebecca! Now eat one of these."

"But this is beyond the call of duty. You've been a help. A friend. So I wanted to come again. To give you this, but to—finish the conversation we had. To make you an offer, officially."

"Rebecca." Priscilla bit into one of the cookies. "I'm not sure it's proper."

"Oh, who cares about proper?" Rebecca knew—they had covered this, the times she'd been to her—that Priscilla had lost her previous job as a nanny for a family that had relocated to the Middle East, a hazard of life in the District. A small stipend from the hospital had been arranged by her daughter, Cheryl. It was a temporary solution. "You'll need." It wasn't about Priscilla needing money, though Rebecca assumed she did; it was that *she* needed Priscilla.

"I surely will." She laughed. "My daughter works here. She pulled strings."

"I didn't mean to assume." Rebecca wanted to have her way. Hadn't it been thus, her whole life? She wanted, and she received.

"I don't know how it might look. The hospital is my daughter's employer. I need to keep things aboveboard." Priscilla looked embarrassed. "It's not that I don't love Jacob!"

"Of course. Perhaps I could—if you're interested. I could speak to the hospital. I'm sure they can be made to understand." It seemed very simple.

"I don't know that there are rules but there are . . . appearances."

"But who cares about appearances?" Rebecca rolled the stool back and forth until the baby stilled. "What can that matter?"

"I should talk to my daughter—Cheryl. I would have to be certain that it won't complicate anything for her."

"It won't. Don't be silly." What were formalities but just that?

"Well." Priscilla picked up another cookie.

"You're a good mother. To think of your daughter." Was she pushing? Perhaps. But she was motivated. She had a need, Priscilla had a need. It seemed straightforward. "Maybe I could speak to her. Cheryl? Reassure her that it's all aboveboard. Maybe I could make a gift to the hospital? I should! To La Leche. You saved me, you helped me so much."

"It is a not-for-profit organization. So it's tax deductible." She sounded persuaded or maybe resigned.

"Why don't we do that." Rebecca nodded. "And I can speak to your daughter, if it would put your mind at ease."

"No." Priscilla shook her head. "I don't think we need to go so far. But maybe you're right. Maybe it's not such a problem."

"It's not."

"You drive a hard bargain, Rebecca."

"So that's yes. You're saying yes to me." Rebecca was whispering, though the baby was quite asleep.

"I bet most people do." Priscilla smiled.

"I know it's short notice, but maybe you can start in January?"

4

SHE WAS AT HER DESK LOOKING AT THE NEIMAN MARCUS CATALOG. It was more engaging than the rejection letters she was supposed to file, including one from the esteemed magazine at her dear old alma mater, a very specific sort of insult. She *knew* some of the readers there, but of course they probably remembered Rebecca at her worst. She'd tarried too long in that city, intoxicated with her own liberty, thinking it viable to spend her time as a student and to spend her youth seducing (yes, that) a professor. Isaiah was unkind, and married, too, but she didn't know much, younger Rebecca. She kept her poems close and took a job at a bookstore in Cambridge. Greg and Lorraine Brooks's 1981 Christmas dispatch: *Rebecca has finished her master's at Boston University but can't get enough of books!*

Now, older/wiser, Rebecca had perhaps had her fill of those. Why not pore over these silk scarves and ostentatious jewels and interesting shoes? It was said Mrs. Marcos had three thousand pairs! Rebecca had seen photographs, an intent woman with a clipboard, dwarfed by teak shelves, making an inventory of wedges, slingbacks, espadrilles, sandals, heels, now the property of the Philippine people.

Rebecca wondered how many pairs of shoes she had. She couldn't guess, in fact, felt done with them, with vanity itself. In the past months, she'd gotten dressed up once. Christopher took her to a dinner at the home of someone he wanted to impress. He was called Bob and he was married to an actress of almost unreal beauty who had been on television, years before. Beside this woman, this wonder (towering heels, white dress, shellacked hair) Rebecca felt dowdy, exposed, as appalled at the loose skin as she was amazed at the fact that it was her body that kept her baby alive, and kept pulling her cashmere shawl tighter around her shoulders, wishing to swaddle herself just as Priscilla had taught her to swaddle Jacob, the constraint a comfort.

Now, Rebecca made excuses. She sat at home in canvas sneakers and red corduroys and talked to the baby and Priscilla. The trousers had been maternity pants and they were quite loose. The weight had mostly melted away as Priscilla said it would, because of Jacob and his incessant need.

Something Christopher had said to Rebecca, when they were looking for houses, stuck with her. "The right amount of money makes anything possible." Words to live by. Priscilla started on the first Monday in January, the sixth, more than one kind of epiphany, the end of holiday festivity. But Rebecca, opening the door to her, felt *Zing!* go the strings of her heart, just like Judy Garland sang. Priscilla in her belted sweater and tan pants, with her strong hands and their soft palms. Jacob always went to her without fuss.

"You have a beautiful home." Priscilla kicked off her shoes in the foyer.

"Oh, we wear our shoes inside." Rebecca was cradling Jacob close to her chest, her knees bent and rocking side to side gently. Priscilla had shown her this trick during one of her visits. Priscilla said it reminded the baby of being in utero, the constant motion of the mother's body.

"I'm making myself at home." Priscilla did not laugh often but seemed often to be joking. "Besides, they say taking your shoes off at the door reduces the germs in the household. Where can I wash my hands?"

Rebecca led her into the kitchen, where Priscilla washed her hands, and took the baby from Rebecca. "Let me show you." She propped the baby's back against her chest, her breasts cradling his lolling neck like those inflatable pillows favored by frequent fliers, one hand under his knees, still bent by habit. With her other, Priscilla made a circle of thumb and forefinger and wrapped it around his ankle. "This is how they do it in the pediatric wards. If the baby wiggles away, you can't drop him."

Rebecca sat with them for twenty minutes that first day before Priscilla cleared her throat and sent Rebecca away. That was why she was there, so that Rebecca could go away.

The office was a purgatory. Nothing happened there. Or it was a church: nothing happened there but you pretended and it seemed like something *might*. Rebecca opened the mail, did a crossword, responded to a letter, skimmed the newspaper, studied the contributors' notes in various journals, angry or irritated about this person's appointment as the Whoever Whatever Professor of Creative Writing or that person's undeserved grant. She'd do this for ninety minutes, then Priscilla would knock and bring in Jacob, and Rebecca would sit by the window and nurse and Priscilla would sit at the desk and chat with her. Then Priscilla would take the baby away, and there would be ninety more minutes or so of quiet, and then she'd knock once more, and then Rebecca would leave the office and sit with her in the kitchen and eat a tuna sandwich and then Rebecca would go back to the office for another ninety minutes and then be interrupted once more, feed the baby once more, then give up and sit in the living room with Priscilla and the baby, and drink a

cup of tea and listen to Diane Rehm and laugh and discuss noth-
ing at all. Rebecca wasn't writing, but everything felt different
and better. Perhaps she'd been struggling not with the baby but
with the loneliness of spending all her time with someone who
could not talk to her.

Priscilla rapped at the door, neither urgently nor meekly.
Rebecca had known it was time, could feel that sense of trickle
or tickle. She closed the catalog and put some papers on top
of it. "Yes."

Priscilla came in, Rebecca took the baby, who smelled
vaguely of Priscilla, who smelled vaguely of vanilla extract,
and sat, holding the baby with one arm and undoing buttons
with the other. She was adept at this now.

"How has the morning been?"

"We played. We read. He napped. I think later we might
walk to the library. It's almost balmy outside, did you know?
Thank goodness. I always get to this point where I can't bear
to look at my winter coat anymore."

Rebecca murmured her assent though she had in fact got
much better at holding conversations while feeding the baby.
At this point she was used to his presence, his pull, his nearness.
Sometimes she liked to bask in it, savor it, as the reverberations
after an orgasm or the lingering taste of a strong red wine, but
Rebecca liked talking to Priscilla and was hungry for the op-
portunity because she had so many questions and these had to
be folded into longer conversations. "Where did you grow up,
Priscilla? I don't know!" Rebecca shook her head as though
this were not to be believed. "You know I'm from Greenbelt.
I'm used to this weather, winter too long, summer too short.
Sometimes I'm tempted to move to Phoenix or something, so I
can feel warm more often than not."

Priscilla tidied the papers on the edge of Rebecca's desk.
"Prince George's area. Well, Charles County. Port Tobacco.

You won't know it. It's country, compared to this." She shook her head decisively. "There's no reason for you to ever go there."

Rebecca sometimes heard in Priscilla a trace of an accent, a tendency toward Southernness, a courtly affect, a slackness around the vowels. This seemed to answer something. "Charles County."

"I hope you're getting some work done, what with our interrupting. You could always pump. That'll make it easier for you to write or get out of the house. Of course, the schedule will change before you know it. Babies keep you on your toes."

Rebecca knew that when Priscilla talked about babies in the abstract she was talking about particular babies—Jamie and Lauren, who had been her charges a couple of years ago, and before that a little boy named David, before that a little girl named Theresa, and before that, of course, her own daughter, Cheryl. The bulk of what Rebecca most wanted to know concerned Cheryl, and this nagging question: How old was Priscilla? It was impossible for Rebecca to tell. Rebecca would herself turn thirty-one in two months. She'd had a baby so much later in life than her sisters had, than you were supposed to, but she had a feeling that Priscilla had done the inverse. Because she was full of a certain kind of wisdom, Priscilla seemed much older, but Rebecca sensed this wasn't the case. Still, she didn't trust her estimates, because Priscilla's blackness was a complication. Hair and skin are the giveaways, but Rebecca didn't understand black hair or black skin. She listened for cultural references, a *when Kennedy was shot* (Rebecca had been at school; her third-grade teacher was named Mrs. Warner), any suggestion that Priscilla was *feeling old*. "To tell you the truth, I like it when you come to visit." The *you* here was understood to be plural but may as well not have been.

"What are you getting done, if I can ask? I've never known anyone who wrote for a living."

"It's generous of you to call it a living." Rebecca grew hot. It was hard to remember, but imperative not to forget, that Priscilla was in her employ, that jokes about money were not seemly. Even among her sisters, money was a subject broached but never boarded, because of the obvious: Judith and Steven had it, Christine and Tim wanted it, Rebecca had gone from having none to having more than she deserved by virtue of luck instead of intensive education. Christopher's parents had invested wisely in London real estate. "I try to think. I read. If I understood my own work better, I suppose I'd do more of it. Or be better at doing it."

"I've never read much poetry, truth be told. I read a lot of mysteries. But I'd like to read some. To understand what you do."

Rebecca was philosophical (OK, flattered). "I don't know." She looked at the baby at her breast, then out of the window. The trees were still bare, but the sunlight did seem stronger. "It's just . . . The thing I like about poetry is that it can mean whatever it is you want it to mean. There's what the poet means, what the writer means, but I'm not sure that matters, ever, and less so even than normal with a poem. It's just you, assembling the words and the images and the ideas and thinking about your own life and the things you know and the meaning is there, somehow, in you, and not where you think it is, on the page."

Priscilla considered this. "Are you thirsty?"

Rebecca shook her head.

"It's interesting. I have this idea about poems rhyming or sounding a certain way, but I know that's not the poetry you write. I read your poem, in that book in the living room, from the University of Nebraska."

The baby had fallen asleep. This was not uncommon; Rebecca rubbed his ear gently, and he suckled, then did not, then did, then did not. She removed her nipple from his mouth, which puckered around the air, a little frown she wanted to kiss.

"Let it dry. Get some air." Priscilla was vigilant.

The best way to forestall blood. Rebecca left the nursing bra unlatched. She felt like Gauguin's Tahitian, in the blue sarong, her single exposed breast somehow more noticeable than her companion's, resting on a bowl of flower petals or fruit. No one, possibly not even Christopher, had seen Rebecca's breasts as often as Priscilla. "I wrote that so long ago. I should be writing more. I thought I'd have a book by now. That's how it seemed, when I was twenty-two—that by the time I was thirty I'd have a book, instead of a couple of poems in a couple of journals that no one reads."

"It's interesting, what you do. It seems interesting, to me."

"I could give you some books. Poets I think you might like. I think you'd like Nikki Giovanni. Or there's some very pretty Wallace Stevens." Rebecca was grasping. She did like Giovanni but was surprised to hear herself say it aloud. Was she recommending Giovanni because Giovanni was, like Priscilla, a black woman? This seemed so idiotic but maybe true. She did think Priscilla might like Giovanni.

Priscilla took Jacob from Rebecca's arms. "I'll get him down. Now, you get back to work."

5

MONDAY WAS THE PUNCH LINE THAT NO LONGER PACKED A PUNCH. Mondays, what was so bad? It had been—what, years?—since Rebecca had gone off to work at that bookstore in Boston, that little island of lost souls where certain types with impressive degrees found themselves upon realizing they weren't tough enough for anything other than books. Neither poetry nor parenthood cared what day it was. Mondays were redeemed, now, by Priscilla's key in the lock, her footfalls in the foyer, her hearty *Hello!* Monday, blessed Monday! Rebecca was free. She had only to hand over Jacob. It was that simple, though sometimes she hesitated. Sometimes after half an hour in the office, she'd take out a photograph of the baby. It felt like madness but there it was. Then an hour later, Priscilla would bring the baby in and Rebecca would feel—better?

Once (only once) Rebecca had closed the door to her office and lain on the floor, rolled-up cardigan beneath her head, and fallen asleep for twenty minutes, waking with a panicked start, her first thought *Where is the baby?* Babies were like that, in the mind at least, wily, capable of slipping away the moment your back was turned, trickster spirits.

But it was Memorial Day weekend. Monday, Priscilla-less, was cause for dread. Jacob woke at eleven, at midnight, at one, at two. Neither hungry nor angry, Jacob was delirious with joy. That, too, is the remit of a child at six months: happiness. They're darling and perfect, able to coo and burble and grab for their feet and twist and wiggle, crazy with the discovery of their physical form. Every baby in advertising is six months old because that's when babies are at their most seductive, the marketing department's ideal.

Rebecca, exhausted, was unmoved. Her third trip to Jacob's room, she'd cradled the wiggling child and wished to throw him out of the window to the driveway below. Her breasts throbbed, her eyes could not focus, and she was tired in a way that transcended the physical. It was not sleepiness, which meant only lack of sleep; it was part of her essence, like using her left hand, like having ears. She held the baby and he stopped crying and fixed her with that stupid smile. A six-month-old was like a drunk who is convinced that his patter is charming.

At two thirty, it became clear that what Jacob needed was not sleep but an audience. Rebecca took the baby to the living room, switched on a lamp, and settled onto the sofa, the baby's head on her knees. He babbled and it seemed like a taunt.

"You're awake." She looked at the baby and the baby looked at her. "You're awake, you're awake. It's nighttime. It's time to sleep."

Jacob turned his head and looked at the dark room. Some cultures believed babies could see ghosts. But a dark room doesn't seem menacing unless you're alone, and she was not alone. These rooms were haunted by Jacob, smiling, genial Jacob, who had never been more awake. She tried stroking the side of his face, which sometimes reminded him that he was sleepy. She sang, trying to engage his attention and wear him out. It made him only happier.

Rebecca switched on the television and Jacob arched his back to see the curious blue light. Rebecca held up a book and Jacob had never been more interested. Maybe he was an insomniac? An insomniac baby, was there such a thing?

She needed to punish him. She put Jacob in the bouncy seat and he whimpered. *Good,* she thought. Maybe he'd cry until he was tired enough to sleep. Then he began to coo, and his happiness was maddening. It was not that she wanted to get into bed, enjoy the relief of the cool sheets, the weight of the heavy duvet, the accompaniment of Christopher's snore. She didn't want to sleep so much as she wanted to erase Jacob's existence, exorcise herself of him. She went into the kitchen and turned on the lights, the halogens a concession, a protest, a tantrum. She peeled back the aluminum foil and ate cold lasagna out of the stoneware dish. She wasn't even hungry. She put the fork down and hurried back to the living room. Jacob sat in his seat, kicking his legs.

She watched an episode of *Three's Company,* and Jacob began to whine. She held him in her arms and he grinned. She watched another episode of *Three's Company* and he fussed to be fed. Having drunk, he seemed still more drunk, burped terribly, spit up on her bare shoulder. Then he seemed renewed, delirious, kicking, turning his head this way and that like a baby possessed. She was afraid, then angry. She turned the television off and put the baby on her shoulder and made a circuit around the sofa, twice, futile as the guards at a tomb, just another ceremony. Jacob laughed, then stilled, then shit noisily, then sighed in what could have been relief or could have been delight in how deeply he'd debased her.

She spread a blanket and put the baby on the floor and he took it for a game of peekaboo. She wiped the stuff from his thighs, the raisins of his testicles, and he laughed, and urine dribbled from his penis and into the mess.

"Damn it." The gummy shit was on her hands, and she wiped them on the blanket and got the clean diaper on. Jacob had never seemed happier than he did that Monday morning at three forty. Rebecca gathered up the shit-stained blanket and left him on the floor and washed her hands in the kitchen sink. It was morning, and she made a pot of coffee. The day had begun or the previous one had never ended. Christopher would be awake soon.

The baby couldn't roll over but he could move. Jacob had scooted about on his back and looked pleased with himself. She picked him up, her movements abrupt. At least those earliest, newborn nights, Jacob had had the decency to cry, to need to be shushed and consoled. This was something else, the way that mania can seem at first to be simply good humor. She was furious.

They had a mechanical swing in the kitchen and she put the baby there and stirred milk into her coffee. "You're supposed to be asleep, Jacob."

The swing groaned. She knew that Priscilla would not come, that there would be no nap on the floor of the office. Rebecca kept a bag in the freezer—the bones of a chicken, the onion that had been going brown, the peelings of carrots, the cloves of garlic that were so tiny it wasn't worth it to peel them—and dumped this into a pot, filled it with water, set it to boil, to make a quick stock. The room filled with steam, a meaty smell, the noise of industry. She found a bag of frozen berries she'd forgotten about and took those out, too; there were fresh apples, too; she'd bake a crumble, with cinnamon, brown sugar, salted oats on top. Rebecca turned on the oven and began to sing to herself. Jacob seemed content—of course he did, what did he need: the swing made him feel he was being held, and he could see her, and he was not being made to sleep, he had all he had ever wanted.

Rebecca slipped past exhaustion to euphoria. She finished her coffee, poured more, looked out at the day, growing inevitably brighter. The only sound was the liquid in the pot and the creak of the swing, but eventually that stopped, because the thing was programmed to run only so long. Rebecca looked over and Jacob was asleep, of course. It was six o'clock.

Christopher came into the room, and she held up a finger, silencing him.

"What are you cooking?" His whisper was confused.

"Turn off the oven in ten minutes. Wake me in an hour."

"I have a meeting."

"One hour."

She went upstairs and got into the bed. Her shirt smelled like chicken soup. She did not sleep, simply turned over and over, twisting her body much like Jacob did, searching for the pose that would bring relief, to no end. She got up after forty-five minutes and found that Christopher had forgotten to turn off the oven and the fruit crumble was burned and ruined. She set it out to cool, fed the baby, changed him, then dumped the dessert into the garbage.

6

CHRISTOPHER WAS TAKING HER ON A DATE. THEY HAD NEGLECTED
each other. Rebecca had read about this, in a magazine, and
so the plan had been hers. The theater in Georgetown was
overly air-conditioned, but it was a relief from the July heat.
(The usual jokes: Washington, D.C., a swamp literally/
figuratively.) There was something familiar about *Hannah and
Her Sisters* that Rebecca was unable to diagnose; though the
movie was entertaining, this was distracting, and it wasn't un-
til it was almost over that she realized that it was the sense of
being a spectator. She was a watcher not a participant, at that
moment of course but also in life. Those nights she and Chris-
topher would end up at mansions in Potomac, Rebecca would
slip away from the conversation and wander, here a grand pi-
ano littered with framed photographs, here a study with that
candied bouquet of tobacco smoked in a pipe, here a sitting
room hung with Audubon plates, here a solarium with bam-
boo furniture and a view of a pool lit from within, watery light
dancing across the dogwoods. The movie's beautiful women
in expensive-looking clothes—they didn't feel like Rebecca,
but they felt like women she had watched. After, Christopher

and Rebecca sat in the restaurant next door, sipped decaf, and ate tiramisu.

"Did you like the film?" Christopher fixed his conversation in the present. He went for observation: the wine they were consuming, the room in which they stood, the achievements of the company that surrounded them. Christopher was adept at the recitation of a person's curriculum vitae; this attended every introduction. To hear yourself described by Christopher was a wonderful thing. Rebecca never felt more a poet than hearing Christopher declare her one.

"I did." She took a bite of the dessert, more damp than sweet. "I like his serious movies more than the slapstick."

"A nice score, I thought." Christopher's mouth was full. "Very charming."

"We're going to the Arena Stage next month. I got us tickets to this Christopher Durang. A bit of funny might be nice, don't you think? The news has been so terrible. It's put me in the most negative mood. Like this movie, did you notice the maid?"

He shook his head. "Was there a maid?"

"She was the only black person in the movie." Rebecca didn't know if it was easy to miss her or impossible not to notice her. The woman had darted through the scene, twice, spoken or nodded maybe once. She wore a uniform. Rebecca was at ease around wealth—presumably she was possessed of it, though its source was a mystery, like an underground river—but she'd never seen a servant in livery. "She had one line. Maybe two. At the very end."

"Oh, in the dining room, yes." He spooned the last of the dessert into his mouth, not asking her leave, though they were, ostensibly, sharing it.

"Setting the table. But she was there, before that, too."

"That's something." Christopher did not sound as though he believed it was, in fact, something.

"Something . . ." She paused, searching. "Something bad, right? She's right there, but she's invisible." Rebecca had the sudden sense she'd gone the wrong way, misspoken, miscalculated. She could see that Christopher did not understand what she meant to say and what felt upsetting now was not the substance of her words but her husband's reaction, and the question of whether it was indifference or confusion.

"She's a maid." Christopher's tone was not dismissive, nor was it impressed. "Isn't that rather the point of a maid? Anyway. The Arena, I think Peter is on the board there. We should see about that."

"Doesn't it seem odd? A movie about New York City with only one black person in it?"

Christopher considered this. "There's also only one Englishman in it."

"That's not the same thing." She was annoyed. "Don't be ridiculous. It makes you wonder. I actually can't think of a movie I've seen about black people."

"You watched that Cosby show. But I take your point. She's quite beautiful, Barbara Hershey." Christopher was teasing.

"I wonder what Priscilla would think." Rebecca did not want to discuss this with Priscilla, but she wanted to discuss it with someone, and besides Christopher and Priscilla, the only person she talked to was Jacob. "A movie with only one black person, and she's a servant. You don't think Priscilla thinks of herself as our servant?"

"Servants don't usually nap on the sofa, do they? Never mind using Christian names and rummaging about in the refrigerator. Anyway. How old-fashioned. We're not old-fashioned people."

When Christopher was born, Churchill was at Downing Street. Was he not a little old-fashioned? And was it not somehow old-fashioned to have someone like Priscilla in the house? She *was* deferent. "I would hate to think that that's how she thought of herself."

"Well, we do pay her." Christopher was logical. "Anyway, I doubt she much thinks about it. She dotes on Jacob. We don't expect her to drink from a different glass, or stand when we enter a room. She comes and goes. She's a part of our household, she's a part of our life. That's the job, when you're a nanny."

"But you think about your job, don't you, even when you're away from the office?" This plagued her: Did Priscilla think about her and Jacob as much as she thought about Priscilla?

"I'm the special assistant to Her Majesty's Ambassador to the United States. Priscilla is a nanny."

Rebecca flinched. "I'm a poet. I think about that."

"That's a *profession*." Christopher was more reasonable now. "Being a nanny isn't a profession. It's a job."

"But it's an important job." Rebecca did not want this to drop. They were near deciding something significant.

"Priscilla is wonderful. We're lucky to have her. But I don't know that she feels as fulfilled by looking after Jacob as you will when the *Paris Review* comes calling." Christopher paused. "But perhaps she does. What do I know?" He yawned. He was either tired of discussing this matter or just plain tired.

Rebecca's coffee had gone cold, but she drank it anyway. Finishing her coffee had something to do with enjoying this date, even though her husband was yawning, even though the movie was now mostly forgotten, just a jazzy riff Christopher would tap his feet to as he drove them home. She wanted to get back and see Jacob but also she did not; she wanted to sit at the table with a warm cup of coffee and say more about the black maid and the nice clothes and how she felt about life, but it was getting late.

7

WHENEVER WORK WASN'T WORKING REBECCA FOUND SOMETHING reassuring in the kitchen (stir, pour, rub the pebble of nutmeg across the back of the plane). Poetry never approached the sublime. It was just more labor, the search for the word, the phrase, the sound, but it was also the search for a starting point, a subject. Worse moments, like today, her life felt too boring. Nothing ever happened to her, or there was no poetry in what did.

Cooking was a relief, like prayer. She liked using her things, the heavy copper pot, the food processor. Cooking was math and miracle: fifteen ounces plus a tablespoon plus three-quarters of a cup, the sum so much greater than its parts. The week before she'd come back from the market with several jars of brightly colored purees.

"Don't waste your money." Priscilla tsked. "I'll show you."

Priscilla had boiled a sweet potato and mashed it with butter. Jacob ate so much they were afraid he was going to vomit. Once, at lunch with her sisters, Rebecca heard herself say that she couldn't *imagine* life without Priscilla, so it must have been true.

Rebecca heard the door swish open then thud shut, the squeak of the stroller's hard tires. "Hello!" She tried to squelch the gooey note that crept into her voice—maybe everyone did this—when talking to the baby.

Priscilla came in, carrying Jacob. The baby kicked his legs happily when he saw his mother. How loyal.

"You're cooking." Priscilla did that, stated the obvious. "We had the nicest afternoon." Priscilla handed the baby to his mother and poured a glass of water.

The boy smelled of the out-of-doors and was soft chubby damp reassuring as babies should be. He did not return Rebecca's embrace but settled into it. His eyelashes brushed against her neck and she felt the milk's urgency. She handed the boy back to Priscilla, dumped the bright green beans into a bowl of iced water.

The baby babbled, approximating conversation, loud, deliberate nonsense. Priscilla squeezed him. "Someone has a lot to say. Going to be talking before you know it, Rebecca. Not going to let you get a word in edgewise."

Rebecca couldn't imagine real words from that gummy mouth. Just because you know something to be inevitable doesn't mean you can summon it. She wouldn't mind someone else to talk to. "His daddy's boy." Charitable, since she knew he mostly saw and therefore imitated her and Priscilla. She was, though, in awe of Christopher's intellect, his ability to remember less obvious facts like which Soviet socialist republics bordered the Black Sea.

"What's cooking?" Priscilla reached for the ceramic bowl of blueberries.

"I'm roasting a chicken. It's too hot for it, but I'm in the mood."

"You're trying to make it feel like fall." Priscilla nodded. "It's too hot, so you're trying to fast-forward. I do the same."

Priscilla reached for another berry, bit the small thing in half, and offered one of the halves to Jacob.

"A complicated dinner seemed more appealing than work. Though I don't know why I would bother, since Christopher is out." He often was, but she and Christopher had plenty of time to themselves. There were times she didn't know how to fill it, their conversation a performance, and Rebecca could not remember her lines, her motivation, the situation, the title of the play, none of it.

"A good meal is like a clean house. A present you give yourself." The boy in Priscilla's arms shivered with delight, worked his jaws, smacking like a ruminant.

Rebecca turned away from woman and baby, suddenly uncomfortable with this intimacy, though perhaps it was the oven, set to 410. This was the key to crispy skin. She hesitated before the bird's splayed body, white with butter. "It seems like more fun than writing, today, anyway."

"Let me show you something." Priscilla put Jacob, his lips purple like a whore's, into his little seat. He'd soon outgrow it. Nine months. He'd been in the world for as long now as he'd been inside her body.

Priscilla slipped a knife from the block and picked up a lemon and sliced it, a single fluid action. "If you put it inside the chicken, it comes out so nice." She slipped the fruit into the bird, put the knife in the sink, and washed her hands thoroughly.

They looked at the chicken like generals studying a map. Then they looked at Jacob in precisely the same way.

"What a doll." Priscilla smiled down at him.

Rebecca was disarmed by compliments regarding Jacob's beauty. Did she have anything to do with it? "Why don't you stay for dinner, Priscilla? We'll eat early, the three of us."

"Why don't I." By some trick, everything Priscilla said sounded like a directive.

Rebecca was an author with no real authority. "You will?"

Priscilla took the baby upstairs to be changed. Rebecca put the chicken into the oven and set the table. To hire a nanny was to invite into the home a spectator. What did Priscilla see/ overhear/imagine/divine/sense/like/dislike/report and to whom (other nannies, neighbors, her own family)? Did she tell everyone that the lady of the house did nothing all day in the spare room, listening to Bach, shuffling papers on the too-small desk? Maybe Priscilla didn't think of them at all, once the workday ended. But if she did, it mattered to Rebecca that Priscilla think highly of her, not only that she not report her worse observations. Rebecca wanted her approval.

Often, Rebecca could not hear the baby, but could hear Priscilla, narrating every single thing she did to Jacob. There was something soothing about this chatter. Sometimes, Rebecca had the strange sense that if she went out, something— Jacob, herself, the house, it was not clear—would vanish altogether. That she would leave and there'd be no returning, like in a folktale with an obscure moral. Mostly, though, it was normal to come back into the house from the library, the post office, and find Priscilla slicing an apple or drying her hands on the blue plaid tea towel, the woman of the house. Rebecca was overcome with the sense of reversal, that none of it—the soft leather sofa, the Robert Indiana lithograph, the Orrefors bowl of dried rose petals—was hers. She would want to slip up the stairs and push open Jacob's bedroom door, be reassured by his placid snores that he hadn't succumbed to crib death. But that would be insane, or worse than, an admission of distrust that would fester. What she had was harmony, and that was too precious to risk.

Rebecca escaped into the office, and when she returned, there were vegetables arrayed on the counter: tomatoes, a fat bouquet of romaine, a yellow pepper Rebecca did not remember buying, glowing like a tourmaline on the jeweler's velvet.

Jacob was in his high chair, gnawing on something. The radio was playing the news. Was she a terrible mother? Rebecca felt, strangely, on the verge of tears.

8

HE WAS TWO. THE CHANGE HAD ACCRUED IN INCREMENTS SO THAT IT was barely noticeable. It was like getting fat, or old, or perhaps all change worked that way. Jacob turned his tiptoed hunch into a proper stride. He forced out syllables, and the adults around him learned to divine their meaning. He was less quick to abandon Priscilla's for Rebecca's arms. This stung but this was what Rebecca wanted. How fortunate to have found someone Jacob loved. It wasn't a competition.

For his entry into the so-called terrible twos, they had Christopher's mother with them. She'd come for Thanksgiving, not a holiday in England, but Elizabeth, widowed now, needed looking after. She was in a subdued state, probably shock though a year had passed, her papery face locked in a bovine expression—and her only son worried. He'd sent the plane ticket. Elizabeth was staying in the guest room at least through the Epiphany. That would be an anniversary only Rebecca noted: the day Priscilla had first arrived at the house on Wisconsin Drive. Rebecca hung framed prints from the Smithsonian in the guest room: a Thiebaud, all those jaunty cakes, as well as a Monet, the lady with the parasol. She bought a clock radio and tuned it to the AM frequency where, in the mornings, you could hear the BBC world service.

That Tuesday, there was grocery shopping to be done, so instead of hurrying to her office—where reading catalogs was less tempting of late; she'd actually been working!—Rebecca lingered in the kitchen making an inventory.

"Time to bundle up." Priscilla was holding the child's sweatshirt open like a chivalrous man with a lady's wrap. The boy darted away from her and she laughed.

"Jacob, put on your sweatshirt." Rebecca's reprimand was never very stern, but it was important to exude authority. "I wonder if the stores are crazy—the holiday and all."

"You should be OK." Priscilla scooped up the laughing child and coaxed his arms into the fleece sleeves. "What are you making?"

"The potatoes. It's not very glamorous, but maybe that's just as well. I need to reserve my energy for someone's birthday party. You'll come, of course?" Rebecca was telling but asking. The party was scheduled for Saturday, despite the fact that after Thanksgiving everyone would be sick of food and one another. "I know it's a holiday. But it wouldn't be the same without you. You should ask Cheryl, too."

Priscilla smiled. Rebecca tried to read something else in it, a tendency she had, perhaps stupid. Sometimes a smile is a smile. She had decided at some point that Priscilla was a mystery to be solved and sometimes found herself choosing to see the mysterious in what was probably not, trying to untangle something that was not knotted. Akin, somehow, to how, in idle hours at that antique desk, she'd search out metaphors for Priscilla's skin color, chocolate/coffee/coconut, all unimaginative at best and offensive at worst, never mind the question of *why* this desire to describe it in the first place. Rebecca knew that it was predictable, that it was *offensive*. With skin, we reach for edibles; they disarm. Black skin called chocolate because the stuff is sweet. Priscilla was sweet, but that was beside the point. Rebecca decided her skin was the color of wet earth, but not mud (ignoble, for wallowing), something elemental, vital.

"Cheryl." Priscilla sounded amused. She handed Jacob a big plastic spoon from the dish rack. He explored it seriously. "I could do that."

"Unless she has to work." Rebecca wanted to give her an option. She finished rinsing the glass in her hands and wiped the marble counter. The advantage was Priscilla's; she had access to almost everything of importance in Rebecca's life. Rebecca was eager—fine, desperate—for some hard facts. That was love, maybe, wanting to know.

"Saturdays she starts at eight. Night shift, double." Priscilla knelt to take the spoon from Jacob, who was near poking himself in the eye. She handed him a book. He put it in his mouth. "But she likes it. She's stubborn. Her own woman, since she was a girl. She used to tell me, *Mommy, go away, I'm playing*."

This made sense to Rebecca; the apple and the tree. Priscilla herself had to have been the same as a child as she was now: placid, unflappable, independent, reassuring. "That sounds punishing. But we would love to have her. You've met my baby, I can't believe I've never met yours." The hard work of being a nurse sounded appealing to Rebecca, the honesty of that long stint, its hard-earned exhaustion. Some nights, Rebecca's mind would spin through the minor events that distinguished that day from the previous, and she would begin to imagine, in horrible, specific detail, the next morning: the warmth of the coffee through the porcelain of the mug, the glide of the drawer as she opened the dishwasher to put away the clean things, the frosty cloud that would spill from the freezer as she chose something for that's night dinner. Then she'd return from this reverie and it would still be night, the morning she'd just lived hours in the future.

"We've all got to work." Priscilla was a realist. "It's as good as anything, I imagine. No job is all fun. Otherwise it wouldn't be a job."

Rebecca wanted to know: What was not fun about Priscilla's job? What could she do to make it more pleasant, for surely its unpleasantness would have to do with her; no one could find fault with Jacob, who was all smiles and soft skin, sweet sounds and glowing eyes, that comforting way he clutched the body of whoever was holding him. *You are loved.* A baby tells you that. That, or *You are needed.*

Saturday was white skies and bad wind. Rebecca's father and mother came with two gifts, beautifully wrapped. Her father was known, in the family, as a particularly skilled gift-wrapper. Judith seemed harried; Steven seemed genially disinterested; and their daughter, Jennifer, was plotting to watch television. Christine and Tim were, perhaps, bickering, though Michelle seemed pleased to join in the general chaos. The doorbell rang while Rebecca was riffling the drawers in search of the birthday candles. She continued searching, knowing someone else would answer it. Moments later, Priscilla stepped into the kitchen. "Rebecca, I want you to meet my daughter."

Cheryl, hesitating at the threshold, looked like Priscilla: broad shoulders, hair worn short, skin the same shade of deep brown, but more lustrous, because of youth and moisturizer. Cheryl wore a long white sweater and fashionable boots.

"Come in, please." Rebecca waved her in like the ground crew does an arriving airplane. "Oh goodness, it's so wonderful to meet you at last." That Priscilla had rung the doorbell struck Rebecca as noteworthy.

"Cheryl." The girl said her own name and held out her

hand, perfunctory but not without warmth. "It's so nice to meet you, thank you for having me."

It was hard not to be struck by familial similarity, especially when you had strong feelings for one of the parties involved. Rebecca considered the outstretched hand. She took her proffered hand, not in the masculine, business-closed manner, but as you would a child's, a parent's. "I feel like I should hug you." She did, felt immediately ridiculous.

Priscilla laughed as she hung her jacket on one of the kitchen chairs. "My goodness." Rebecca always felt that Priscilla was hovering around some form of direct address—ma'am, something—but stopping short of whatever noun she was reaching for. "And where is the birthday boy?"

"He's around here somewhere. Oh, Priscilla, he'll be so excited to see you. His big cousins and you, his favorite people. He's not going to believe his luck."

"I'll go say my hellos then."

"Go, go." Rebecca shooed her away. "Cheryl, keep me company. I need to find these stupid birthday candles. The kind of thing you use twice a year, I can never remember where I stash them." Rebecca could hear the enthusiasm in her voice. She was talking to this woman as though she were a girl, but Cheryl was near her own age. "It's so good to meet you at last. Your mother talks about you all the time."

Cheryl sat down. "Yes, I've heard so much about you. And Jacob, of course."

"Cheryl, we have mineral water, there's grapefruit juice, and I'm going to make a pot of coffee. Or there's tea, if you'd rather. My husband is English; we always have tea."

"Just some water will be fine."

Rebecca handed her a glass, noticed her manicure, nails trimmed short, the color of flamingos. "I love your nails," she said. "I'm glad you were able to come. I know you have work. I don't know how you do it. You're a superhero."

"I have to be in around eight." Cheryl sounded resigned, but also pleased with herself. "Just once a week, it's not bad."

"Well, I'm impressed." Rebecca couldn't imagine it. "Anyway, we have you now, that's what matters."

Cheryl was taking in the yellow kettle, the scarred butcher-block countertop, the ceramic crock stuffed with well-used spoons. "You have a lovely home."

"It's a disaster." It wasn't, though, and Rebecca knew it. She kept an orderly kitchen and her standards, already high, were exacting during her mother-in-law's stay. "But thank you. Do you live in the District?"

"I live with my mother." Cheryl sipped her water. "I thought you knew."

"I didn't." Priscilla lived in Silver Spring, forty minutes by Metro bus. Rebecca couldn't picture the place, didn't know if it was a house, an apartment, a town house. She didn't know if there was a man there. "That must be nice. I bet your mother is a great cook. She's totally spoiled me by making me lunch. Before, I'm embarrassed to say I mostly ate cereal. Now, salads, with tuna, and garbanzo beans, and diced celery. Above and beyond the call of duty, your mother. Jacob adores her. We all do."

Priscilla reentered the kitchen, shaking a little cardboard box of candles. "Look at what I found."

"You're a genius, where were those? I've been in every drawer in the house."

"The sideboard, with the fancy napkins." Priscilla's always-gentle reproof. "Cheryl, come say hello to everyone."

Cheryl smiled at Rebecca and followed her mother into the dining room. Rebecca spooned the coffee into the gold filter, losing count, as she always did.

Jacob could relish the gifts but not unwrap them. Priscilla assisted in this task while Rebecca took photographs. Christopher sat beside his mother and shared the occasional chuckle. Lorraine and Greg watched appreciatively, Steven wandered into the next room to watch television, the ambient roar of a crowd at a sporting event. The boy's aunts sipped chardonnay and applauded at every present that was revealed—now a wooden truck, now a Dr. Seuss book, now a plastic doctor's kit.

After the bounty had been revealed, the kids ate cupcakes and ran in and out of rooms, bumping into things; the adults drank coffee and talked about Paul Simon, the senator not the singer, though inevitably talk of the one led to talk of the other. Jacob, practically vibrating with energy, fidgeted on Rebecca's lap, then fell asleep.

"I'll take him." Priscilla lifted the boy's hot, sticky body off Rebecca's.

"You don't have to." Rebecca's protest was halfhearted. It was tiring, Thanksgiving and beyond, especially when you added into that having a guest. Under normal circumstances, home would be a respite from the holiday's itinerary: slip off shoes, bra, watch; turn on the television, drink some wine, pick at leftovers; shower for too long, slip into bed naked and still damp, wait for Christopher, his attentive tongue at her ear, and now that they were his alone, again, her breasts. But his mother lingered. They slept beside each other mostly chaste as pensioners, though one night Christopher had quietly eased himself on top of her, into her, stifling his heavy breath with the percale sham. Elizabeth seemed to know it (guests know it) and was quiet to the point of mousiness; she tarried in her room with a cup of tea in the morning. She seemed amused, but only vaguely so, by the sight of Jacob fiddling with his breakfast. Some days, Elizabeth explored—she was spry enough to be sent off to Dumbarton Oaks with a bus map and bottle of

Evian—but other days she sat and read until Christopher hurried home at six. Those days, Rebecca was unable to work. Jacob would be asleep, Elizabeth would be paging patiently through *The New Yorker*, Priscilla would be eating canned minestrone, her pencil scratching as she did the crossword, but to Rebecca it was a cacophony, the accrued sounds of all these people existing at one time. She missed the harmony of her days with Priscilla and Jacob, and wished Elizabeth away, and hated herself for it. An old widow deserved pity.

Priscilla, efficient, was back in time to hear Christopher assert that Bush would be the first vice president in a century and a half to get the promotion. Priscilla put one discarded cup inside another—Judith and Steven had left; Christine and Tim had left; they were, frankly, tired of one another—then, thinking the better of it, sat. "The governor, Dukakis," Priscilla said. "He seems like a good man."

"Quite so." Christopher peeled the sticky paper from the base of a cupcake. "You're right, Priscilla. He's a decent sort, which is why it probably won't be him, in the end. I don't know how much decency matters in politics now."

"The cupcakes turned out well, didn't they?" Rebecca took one, had already had one, but what did it matter. She wanted to savor the day's success, and she wanted everyone to leave her alone. "I've had too many already."

"The children loved them." Priscilla was piling dirty napkins one atop the other. "I ate two, too, so go ahead, Rebecca."

"Leave it." Rebecca was scolding, but kindly. "You've been running after the children all afternoon, and it's supposed to be a party."

"The kids certainly had a nice time." Lorraine had more to say. "But the way Jennifer is with the television. It can't be healthy. It's just because Steven won't allow it at home. Whatever is forbidden takes on this terrible allure for kids."

Greg shook his head. "Well, never mind."

"Don't think she didn't notice her dad was in there watching the thing. I mean, talk about setting an example." Lorraine fixed her eyes on Cheryl.

Cheryl sipped her tea and said nothing.

Rebecca felt a pang of something for her ever-disappointed mother. She knew she ought to clear the table, knew the afternoon had come to its conclusion, knew Cheryl had to go to work, knew Priscilla wasn't being paid to keep them company, knew Christopher would be crabby if he didn't have time to read the newspaper and smoke a cigarette, knew Elizabeth needed a lie-down for an hour, then a cup of tea, and knew that for that hour that Elizabeth's nap and Jacob's nap overlapped, the house would be deliciously hers again.

Priscilla seemed to sense, too, that the spell had been broken, and she pushed away from the table, and Rebecca did not object when she began to clear.

"You can take this, dear." Elizabeth placed the gilt-lipped china cup onto its companion saucer and slid them in Priscilla's general direction.

"I'll do that." Rebecca plucked the cup up, milky tea splashing as she did.

They were at home in the kitchen, she and Priscilla, and circled the room in a practiced choreography, Priscilla scraping scraps into the garbage disposal before placing the plates into the dishwasher, Rebecca tossing the blue napkins that had been twisted into sticky balls into the trash.

Rebecca's ears were hot and her throat dry; she was angry. She wanted to offer some explanation for Elizabeth's rudeness, but the slight was too great, and it was not hers. Priscilla herself seemed much the same as she always did: unfathomable, maybe even happy. Rebecca worried about her tendency to think of Priscilla as some impossible-to-solve mystery: at worst, it was some misguided sense that her blackness rendered her other, instead of human. Less bad but still troubling was the possibility that Rebecca simply didn't understand other people that well, in which case, what did that say about her work, never mind the entirety of her life?

In the end, Rebecca said nothing, because she couldn't think how to tender an apology she was sure Elizabeth would not have offered. She began to watch more closely. Elizabeth would leave her empty cup on the table beside her favored chair in the living room. Naturally, it wouldn't stay there long; Priscilla would ferry it to the kitchen, where it belonged. Elizabeth would hold hands outstretched to receive the baby, but in a particular way—gripping the baby under his armpits, as you might lift a puppy from his mother's teat—that limited her contact with Priscilla's body. Or so Rebecca thought. She noted the odd triangulation of the conversation; Rebecca might begin with a general observation, Elizabeth would respond to her, specifically, sometimes even using her name, for emphasis, while Priscilla took it in, rarely interjecting.

Rebecca could not talk to Elizabeth, certainly not to rebuke her. The law made her a daughter to Elizabeth, but Rebecca was not the sort of daughter to speak directly even to her own mother.

At some point toward the end of December, Elizabeth began to wander, over dinner. Perhaps it was the wine.

"You remember we had a nurse?" Elizabeth studied her only son from across the table. "When you were small. So small, I wonder when memory actually begins. It seems to be different, for different people, though I think sometimes people lie."

"A nurse?" Christopher chewed. "I'm not sure I do remember. I recall wanting a dog." He grinned at his wife. "We had cats. Terrible things that ignored me utterly."

"I've a friend who swears she remembers her nursery, seen through the bars of her crib." Elizabeth's smile was near a grimace. "It can't be possible. I myself can barely remember last year. Maybe it was the shock of losing your father."

"A nurse." Christopher again, this time not a question but the beginning of a reminiscence, though it could have been an act. He was dutiful. "Vaguely. Maybe."

"A sweet girl. Catherine, or Charlotte. Or. Something with a C. No, Charlotte was your father's cousin. You wouldn't remember, she died when you were small. Catherine. Or Kate." Elizabeth swirled the wine in her glass, which made her look villainous, but also made her look small, elderly, frail, regretful.

"It's good to have help, when they're young." Rebecca intended a barb: Elizabeth had never had a *career*. Rebecca needed help because she had things to do. If she'd been a painter, or a sculptor, or an engineer, or a composer, this would have been a given. You need to stretch canvases, mix clay, sketch plans, feel out notes on a piano. Poets did the same stuff, but no one saw. What had she done, Elizabeth; whatever well-bred London wives did during the day. Rebecca kept going into that office. It had been only pretend, initially, then it had become something else. Rebecca made herself a poet the only way she knew how: by being one.

"I've noticed your girl sits with you. When you're having your lunch." Elizabeth's smile was inscrutable. "That wouldn't have been done, in my day."

"A lot of things wouldn't have." Rebecca looked at the napkin on her lap.

"Times have changed." Christopher, the diplomat, sounded as though this was both a good thing and something to lament. "And of course, America is its own place, Mum."

"They certainly have." Elizabeth smiled. "And it certainly is. America. I'll never get used to it, myself. Christopher, I don't know how you do it. I couldn't imagine coming in from a walk and finding a servant napping, as an example."

"Priscilla isn't a servant." Rebecca was understated. Dramatic flourish never seemed wise in hindsight, however tempting. "She's not a servant," she said again.

"Oh, yes, I've noticed." Elizabeth sliced into her chicken. "This is quite good."

"Priscilla is . . ." Rebecca wasn't sure how she was going to finish the sentence. Christopher changed the subject. Two weeks later, Elizabeth went back to London.

9

FROM THE KITCHEN SINK, YOU COULD SEE OUTSIDE. WINTER, HANDS warm and soapy, Rebecca could watch the snow collect on the deck, and in the summer she could see this: Priscilla, the plastic swimming pool slack between her legs, the woman and her summertime brownness, the Adirondack chairs and their seashore whitewash, and Jacob, pink as a koi, urgent and nude, a child's impatient calisthenics. It was beastly hot outside but Christopher set the thermostat so low she kept a scratchy shawl (a gift from him; his work entailed the occasional trek to Islamabad) flung over her chair. She was taken in by the sight of the boy, her flesh remade into that bulge of tummy, the swell of his bottom. He was young, still, so she knew, over time, it would fade, this sense of awe at his physical being, his astonishing beauty, the simple fact that he'd been made of her body. Love faded, that was its nature, but the half-life of maternal love was an eternity compared to anything else Rebecca knew.

She needed to shower, needed to dress, needed to be ready because Christopher needed her, but Rebecca slid the glass door open and stepped into the evening, which shimmered with heat.

"This darn pool." Priscilla puffed. "It'll be worth it."

The grass felt damp under her bare feet. "It makes me wish we had a real pool. I'd get in." The money would not be an issue, but it was dangerous, Jacob was still so young.

"You should be going." Priscilla put the pool on the ground and twisted the nozzle on the hose.

Jacob squealed, satisfied, and stepped into the pool, unable to wait, scooting his bottom around on the damp plastic.

"Careful." Rebecca handed the boy a toy truck. "I should."

She did not move, though. Somehow the thought of putting makeup on made her feel tired. "I don't want to go." Maybe it was an off-the-cuff admission, or maybe Rebecca was trying to bait Priscilla, wanted an invitation to unburden herself.

"I have something I need to tell you." It was probably impossible to say such a thing and not sound strained.

"What is it?" Rebecca paused. "You're not quitting?" There was always that chance. Only weeks ago, Cheryl had married. Ian was a salesman at a luxury car dealership: midlife crises and year-end bonuses. Christopher had been pleased to learn about Ian and had months ago bought from him a navy blue BMW; Rebecca had been pleased to learn about Ian and had sent the couple two hundred dollars as a wedding present. Rebecca knew that Cheryl was pregnant, and Rebecca worried that Priscilla would want to give up work to be a full-time grandmother.

"I'm not quitting." Priscilla was as serious as she was capable of being, or as she'd ever been, with Rebecca. Their intimacy was lived, not spoken. Almost actual friendship, though what of the neat stack of twenty-dollar bills Rebecca left on the demilune in the foyer every Friday afternoon? "I am pregnant."

The pool had filled an inch, two, three. Jacob pushed at the water with his palm, examined the spouting hose. Rebecca lifted it out, twisted the nozzle, and the yard was quiet. There was that metal in the mouth: adrenaline. She couldn't say why this was her response. Priscilla's body looked the same, that familiar soft hardness, that compact power, that unfussy grace. Priscilla's femininity was more like utility. She was able to do so much, even inflating that stupid pool. "You're pregnant!" Rebecca forced in a note of joy, because that was warranted.

Priscilla laughed, nerves not humor. "I didn't think it was possible, but seems like it is." She waved her hands at her side, brought them up to rest on her belly.

"But . . ." Rebecca couldn't ask the question she wanted to, and let the conjunction hang. But: you're old/you're not married/you're forty-two or forty-three/you work for me/ what about Jacob/what about us/what about Cheryl. That last was the way to go. "Cheryl."

Priscilla's abashed smile said that she knew the absurdity of the situation. "She's going to have a brother, I guess. And he's going to have a niece or nephew."

Rebecca felt joy, more real, now. She took Priscilla's hand, which did not seem any bigger. During her pregnancy, her hands had swelled. "Congratulations."

"Don't sound so final about it." Priscilla said. "I'm not going anywhere."

"We'll figure things out." A vision of Jacob and a new baby, then the same age, by some magic, best friends, black limbs and white limbs splashing in that very pool while she and Priscilla looked on. A fantasy, that was all.

She kissed her son and went inside and showered. Christopher came home and they drove to Great Falls in the BMW he'd bought from Priscilla's son-in-law.

"I have some news." She wasn't sure how to frame it, but he needed to know.

"What's that?"

"Priscilla is pregnant."

Christopher let out an impressed whistle. "That's something."

"Isn't it?"

"Medical marvel, I rather think. But good for her." Christopher chuckled. "I didn't know she had a—well, is she married? I don't know, I guess?"

"You'd know if she was *married*." Rebecca was not sure that he would, though.

"I thought I knew that she wasn't. But—well, the one doesn't have to do with the other, I suppose. She's happy about it?"

Rebecca thought she'd seen in the woman a shadow of worry, but she nodded.

"Jim and his wife, they used a service to find their nanny. We can ask Molly tonight. I remember him saying they liked her."

"What do you mean?"

"They pay her on the books. He takes the long view. You can't say Jim's not confident. In his imagination, a decade from now he's the attorney general. What does Molly do? I can't remember."

Rebecca couldn't picture Molly—she got as far as brown hair, lots of turtlenecks. "I don't know."

"I have the strangest feeling that she has something to do with BCCI. I heard the name *Molly* and it must be the same Molly. It has to be. I forgot that she was an analyst—you remember, she was so hugely pregnant when we first met them."

Rebecca had a vague memory, Molly, majestic, mammary, forgotten because other people did not interest her, and somehow in the years they'd been together Christopher had not realized this. "Priscilla is pregnant, but she's not quitting."

Christopher glanced at her, then back at the road. "What?" He frowned. "What was the exit again?"

Rebecca consulted the directions she'd scrawled on an envelope. "Forty-four. And just to clarify, we won't need a service. Priscilla is pregnant, but she's not quitting."

"Don't be ridiculous, Rebecca. The woman's going to have a baby of her own and then come over every day and look after our baby?"

"We haven't got that far yet."

"Keep your eyes open for that liquor store—there's one just as we get off."

"I just wish you wouldn't imply that we need to replace Priscilla."

"Why are we still talking about this, Rebecca?"

"You're the one who said we should talk to Molly about her nanny service."

"You're the one who said our nanny is fucking pregnant."

"But that doesn't mean—"

"I can't tell you how uninteresting I find this as a topic of conversation."

Rebecca looked out of the window. "Well, that's too bad. Because it interests me. Priscilla is—I mean, because of her—" She'd just finished it. A book! It was the promise she'd made herself, so many years before. It was a bit late but it was there nonetheless, unruly stack on her desk.

"I know that for some reason you've decided you *owe* this woman your every success. As if I haven't been paying her, week after week. A small fortune."

"For your son. Not that it matters. You told me to hire her! You told me it was a good idea, to return to my work."

"And it was, wasn't it? Not that I need any thanks."

"I'm sorry. I'm just—it's sensitive. You don't know. You're out of the house, at the office, but I need things to run *smoothly,* and Priscilla has brought order to everything. And I like her, is that wrong, that I like being around her, that I feel better?"

"I think you're being naive. If you think that her having a baby won't make things more complex for her. Just as it did for you."

"She won't leave us. I'm sure of it. We'll work something out."

"You're an optimist, then, Rebecca? After all your poems about Orpheus looking back to hell."

"Hades isn't hell. There's the liquor store." She pointed out the window, and he slowed the car. They never rightly determined, that night, whether she was an optimist or he a pessimist. They bought two bottles of rosé. Christopher spent much of the night talking to Molly, who was the analyst Molly he had heard tell of, while Rebecca looked at their ugly abstract paintings and made immediately forgotten small talk. Then they drove in not exactly companionable silence to their own home, which was so cold, the air-conditioning humming the way a heart beats, ceaselessly, reliably.

10

THANKSGIVING THAT YEAR WAS A CATERED AFFAIR AT JUDITH AND Steven's baronial table, a crew of smooth-cheeked boys in black button-down shirts called in for the night. Rebecca slipped each a twenty-dollar bill—surely their mothers missed them. The day coincided with Jacob's birthday, so that was put off to Saturday, and after all this *together,* the clan went their separate ways. One of those Sundays: knocking against one another in the confines of the cold house, tripping up and down stairs, listening to *A Prairie Home Companion,* brewing pots of tea, eating snacks they didn't want, switching on the television, taking an early bath, changing the bed linens, making a grocery list, until Cheryl telephoned.

For a moment, Rebecca didn't know who Cheryl was. The emergency in her voice was explanatory. Christopher was adept enough at the bath and bedtime rituals, so Rebecca pulled on a sweater and drove to the hospital. Unsure what else she might offer Cheryl, Rebecca brought a sandwich, made of leftover, joyous turkey.

Cheryl should have been beatific, with all that pregnant fat. She looked stoic. But she was a nurse: she'd seen it all. *We're doing our best for her,* everyone kept saying, and it seemed to Rebecca to be true; this was Cheryl's hospital, this had been Priscilla's workplace. Special treatment! Rebecca squeezed Cheryl's dry hand. This was where Jacob was born, surely nothing bad could happen here.

They looked in the nursery window, because who could resist? Tiny, uncanny creatures in every hue: peach, salmon, mustard, cocoa. Looking at the babies made Rebecca hungry, a desire to eat that was maybe a desire to survive. *Wake up wake up,* she said to herself, the most common prayer, though on some level, Rebecca knew Priscilla would not. A woman of forty-three flying close to the sun on wings of wax, and the world a placid pastoral, barely registering her fall to sea. Rebecca was *mad at* her: Priscilla had tempted fate. She should never have had this child, but there he was, and he was a love.

"There's nothing to say." Cheryl seemed to sense Rebecca's desire to say something.

Rebecca turned to her left, took Cheryl's chin in her hand, and eased the woman's head onto her own shoulder, and Cheryl was made a girl again. "I brought you a sandwich," Rebecca said. They sat beside each other, then Cheryl was called away, and when she came back, it was to tell Rebecca that Priscilla was dead.

The only telephone call they might have made was to Ian, who had only just left them, because it was late, and he had to work in the morning. "Let him be." Cheryl held up a hand and Rebecca thought of Diana Ross, stopping someone in the name of love. It was an absurd thing to think, but it was an absurd situation.

Cheryl wept, brief, dignified tears. She shook her head to dispel them. "You should go."

They sat in the cafeteria with waxed paper cups of tea and

jelly doughnuts. Rebecca, never knowing what to do, had decided to buy something. "Your brother is beautiful." They had taken turns holding him. The nurse had urged it but they both knew: the baby needed to be touched, a human needed to be touched.

Cheryl took a bite of her pastry. "He is."

Rebecca considered her doughnut, its rich gut of red. "How are you feeling?" She meant not the situation, but the pregnancy. How they felt about the situation was clear. "You sure you don't want me to phone Ian?"

She shook her head. "There's no point ruining his night's sleep." Cheryl's strong jaw (it was her mother's strong jaw) made her look some mixture of resolute and resigned, the sort of woman depicted in art from the era of the Great Depression. "I know him. He'll be up at five. He'll come here before work."

"You're sure?"

"She'll still be dead tomorrow morning."

Rebecca was not offended. Of course Cheryl had earned the right to snap. "Maybe you should come home with me. You don't need to stay here."

"I know that." Cheryl took another bite. "I'm going to stay here. Thank you."

Rebecca tried a different approach. "Cheryl, when are you due?" She pantomimed a hand over her belly. No matter what, the cells kept dividing. A baby (life!) was the only force as unstoppable as death.

"Two weeks, give or take." Cheryl was massive with it. "She's moving all day. Seems like she never sleeps. Rebecca. I can't do it." Just a whisper.

"Never mind, now." Rebecca offered her hand. She was not sure that Cheryl liked her. It seemed fairly clear that Cheryl was *unimpressed* by her.

"When, then?" Cheryl pushed away the food. "Shit." This came out as a whisper, a reasoned judgment rather than impassioned utterance.

"I'm so sorry." The tears welled up in Rebecca's eyes. She blinked them back, because they felt theatrical.

"I'm going to have a baby. What am I going to do—with my brother?"

There would be others, besides Ian, to come tomorrow and be with Cheryl, friends, colleagues, peers, intimates Rebecca could not guess at, like the man who was the father of that small baby with hair like a lamb and skin like a hazelnut. Rebecca imagined them, a loving group, passing the baby like a baton. "Don't worry about that now." Rebecca hoped her charade of nonchalance would be reassuring instead of maddening.

Cheryl took her hand.

"But when?" She was so calm. "When should I worry about it?"

"It'll be fine." Some of life's situations—what else was there to say? You had to believe the *deus* would emerge from the *machina* or you had nothing.

"I wish I had that sense that the world is going to work out fine in the end. I've never seen that happen." Cheryl released Rebecca's hand.

Rebecca chose to hear this as a comment on the scenario, not personal insult. But maybe that would have been right, too. Maybe Rebecca's life was charmed, as Diana's was charmed; maybe some lives contained nothing more to worry about than being wed and bred and having perfectly set hair while other lives brought you here, to the hospital. Maybe Rebecca had only platitude because Rebecca had never had a problem. "You're going to have a baby. It's a happiness that'll make you feel like everything in the world is just as it should be."

"This was not how it was supposed to be—" Cheryl was angry. "Fate is the laziest way to explain terrible things."

"I'm sorry." Why did Rebecca feel at fault and why did she think she could fix everything? "Why don't I take him home?"

Cheryl laughed. "Why don't you what?"

"I could." It seemed, suddenly, quite clear, that Rebecca could be that *deus*. "He needs to be fed, and rocked, and looked after. He needs to be kissed, and sung to, and bathed. I know how to do all that."

"He's my brother. It's my—responsibility."

Speech and thought moved at different speeds. "Cheryl, it's not that you can't do it, it's that—I'm right here. We have a crib. It's not even an imposition."

"So what, you'd just take him home?"

"Let us help." She waited. "At least for now. We'll talk about later—later."

"I don't want to be someone who needs help." Cheryl frowned. "But maybe I am."

Two days later, after some cajoling, Auntie Christine came to the house on Wisconsin Drive bearing a bucket of chicken, a rented videocassette, and cousin Michelle, whom Jacob always enjoyed seeing. Rebecca found the infant seat in the basement and buckled it into the car. She found Jacob's old bassinet, Jacob's old blankets, Jacob's old onesies, and washed these, folded them neatly, piles of white cotton, smelling of nothing. The children watched *The Muppet Movie* and Rebecca drove to the hospital, "The Rainbow Connection" echoing in her head. She disliked the Muppets, all their earnest, homespun pathos. She brought the baby home. His hair was soft, his skin mottled. He rarely opened his eyes, and his mouth was a displeased frown. He was perfect. His name was Andrew.

PART TWO

11

SHE PUT THE BASSINET IN THE SAME SPOT AS BEFORE. IT WAS ALL SO familiar and yet all so different, governed by the logic of a dream, the sort that seems like it might be recurring, but how can you tell because it's a dream? Though she thought of Jacob as *baby* this was an actual baby. He fussed and she picked him up. It was all rote, required no thought; she lifted him to her, both hands, his little body slack as a cub's in the mouth of a lioness.

Downstairs, she filled the bottle from the pitcher of filtered water. You had to do that first, so the volume was correct. She added the scoop of powder, which crunched like snow and smelled like metal. She shook it but let it sit, because you had to, or the baby got gas.

"'What good is sitting alone in your room?'" She sang, because a baby liked to be sung to, she remembered that, even if it had been three years. "But you can't sit, can you? Can you?" You had to talk to babies. They said that a child had to reach school age having heard a million words. This was part of the responsibility she'd taken on, part of the favor she was doing. "'Come hear the music play!'"

Andrew yawned, then his tongue slipped from his mouth. She knew, somehow, that he was hungry, an intelligence she was surprised she still retained. Rebecca sat at the table and held the bottle, and Andrew drank.

She had always imagined another baby, that's why she'd saved those darling, monastic garments, so soft and white. Princess Diana had done it twice but she'd done it for the kingdom. Rebecca just wanted it for Jacob. Having a sibling gave you the temporary illusion that you weren't alone in the world. "We're not alone in the world," she whispered, six more words on their way to that million. The sound of his drinking was surprisingly loud.

The marble counter was cluttered: the glass lids of pots, the ossified twist of a tea bag, a dirty bowl and spoon. Rebecca had always planned on a plan, not this—instant infant. It was like something from myth, like she'd crept up some sacred mountain and spirited him away, a baby touched by God but also cursed, so that the rest of her life dissolved into disorder. Well, he was very cute.

"You're all done! Already!" The baby looked stunned, more often than not; perhaps as he should, the world was a stunning place. She lifted him to her shoulder and rubbed her hand in circles along his back. Her milk was gone, but Rebecca could sense the machinery of her breast at work, like dormant gas lines in the ceilings of turn-of-the-century homes; a sense of dampness, the itch in an amputated limb. He belched, quite loud, and she laughed. She lifted him from her shoulder and studied his face. His eyes could not focus, rolled about seeking a direction like the needle in a compass.

She heard feet falling, heard the television switch on. They'd decided a bit of *Sesame Street* was not so bad, that Jacob deserved a concession. Andrew was like a surprise party that none of them could leave; the day he'd arrived, Jacob, defiant, stood behind the living room curtains and shit his pants. Rebecca had put the baby down, stripped Jacob nude, thrown the soiled underpants into the garbage can. She'd started saying *I love you* more than usual, and there was a *still* implicit in it.

Christopher came into the room. He was tall, slightly stooped, and somehow avian, like a stork, graceful even though its legs bend backward. He was not frowning but she knew that he was not happy. "We're awake."

It was not so early; it was nearly six. "Yes. We're awake." Rebecca kissed Andrew's prominent forehead, which was made the more so by his hesitant hairline, foreshadowing the middle-aged man he'd be.

Christopher began to peel a banana. "I'm letting him watch *Sesame Street*."

"Fine." Rebecca didn't want to hear more about what she knew Christopher was getting at, that *I*.

He delivered the banana, returned, and switched on the electric kettle. "So."

"It's a mess in here, I know that's what you're thinking. I'm going to ask Marie to come Mondays *and* Thursdays. Don't you think? And maybe she can help with the laundry." The laundry was relentless. If one baby was a balancing act, two was a war.

"So. What's the plan here, really?" Christopher filled his mug.

"The plan?" She hadn't, technically, consulted him, before making her offer to Cheryl. This was a mistake, Rebecca knew, but sometimes you made a mistake and just had to forge ahead.

"I know this seemed the right thing to do." He fiddled with his hand like he was physically looking for the right word. "But it's an extraordinary situation."

The day beyond the windows looked bright and clear, and

she wished to throw them open, let in the frigid December air, let it cleanse the house, let it rouse her into true wakefulness. Rebecca stood and bounced, because babies like it when you bounce. She pulled Andrew close, proximity approximating what—pregnancy? She had to give him more than that million words; she had to give him *love*.

"Rebecca." Christopher hesitated. He sat. "Sit."

"I can't sit." She began to laugh. "Sit. Like a dog? Don't tell me to sit."

"I'm asking—"

"I can't stand it. Get it? Stand. Sit." She laughed joylessly, but then it began to seem truly funny and she laughed sincerely. From the next room, she could hear the jaunty music from Jacob's show, and this seemed appropriate. "Should I call Cheryl and say, *Oops never mind here's your brother back?*"

"No one is saying that."

"She *just* had a baby, Christopher. This is the least I can do." Rebecca had gone to see Cheryl and Ian and the baby they had named Ivy. Vague grief had blunted the sharp joy they should have been feeling. The celebration was muted. Rebecca had taken balloons. They seemed ridiculous instead of festive, a taunt.

"I was as fond of Priscilla as anyone." The verb tense was disarming. "But this is—it's too great. To ask."

When Rebecca had imagined their second child, she'd imagined Priscilla. It was only now, truly without Priscilla, that Rebecca understood. The crumby plate on the side table and the Legos on the floor, the misplaced dish sponge and the expired lightbulb in the foyer, the wooden train and the balled-up tissue and the unfolded blankets and the need for butter and the discarded rubber band from the weekend's newspaper on the kitchen floor, yes, all of that, plus Jacob and everything he needed, plus Rebecca's work, to whatever extent that mattered. Priscilla stood between chaos and the rest of them. A little mess didn't matter, but Priscilla was *order*. You couldn't get through life if there was no logic to it, and there was no logic in any of this. "No one *asked*. I offered. Think of what she did for us."

"You meant well. You meant a kindness." He was gentle.

"I didn't know what else to do. I didn't know what else to do." Rebecca had never felt more honest.

"But, Rebecca. What's the . . . ?"

"God laughs, remember? Plans make God laugh hysterically." She had sketched a plan, though, she and Cheryl. *A few weeks,* they'd said. Babies changed a great deal within a matter of *a few weeks.* Priscilla herself had made those first *few weeks* so much easier for Rebecca, now it was her chance to do the same for Cheryl.

"Perhaps I should talk to Ian. Man to man. Find an arrangement."

"Man to man!" Rebecca chuckled. "We're not making a *deal,* Christopher. It's a baby, not a—" She faltered, not knowing any nouns relevant to his work. "He's a person."

"I just meant that perhaps he and I could speak frankly. Put aside some of the emotion."

"I am too tired to laugh as hard as I should be laughing right now."

Her husband liked a tidy room. He liked a tidy life. "It's a terrible situation, but it's not our terrible situation." Christopher was doing his best; his best was *reasonable.* "We can help, certainly. It would be a bit like having twins, I expect? Twice as much work, and expense, but people survive that."

"You want to—give them a check?"

"I'm just thinking out loud."

"Jesus Christ." She squeezed the baby closer. He was too young to protest this.

"We could send them her wages. Priscilla's. On a weekly basis, for some period—"

"This is a horrible idea and an unbelievable insult."

"It's testament to how highly we think of them, of Priscilla. But life has to go on, Rebecca, and I don't think it can go on like this."

"You're missing what you had. The ordered life. The happy wife. Don't you see—we had that because of Priscilla?" This was a debt owed.

"So, how does this end?"

The anger or irritation or whatever it was she was most feeling dissipated as the baby dozed in her arms. The day was filled with these moments of respite and you had to seize them, because they were brief. She understood what Christopher was asking, and understood that it was reasonable to ask, and that it was unreasonable that she had no answer save the one she offered. "I don't know."

They were silent and then, like an actor late on his cue, Jacob called out. "Mommy! Mommy! Daddy! Mommy!"

Rebecca left the baby in her husband's hands, even though he had to be at work, and went to see what it was Jacob needed of her.

12

THIS HAD ONCE BEEN HER FAVORITE PLACE. THE SOUND WAS AS transporting as one of the popular songs of one's youth: the chorus of human noise over the steady canned music with the flourish of the fountain's plash echoing back from the soaring ceilings. The smell was cinnamon from something baking and the bouquet of all those cosmetics and that odd chemical newness of merchandise. The wide marble hallways were meant to conjure great urban boulevards and were lined with glass façades displaying the artful or the alluring. Those first few months with Christopher, Rebecca discovered that the diplomat's consort required certain things that the nursery school teacher's assistant did not possess. Silk dresses, shoes with a heel, smart handbags, that Paloma Picasso perfume in a bottle the shape of an eye, the occasional, modest piece of real jewelry. So she'd gone to the mall. She'd spent a small fortune, which was all she had, but Rebecca, at twenty-nine, had lived at home, and her parents did not ask for rent.

White Flint Mall for a White Christmas. There was desultory snow, dry and halfhearted, but Jacob was old enough to understand Santa and the notion that it was better to give than to receive. Christopher took the boy to I. Magnin and Rebecca sat in the food hall, Andrew nuzzled against her chest, hot and sleepy. She had a cup of tea and a copy of the *Indiana Review* that she'd been waiting for even if rereading her poems was like prodding a cut to marvel at the pain. It was nice to see her name in print but she wanted to make art with meaning and just kept coming up with this? Still, she flipped to the little paragraph at the back and relished the biographical notice: *Rebecca Stone is the winner of the 1988 Yale Younger Poets Prize*. She was thirty-three but in Yale's estimation that was young enough.

She remembered well the day she'd received the fat envelope from New Haven. She'd stopped work early, retreated to the kitchen, singing along to Liza Minnelli, marveling at that voice. Was that genetic inheritance? Did it matter who your mother was? Her happiness contained no embarrassment.

"You're in a good mood!" Priscilla had laughed; even Jacob had laughed.

Rebecca explained why, then took down the bottle they'd opened with the previous night's dinner. Priscilla sat and Rebecca poured and the boy played at their feet and by some magic (in vino veritas!) they pushed past small talk and into something else and Priscilla told Rebecca the story of her own mother.

"It was a long time ago." Priscilla had tried to explain it but not to excuse it. "Cheryl's twenty-five. It was twenty-five years ago. I was seventeen, was all. My mother wanted something different for me."

Since the woman's death Rebecca had been waiting for epiphany. She had only this: that without Priscilla, she didn't have a person in whom to confide her sadness about Priscilla's death. That was quite stupid, or something like a koan. Rebecca reached for her tea, careful not to spook the sleeping baby. Was *spook* racist when a verb as it was when a noun?

That day, Priscilla had told Rebecca about the girl she'd once been. "I worked so hard at it. My mother, what she was saying, is that I was supposed to be *better*. So I made myself better. It's hard enough when you're a woman. When you're a black woman, the world says you're not good, be better. And my mother *believed* it. She should have protected me."

Rebecca at seventeen had been patchwork jeans and Judith's hand-me-down *Bell Jar*, chemistry class and a strong feeling about Duane Allman. Priscilla at seventeen had been alone with a baby. Priscilla at forty-two or forty-three had had another baby and what remained unknown was what Rebecca at forty-two or forty-three would be. Rebecca gently tipped the child's head to the side, but his eyes remained closed, his breathing steady.

She had never thought that she'd *win* the prize. She only sent in the manuscript because James Merrill was the judge. She thought he might understand her work, and she'd been right. But now that work belonged to the *before*. This was now and Rebecca should get up, throw away her tea, walk down the hall toward the department store, but the days had been quite awful and just to sit felt like an achievement. Jacob's voice had a new, jarring note of complaint in it. Winter was so indifferent, cold at midday and dark shortly thereafter, and Rebecca was supposed to decorate a tree and buy presents and devise activities and make bottles and wipe bottoms and cook dinners. Christopher, worn down at last by her jokes (*death by a thousand Cuts*), was trying to swear off the Silk Cuts.

"My mother, she took the moral view. It was immoral, you see?" Priscilla had said. So what was moral, and how would you know it? Maybe Merrill was right and Rebecca should push the plastic lid of the teacup across the laminated table, near enough a Ouija. Failing that: Should she ask the woman walking past with her shopping bags, the man playing "Santa

Claus Is Coming to Town" on the white lacquered piano, her mother, her sisters, her husband, her son, James Merrill himself, Diana, Princess of Wales, Yale University Press? The baby strapped to Rebecca's chest had been left alone and this felt like a test.

There was no sense, there inside the huge building, of the world outside. It was all simulacrum, an arcade as Arcadia, far removed from the dry snow, the white sky, the winter's insistence. She put the *Indiana Review* back into her bag and threw away her unfinished tea. At the end of the corridor, she could pick out Christopher and Jacob, hand in hand, then not, as the boy rushed toward her. Had she really spent so much time there once? Had her principal preoccupation been dressing for a garden party at the embassy?

"Mommy, Mommy, we bought you a present."

That high girlish voice broke your heart. Rebecca regretted having found Jacob unpleasant the past couple of weeks. Wasn't it to be expected? "Did you? I'm so excited." She kept one hand against the baby's head, and with the other, stroked the boy's soft hair. Her body had beaten her mind to the realization that she could do this, be mother to them both, at the same time.

"It's a scarf."

"Don't tell!" Christopher swung the pin-striped shopping bag.

"Can we get a cookie? Daddy said we could get a cookie."

"Guilty. I did say that." Christopher smiled. "Did you have a bit of a rest?"

Maybe the holiday spirit had defeated his need for nicotine? "I did, thanks. Just sat and had a cup of tea and thought about nothing." This was a lie, but sometimes you had to lie. The family turned around and went back toward the food hall, for the promised cookie.

13

IT WOULD BE GOOD, IAN HAD SUGGESTED, TO GET THE BABIES TO-gether. *Good*. Rebecca was interested in doing what was good, even if it was a nuisance to stuff the boys into their winter gear and into the car. It was hard to buckle the car seat's straps over the bulge of the infant snowsuit.

Cheryl and Ian's house was suffused with silence. Child care's industry was best conducted in meditative quiet, amid the smells of talcum and soap. Rebecca curled into the crinkling leather sofa, pulling her stockinged feet up beneath her. Jacob was breaking the spell, playing a noisy game of truck. He did that: prone, cheek to the carpet, *vrooming* an incantation. Ian, patient Ian, on his day off, packed the big boy into the car and drove to the lot where he spent forty hours a week, with the promise that Jacob could sit inside lots of different, brand-new vehicles. Rebecca handed Andrew to his sister, and Cheryl handed Ivy to her. It was like a minuet or some other old-fashioned dance routine.

"He's doing well. Great, actually." For some reason, Rebecca was whispering. "We had to bump him up to four ounces. He would finish the three and still be pulling at the bottle. And he sleeps. I have to keep him awake to burp. I know he's a baby, but, Cheryl, I swear, he glares at me when I do it. Glares."

Cheryl jostled the baby. He was so fat and imperturbable he practically dared you to. Ivy was only sixteen days his junior but a different kind of baby altogether. Rebecca held on to the little thing, as brown and nervous as a common bird, all bones and heartbeat. "Good. He's pretty damn cute."

"Who could disagree?"

Cheryl yawned. "I knew I would be tired, but I didn't think it would feel this way. I can work a double overnight and still get an IV into a vein, but this is—yesterday, I put the cordless phone in the refrigerator."

Rebecca laughed. Ivy flinched at the sound, and Rebecca held the child closer, rocked in that pilgrim's rhythm that comforted an infant, and Ivy dozed. They slipped so easily from waking to sleep at this age. It made their grasp on life itself seem so tenuous.

"Rebecca." Cheryl held the baby, her brother, up to her mouth and kissed him quietly. "I haven't said thank you."

Rebecca shook her head. "You have. Anyway. You don't have to thank me."

"I do. I haven't, appropriately. Thank you. Thank you for this."

"There's nothing to—"

"But there is." Cheryl's tone was sharp even as her words were not. "Please listen. Accept my thanks for this thing you're doing."

Rebecca was quiet. "You are, of course, very welcome." Cheryl was in a fragile state. She deserved to be listened to.

"I can't imagine the future right now." Cheryl's eyes were dry, but there were tears in her voice. "I'm not sure what to tell you."

Rebecca thought of Priscilla as a teen, severed from her

own mother, then Priscilla as an adult, not quite mourning that mother. She remembered, as how could she not, her first days with Jacob, when she had felt alone in the world but for a woman at the hospital whom she didn't know at all. "We don't have to think about the future at the moment."

Cheryl was determined. "We'll make a timetable. Three months. I know that's a long time. But by three months—"

"Six, even. They're not even truly alive, awake, until then."

"That's June, Rebecca. That's awfully far away."

"I don't want you thinking about timetables. Just concentrate on the matter at hand. On Ivy." She wanted to ask, but somehow could not: How was the breastfeeding, the sleeping, the pain, the blood, the bloom of sadness, the surprise euphoria, the balancing, the business of motherhood? Somehow it was too intimate.

"I'm very lucky." It was true, wasn't it, that even now, with her great bad fortune, that Cheryl was one of the lucky ones? "I know that."

"Just"—Rebecca felt it was simple—"put this out of your mind. Enjoy these moments. I know they're not very enjoyable. But that's what I found—that when I gave in to motherhood I found it a lot simpler. Until you go back to work, until you go back to real life, just let Ivy take over your reality. That's what matters."

"Rebecca, you're an idealist." Cheryl shifted. "Don't think I don't appreciate it. Your optimism. It comes easily, doesn't it? I can't find my way to that. I guess that's why people go to church, huh? To learn that, or to have some reason to feel the way you feel, like everything is just—going to be fine. Would you take him?"

Rebecca reached up and now she was holding both babies. It was surprisingly, strangely, simple. Two arms, two babies. She sank back into the sofa under the insubstantial weight of these two lives. "Maybe that's all I know how to do. Pretend like everything is going to be fine."

Cheryl stretched. "Whatever works. Can I take a shower? Would you mind?"

Rebecca shook her head no. She placed Andrew, asleep, on the sofa beside her, put Ivy, asleep, into the bassinet by the fireplace. Cheryl went to take a shower and Rebecca righted the cushions, tidied the newspaper, loaded the dishwasher. She worked in silence, and it was as though a spell had been cast, the four people gathered under that roof locked in enchantment, a state of suspension.

14

A FEW MORNINGS—FORGIVE HER—REBECCA THOUGHT SHE HEARD Priscilla's happy *Hello* at the appointed hour. Of course she did not. This psychological break was recourse, since prayer was not available to her, but no matter how fervently she wished it Rebecca could not will it to be true. Rebecca gave Andrew his second bottle of the day and the kid was stunned into sleep. She put the bottle on the table beside the rocker and eased him gently into the crib, shushing and shushing as she did. She lingered cribside, her fingers spread wide, the weight of her reassuring hand on his back, and she marked the transition from shallow to deeper breaths, the way his legs folded up under his torso and his bottom lifted to the air. She tiptoed, closed the door quickly because if you did it slowly it would creak, and once in the hallway she realized she had, once again, forgotten the dirty bottle.

In the living room, unattended, Jacob waited. Andrew's naptime meant Jacob's me time. Oh, they had spoiled him with the undivided attention of three adults, and now Jacob was bereft. "Read with me!"

She sat. Reading, fine. It was easier, because the words were within her from so much repetition, and she could lie back, hold the book so he could see the illustrations, and mumble through it like a lapsed Catholic doing an emergency rosary. She owed him her attention; Jacob had a loss, too. She'd explained it, trying for the truth. *Priscilla isn't coming back*. He didn't understand because he was a baby, too.

"Read it louder."

"Shhh. Baby Andrew is sleeping." She didn't know if the baby could hear, and doubted it would bother him if he could, but the silence was for *her*. She reclined on the sofa, pulling the boy's small body atop hers. She needed to gather her thoughts. Of these there were too many. Priscilla had managed the naptimes and the story reading, and Rebecca had given her afternoons over to thinking, and lots of thinking led to some writing, and of course, wasn't it the way, that now she was positively pregnant (ha ha ha) with thoughts but without the time to do what came next. Well, she had been the one who lamented that nothing happened in her life. Now something had, but she certainly didn't have time to make that into a poem.

"I want the truck book."

"The truck book is—" She sighed and pushed herself up into a sitting position. "Where is the truck book?"

Jacob shrugged. "I want the truck book."

"It must be upstairs. Let's play downstairs so we don't wake Baby Andrew."

"I want the truck book!" Jacob screamed.

"Jacob! Lower your voice this instant." The sound of his scream was terrible, a screeching thing, full of pique, sarcastic, fake, cruel. She hated it when he did this, worried that there was in him some tendency toward hotheadedness. "The baby is sleeping. We can't go upstairs to get the truck book. Let's make a city with blocks."

Jacob pushed off the sofa and threw the basket of blocks to the ground, satisfied. "The baby is stupid."

"We can do lots of other things instead of reading."

Jacob sneered. "Make a highway. Make a highway for trucks."

Rebecca pushed off the sofa and sank to the floor. The room was a mess; she could choose not to see it, but she was still aware of it. "Let's call our city Jacobtown." Often, she could sit and narrate his play and this would be sufficient. But he knew when she wasn't paying attention, when she was humoring him, and this made him angry. It wasn't as though she could do the work she'd normally be doing, while sitting here on the floor, knees bumping up against the coffee table. Nor, though, could she give in to the reality of Jacobtown. She just shut off, or down, the way the refrigerator ceased its hum for half an hour or so when it had reached its favorite temperature.

They played for a few minutes, then Jacob was not interested in blocks: he wanted to make a train.

"I have an idea. Let's go in the kitchen—"

"No!"

"And we can build a train track—"

"No!"

"That goes under the table."

"No!"

"It's a big tunnel—"

"No!"

"No, I'm sorry. I made a mistake. It's a *subway*. A New York City subway. The J train. The J stands for—"

"For what?" Jacob stood, his hands on his hips. It was a silly pose, but contained defiance.

"Jacob!"

He was mollified, especially when he dumped the box of wooden tracks onto the kitchen tile, which made a terrific clatter for which she did not even bother scolding him. Rebecca put the dirty coffee cups in the dishwasher, found a roll of paper towel with which to replace the cardboard tube that had been taunting her for days. She took the plastic mixing bowl full of Andrew's dirty bottles to the sink and began unscrewing them. They smelled horrible, old milk and heavy metals.

"Next stop is Tenleytown! Tenleytown." Jacob was distracted.

She had to move quietly, because he had forgotten her, momentarily. She set the pot to boil, scrubbed the bottles and their innards with the soapy brush, dumped the lot into the bubbling water. She marked the time on the clock on the stove, set the tip of the tongs into the water to make those sterile, too, then lifted the components out and onto a dish towel. Here was where her plan went awry, surely, because the cotton towel was clean but not sterile. No matter. It was something, and Andrew seemed healthy.

"Mommy." Sometimes his words were so clear, his affect so unlike the baby he'd been for so long. Sometimes he talked to her just the way her mother had talked to her, just the way Christopher talked to her. "Come and play."

She didn't want to play. Play was work, a child's work, and it was important—this was how you learned to exist in the world—but it was work that she was done with. She wanted to be *alone* for half an hour, and to take a shower, and come downstairs and find the place magically tidied (not spotless even; just all the wooden train tracks in a box and out of sight) and drink a cup of hot coffee and then go into her office and turn on Dvořák and sit at her desk and just—well, what would come after that didn't even matter. "I have to finish the baby's bottles."

"Don't do bottles. Play trains. This is an express train."

He wasn't whining, nor was he yelling. He was asking for what was his by right: her attention. "OK, the bottles are almost finished." She dumped the rubber nipples into the soup and they bobbed about crazily. She had forgotten how long she was meant to boil them. She waited two minutes, then three, and that seemed sufficient to keep bacteria at bay. She plucked them out one by one, then turned off the stove.

Those days of leaving her work as a mother for her work as a poet were behind her. Of course she could hire someone. Some efficient whisperer with a West Indian accent, some rotund nurturer who smelled of menthol cigarettes, some eager Emily with a degree in early childhood education, to build towers with blocks, to rub balm into the baby's bottom, to ensure the bottles were germ-free, to sing songs and impart the alphabet and give baths and lead excursions to the library. That made the most sense, but it also made sense, at least to her, to choose otherwise. It wasn't punishment, exactly, but it was something like penance: Rebecca owed something to Jacob, to Andrew, to Priscilla. She owed nothing to poetry.

Soon, the baby would be awake. He'd cry, then she'd go upstairs, and change him, and bring him downstairs, and he'd have another bottle and Jacob would have a peanut butter sandwich, or macaroni and cheese from a box (if you added peas that made it healthy). She'd think of something they might all do together, or she'd hold the baby in her lap while Jacob continued at his trains or his trucks, or she'd turn on a CD, or switch on a cartoon. She'd read a board book to the baby then a big kid book to Jacob, then someone's bowels would move, or both of their bowels would move. Or someone would need a clean shirt, or spill apple juice, or fall down, or weep. Then Jacob would get sleepy, and Andrew would get sleepy, and she'd try to decide who to coax into sleep first, and Jacob would nap for an hour and Andrew would nap for two, sometimes three, their naps a Venn diagram, and Rebecca in the seed-shaped overlap at their center would sit at the table and survey the kitchen and do absolutely nothing. That was what would happen, soon, but it was not happening now, so she sat down and marveled at the trains under the kitchen table, trying not to notice that the floor was sticky with something unpleasant.

15

REBECCA PREVAILED UPON HER OLD COLLEAGUES TO ADMIT JACOB
to school early, which was against the principles of the school,
but when she told them *why,* those principles were set aside.
Her days thereafter were the relief of discovering that instead
of breaking both legs you'd only broken one. Rebecca now
had to pack school lunches, but when Andrew napped (ninety
minutes in the morning; two hours in the afternoon) she could
crawl into bed and sleep and sometimes—shame—weep, de-
pression *sans* partum. *Poetry* magazine bought a poem, but
what did she care about poetry or *Poetry?*

On a February day that was unremarkable otherwise, the
sky gone purple, the world cold, they all put on nice clothes
and gathered at Ian and Cheryl's house to make conversation
about nothing in particular and remember Priscilla's life. This
was a strange but necessary human ritual; Cheryl needed it to
heal from death but had had to postpone it while she healed
from birth.

Rebecca wore black because she didn't have the temerity
to break with convention, but it seemed unfair, the insistence
on joylessness. She thought of the way they buried people in

New Orleans, with menacing jazz and furious dance. Priscilla had made her so *happy* it was disappointing to not be able to allude to that, now.

Rebecca tried to make herself useful. She answered the door for neighbors, Ian's extended family, the contingent of nurses from the hospital. She collected abandoned plates, put more crackers out, snuck into the kitchen to make a fresh pot of coffee.

Cheryl was there, wiping the counter with a paper towel, distracted.

"You OK?" Rebecca wanted to touch her but did not.

"I'm fine." She crumpled the towel and threw it in the garbage can. "Lost in thought, for a minute."

"I don't mean to intrude. I was just going to make some coffee."

"Thanks." Cheryl sat at the kitchen table.

Rebecca filled the chamber of the coffeemaker. Then she turned to face her host. "What if we keep him?"

Cheryl rapped a fist against the table. "What if." It was not a question, there was that.

"We could do it, Cheryl." Such occasions, people proffered flowers, casseroles, but Rebecca had only this. "We could make some kind of arrangement."

Cheryl stood. "I should put out those cookies the girls brought."

Rebecca handed over the plate of cookies, delivered by Cheryl's colleagues. "I'm sorry to be so abrupt."

Cheryl looked at her. "This is not the day, Rebecca." She carried the cookies into the next room and Rebecca waited until the coffeemaker had finished its hissing and dripping, red-cheeked, hot with shame.

It had settled or festered, what Rebecca had said, because

Ian and Cheryl came to lunch the first warm day in March and Ian mentioned McDougal.

"I met a man. A lawyer." Ian sounded apologetic for changing the subject.

Christopher toyed with his pasta. "You need a lawyer, Ian? You could have come to me. This city is lousy with lawyers."

Ian cleared his throat. "He does trusts. But he's done adoptions."

Rebecca placed her fork on the edge of her plate. "I see." Her heart did something now, something she had no longer thought possible. It swelled. She could fairly hear it pounding. She didn't want to eat, she never wanted to eat again.

"I know we talked about an arrangement." Cheryl was concise. "Ian sold this man a car. He gave him his card. It seemed prudent. To call. So I did."

"An arrangement." Christopher nodded.

"We discussed it. Briefly." Rebecca stood and retrieved Andrew from his little seat on the floor. "We ought to come to some kind of terms."

"Terms." Christopher spoke through his food, dispassionate.

"I hope I haven't—done anything wrong." Cheryl was not smiling.

"He's a good man." Ian pushed his own plate away. "When it's time. If it's time. McDougal. I just had a feeling about him."

Christopher drank his water. "I think it's best, when working with lawyers, not to rely too much on feelings. But it's good, I suppose, to have a good feeling about a man."

Rebecca understood. She held Andrew close to her breast as though he were a life preserver. "Why don't I put on some tea?"

They picked it up, as a correspondence game of chess, after

their guests had departed, the children fed once more, bathed, read to, tucked away for the night.

"McDougal." Christopher poured himself a drink.

"I'm sorry. I should have prepared you."

"What on earth are you doing, Rebecca?" Christopher splashed water into his whiskey. "What promises have you made?"

"I haven't made any promises." She sat at the kitchen island, on one of those stools that were so tall her feet swung helplessly, like a child's.

"Isn't this—this whole thing—a promise? You think I don't realize what's happening?"

"I just wanted to make everything better. For everyone."

"It's not your job to make anything better."

"Then what is my job? Writing poetry?" She had wished, once, for something to happen to her. She had thought it would give her something to write *about*. "I can do this, I can make this better."

"Maybe it's our family so you should discuss it with me. Maybe it's their family so you should just stay out of it."

This was important to admit. "I should have—discussed this with you. Before. But it's been so hard to find the time."

"And you didn't want to. You want something, you seek it out, it doesn't matter who else might be affected."

"I don't think that's true." She felt, herself, like having a drink. She would regret it, wake thirsty and depleted to Andrew's steady wail.

"You wouldn't, naturally. What if it's not what they want? A white family with a black child, that can't be what they want."

"Don't be silly, Christopher."

"Don't be willfully naive, Rebecca. It's not . . ." He paused.

"He needs—it's important, the child's roots, to maintain—what is *natural*."

"Don't give me nature, please. If you object, fine, but don't tell me it's because of what the universe wanted. Just admit what it is. You don't want a black child, say that you don't want a black child."

"You think so little of me." Christopher tugged on an earlobe, a tic that had developed as he'd tried to smoke less. "Or maybe not at all. Maybe you think only of yourself."

"I am thinking of Andrew."

"You may well believe that."

"Why are you—" But she knew. "So let's discuss it."

"I'm so pleased." He drained his drink and set it back on the counter. The ice clattered and the sound was angry. "You'd deign to discuss—with me—whether or not we'll have another child. Whether we'll adopt a child. The child of a stranger. On your whim."

"It's not a whim. And she's not a stranger."

"Why do you presume that this is your responsibility? Why do you presume it's your right? How can you know that they wouldn't rather have some money? I proposed that and you were so—righteous. But how do you know, for certain, that they wouldn't rather have some financial help than give up the baby? He's her brother. He's nothing to you. Or maybe you don't like to hear that, but you'd be nothing to him."

She took this as it was meant: a blow. She tapped her fingers on the table, impatient but still intent. Fine, she was nothing to him. A mother is nothing to her children. "How can you think they'd rather have a check than a loving home, a family—fine, a different sort of family but that's what we'd all be."

"How can you think that you know what it is they would want? Have you ever asked anyone what they wanted?"

"So, you don't want the baby. You want me to go upstairs, pack a little bag up, and send him away."

"To his sister. Not to Fagin, for Christ's sake." Christopher poured another drink. "I don't want you to send him away."

Rebecca was quiet. "You don't."

"This is an impossible situation."

"He's ours, Christopher. Let's make him ours. Let's adopt him. Let's say it's forever. He's my baby. My God." The tears came, which was maddening. She felt like such an idiot, such a *girl*, crying, now. "He's my baby. I can't live without him, you can't take him away, he doesn't have anyone but me. But us."

The room was quiet. "Why wouldn't you just ask me?"

She didn't know. There was no answer.

Christopher dumped his drink into the sink. "I'm going to bed."

It went unsaid, in the parenting books, in the chatter on the playground, in the warnings from her big sisters, that the baby needed you but also you needed the baby. They were reassuring. You could hold on to them and it was like you were holding on to life itself. You could hold on to them and nothing else seemed to matter, not the vanishing of species, not the signs of war, not the anger of your husband, the various depredations of contemporary life. A baby was so weak—why should it make you feel so invincible?

Rebecca walked upstairs and took the baby from his bassinet, though you were not supposed to disturb them when they were sleeping. Even the sound of Christopher in the shower was angry. Andrew stirred and began to cry.

"I'm sorry," she said. "I'm sorry, I'm sorry." She took him downstairs and sat on the sofa with him and he fell asleep and she just held him, like that, asleep in her arms, and felt renewed.

Christopher was asleep when she crawled into their bed, and asleep when she crawled back out of it. Rebecca stood in the kitchen doing that whole ridiculous routine with the baby's bottles, and Christopher came into the room, his hair matted, his eyes tired.

"How did you sleep?"

"I don't know." She didn't have an answer.

"You think I don't know, what you were trying to do, all this time. And what's worse, Rebecca, is that you think I don't care. You think I'm some kind of monster."

"I don't."

"Have you thought of me, though, at all?" Christopher poured a coffee. "I don't think that you have."

He was right, was the terrible thing. Maybe she was wrong about everything and there was only some finite amount of love in her, if not in the world, and she'd apportioned all of hers to Jacob and to Andrew and now here they were. "Can we talk about it? What comes next? Can you forgive me for not talking to you about it sooner, and can we talk about it now? Right now?" Andrew was in the little mechanical swing that had been Jacob's and she looked at him and he looked right back at her as though aware they were discussing him.

"Let's talk about it."

"Is it so crazy? Really?" Rebecca had not planned an argument but one emerged. "We were going to have another child. Weren't we? I always envisioned another."

"But a person doesn't—" Christopher hesitated with his coffee. "It is a little crazy, since you ask. It is. You must admit that."

"It just feels right. Inevitable, somehow. It feels like—so crazy that it's not crazy at all."

Christopher looked out of the window. "It's animal, don't you know? A baby works on you, by some magic. You see them, they're so small, they need everything, and your brain tricks you into giving them everything, and we call it love."

"What do you mean?"

"I've been here, with you, haven't I, all this time? Since December. Months. But you think because Jacob came from your body that you love him more than I do. And you think you're the only one who cares about what happens to Andrew."

"No."

"You think because you brought this baby, this stranger's baby, this black baby, into my house, that I'm going to say no, we can't give him my name, we can't care for him, we can't send him to college. You think that this baby, you think that *Andrew*—that I haven't been here, all this time, his entire life. Falling in love with him."

"I don't think that."

"You thought I was going to object. Maybe I do object. Maybe the small part of my brain that is still able to be rational about things knows that this is a big fucking mess, an impossible mistake. But it's too late, isn't it? We've already—it's too late."

"Too late for?"

"It's too late to talk about reason." Christopher stood and patted his pocket in search of a lighter. "Call the lawyer. Make it happen. He's our son. Jesus Christ, Rebecca." Christopher left the room. She called McDougal two hours later.

16

before bed, over the fact that Christine and Tim had called their second child Michael when they already had a child named Michelle. *But it's the same name?* Christopher had been more flummoxed than amused, but Rebecca still found it quite hilarious even though he was, her nephew, very sweet, pink and wrinkly, creaky and complaining. She held him and Christine held a cup of tea and their mother held Andrew and Judith held the floor. The bigger kids were in the yard, watched over by the husbands who were drinking Dewar's and feigning camaraderie. The women were where the women always ended up but never mind because the kitchen was a household's actual seat of power, especially Judith's, with the Jenn-Air stove that glowed red when hot, the complex bronze cappuccino maker, the wine fridge.

"All of which is to say, what I'm trying to get the hospital to understand is what you're saying—it's not surgery. It's the body doing what the body does. It's the eighties for God's sake. The future." It all had the sound of a stump speech, which it was. Judith had gone into obstetrics because it was mostly men and she wanted to effect a change.

"Mmmm." Christine's response was neither approval nor disagreement. They all knew how to deal with Judith. "Well, it's over now. And he's here. And I'm never doing that again." She lowered her voice. "Tim's getting a vasectomy."

"Never mind." Lorraine nuzzled Andrew. The mother who made her daughters march for the ERA, who had happily left her kids in a nun-run day care to go back to work, who had leveled with her daughters about Maude's abortion, had become a grandmother squeamish about labor and delivery, a woman who wept when her youngest, near spinster, married at last. "Let's talk about something else."

Because it was Lorraine's birthday, the daughters were amenable.

"Chris, I brought you some clothes. They're in the trunk, don't let me forget. I should just ask Christopher to get them now while I'm thinking of it."

"Clothes?" Judith was confused.

"You wouldn't know about hand-me-downs, I guess." Rebecca meant that Jennifer was an only child, but also she meant the grandeur of the place (seven bedrooms!). Steven worked at Legg Mason. She nodded at Andrew. "That one is out of the six-month stuff two months early." Rebecca rocked the newborn carefully. He was so small, compared to Andrew, compared to Jacob, so flawless, so pink. He began to cry.

"Thanks, Bec. I was reusing some of Michelle's things but Tim is—well, he doesn't approve. I can hang on to them for you. I mean—you'll want them back, I guess?"

Rebecca knew that Christine was not digging, as Judith might; she was flustered. They all were. No one knew what to say about Andrew, for fear of it coming out wrong. "As it happens." She didn't want to make a scene. It was her mother's birthday. "I don't think we'll need the clothes back."

"It's nice, you girls having one another, your kids growing up together. I always wished your uncle Bruce and his kids didn't live across the country." Lorraine wiggled a finger and Andrew reached for it, tantalized.

"I think we've—well . . ." Rebecca faltered as Michael began to cry. *The body doing what the body does,* Judith had said. A tidy précis if not quite true. Motherhood was in the body, but it was not only in the body.

"I'll take him." Christine pushed the teacup away and unbuttoned her shirt. "He's hungry."

Rebecca handed the child to his mother, carefully, fearfully, though she knew they were designed to withstand almost anything. "It's Mom's birthday so I don't want to make this all me me me, but you should know that we've, we all—Cheryl, and Ian, and me—we've decided that Christopher and I are going to keep the baby. Andrew, I mean."

Christine looked up from the child at her breast. "What? Sorry? "

"We've been talking, and we think it's . . . I think it's the perfect arrangement." Rebecca felt relieved to have it all out. "We're meeting with a lawyer next week." She itched with that particular urgency to hold the baby—to hold *her* baby. She was still trying out that possessive.

Lorraine—maybe sensing her daughter's need—handed Andrew back to Rebecca. "I'm a little surprised, honey. I don't know what to say. You've discussed this? "

"It's good news, Mom. It's something to celebrate! Or, you know, it will be, when we sign the papers and get everything sorted out." Rebecca felt hot. "I'm sorry, I didn't mean to make this big announcement, but happy birthday, you're going to be a grandmother for the fifth time."

"So you're seeing a lawyer, but you haven't yet? " Judith was concerned. "I don't need to tell you, I don't think, that you can't have any of these sorts of conversations without involving a lawyer. You can't—make promises. You don't know these people—"

"I know them, Judith. Cheryl and Ian? I know them, you know them. Let's not overreact."

"No one's overreacting. But Rebecca. You do have a tendency—"

"What tendency?" She smelled the baby's hair.

"Rebecca, this is a big choice. Life-altering. This is what you want? What *Christopher* wants?" Lorraine leaned toward her over the counter. "Of course, the baby is lovely. Andrew is lovely. But this is a major thing you're talking about, it's not like—getting a cat."

"Yes, Mom. Of course we've talked about it." She demurred. They were her sisters and her mother, but Christopher, Jacob, Andrew: *they* were her family.

"I think it's wonderful. It's the best possible outcome." Christine lifted the baby off her, eased him up in her arms. "Who would ever have thought. It's the craziest story! It's like—fate."

"I don't know if it's fate." Rebecca had been down that road. Fate was a grandiose term because no one wanted to admit that bad luck existed. "And I don't know if I have a *tendency*, I don't know what that means."

"Don't be insulted." Judith was slicing a cantaloupe; it smelled of garbage. "We worry. You bounce. You know it. You had that whole thing with your teacher, in Boston. Then you come back here and you say you're going to be a poet and you live with Mom and Dad and you teach at the school—I mean. Christopher is wonderful, you've got a beautiful kid, that gorgeous house of yours, you won that prize. It took you—well, you've got all this and now you want to adopt someone else's baby, a black baby?"

This was what Rebecca expected from her oldest sister.

No transgression would ever be wholly forgotten. Her words were calm. She couldn't be bothered. "I've looked after him, his entire life."

"Of course." Judith swept the knife across the board, balancing the fruit on its edge, then tossing it into a bowl. "You know, Priscilla looked after Jacob all his life. So if you'd died, would you imagine she'd adopt him?"

"Jude. Let's not—" Christine tried to preserve the peace.

"Don't be crazy." Rebecca shook her head.

"He's very sweet, of course, Rebecca, but he has a *family*." Judith shook her head as if it were not to be believed.

"Yes. My family is his now. This is happening so maybe pretend to be excited about your new nephew." Rebecca thought that might do it, that some words did have power.

"I think it's possible to be excited but also to be reasonable." Judith had slipped into her stern and steady bedside manner. "What if there's some disagreement? Or it turns out they want money, or they're going to change their minds? You don't know anything about these people. What if there's a family history of schizophrenia. What if there's AIDS?"

"Let's not." Lorraine stood up. "Judith. Come on. Rebecca, honey, I'm amazed. I'm a little in shock. We adore Andrew, obviously." She put a hand on the baby's head.

"Obviously," Rebecca said.

"This is what Christopher wants, this is what you want?" Lorraine had not gone pale, not exactly, but there was a clear effort to retain her equanimity. "It's . . ."

That last word hung there, and none of them expected their mother to finish her sentence. What was there to say, anyway? "This is what I want," Rebecca said, and as she said it knew that she always got what she wanted.

17

THE PICTURE ON THE DESK TOLD THE STORY OF HOW MCDOUGAL
had once been a handsome boy and was now an unremark-
able man. Matriculating McDougal, in ill-fitting suit, beaming
under the arm of his father, was a ghost of the man before her,
who was heavier, softer, and beginning to lose his hair. He was
kind and efficient. The things he explained—the petition, the
letters, the background check, the social worker who must be
engaged—seemed simple and reasonable. The ladder of the
law had no top and no bottom, but every rung was paperwork.

"I brought this letter, from the doctor's office." Re-
becca produced the paper that said it plain: Andrew John-
son had been seen by Doctor Anderssen the day after he'd
been discharged, then a week after that, then at a month, two
months, four months, and six months. He'd been poked with
life-preserving sera and pronounced hale.

"That's good." He nodded. "When the social worker
hands over her report, which should be soon, we'll go ahead
and schedule an appearance. Now, the courts are tied up. This
isn't life or death, so it's going to get lower priority. You'll
just have to be patient."

She didn't like being told to be patient. This felt like life or death to her. "I can wait."

"There's absolutely no reason to rush, and no reason to be fearful. This is a noncontested adoption. The baby's sister would be, in any court's estimation, his legal guardian. And she wants this."

"Yes. I know." Rebecca relished this. That their arrangement was so amiable meant something, just as the fact that Jacob was conceived in love meant something.

"You've worked out a formal agreement. That's—above and beyond. Monthly meetings, weekly phone calls, it's more amicable than any custodial suit I've been part of. Judges see this, in divorces, everyone's at pains to prove they can get along. You're going into chambers with Cheryl. You're on the same side. So, I can see that you're worried, but everything is going to be—there's no reason I can see that things won't work out for the best for you, for Cheryl, and for Andrew, most importantly."

"We haven't been able—you asked about paternity. And we haven't been able to establish anything." There had been not far to look. They had discussed it, however uncomfortable a discussion it was. Cheryl said she knew nothing; she would swear to it, would have to, before the judge. Rebecca had run over every conversation she'd ever had with Priscilla, though they were a jumble in her mind now. Never once a mention of a man. Not her own father, certainly not Andrew's. It truly felt mythic, a baby conjured by nothing but the force of his mother's body.

McDougal ran a hand through his hair. "So, it's a snag. But it's a very minor one. Cheryl—she wasn't able to provide any further leads?"

"Nothing."

"Andrew, at birth, did not have a father recorded on his

birth certificate. That's fine. Standard. Maybe even statistically the fact in the majority of births inside the District. It has no particular bearing on things. The State of Maryland, like most, invests most parental authority in the mother, anyway."

"But. What if? What if we find out that he's out there, that he just doesn't know what happened, to Priscilla, to the baby?"

"Let's say that's true. It's been months. He could have found out, if he wanted to. He doesn't want to."

"How do you know?"

"Even if he does. It doesn't matter."

"How can it not matter—who his *father* is?"

"The child is—Andrew is . . . He is, as far as we can tell, he's African American."

"Yes."

"A hundred percent, let's say."

"He seems so. How can you tell these things?" She thought of Kate Chopin.

"You can guess. So let's guess. Typically, parental rights pend for thirty days. These are maternal rights, most often, because fathers so rarely enter the picture in cases of adoption. So there are thirty days during which a mom can say—hey, I've changed my mind here. It's rare, but it happens. But it won't happen here, because there's no mother. There's Cheryl, but she's not going to change her mind."

"No, she won't."

"So say, theoretically, that by the time we go to court, this father makes himself known. He would have that thirty-day period. But I think he'd see that this is a great outcome. I think he'd be fine with it. But say he wanted to stop it, for whatever reason. He'd be going against your wishes, the wishes of the woman who has spent the past five months taking the baby to pediatric appointments and buying him formula and diapers. He'd be going against the wishes of the baby's de facto guardian, his sister, their mother's surviving child, who also happens to be an adult. A *professional*. A nurse."

"But maybe he would object. Maybe he'd say a white woman has no business."

"Rebecca, there is not a judge in this state who is going to privilege the objections of a black man over those of a white woman. Not one."

She had never considered that being a white woman was, when weighed against being a black man, superior. That a judge would be more inclined toward her for simply this fact. This theoretical man, Andrew's father, crept up on her, over the course of Rebecca's otherwise unremarkable days. Changing diapers, loading dishes, then there he'd be. She'd look at the baby's flawless face and try to decide who it was she saw there, whether it was Priscilla or the man who'd conspired with her to create Andrew. He just looked like a baby, he just looked like her baby. She both pitied the man and hated him, was grateful to him for having existed and hoped he would never materialize. Whoever he was, he would never be able to take what she now thought of as hers.

One uninteresting day in April, Christopher came home and handed her a manila envelope. "Take this to McDougal."

"What is it?" She put the envelope on the kitchen counter and broke the spaghetti into a pot of boiling water.

"It's the will. I've had it revised."

She unhooked the little prongs that kept the envelope sealed.

"It can't be executed while the adoption is pending. But I want McDougal to see it. To be able to show the judge. If he needs to."

"Show him?"

"That after those thirty days are over, after Andrew becomes Stone, he becomes Stone. That when my mother dies, he will inherit twenty-five percent of her estate. That when I die, he will inherit fifty percent of my estate."

She was unsure what to say. She had misunderstood Christopher. *Becomes Stone,* like something out of Ovid. "Yes. I'll take this to McDougal."

They were given a court date in May. They gathered in a windowless conference room, and Rebecca was disappointed because she'd been expecting mahogany and grandeur, maybe a mural. McDougal directed them to answer the judge's queries honestly and told them those queries would be mostly about their paperwork.

"Your petition is up to date?" This was the judge's clerk, her lips tight as though suppressing a smile. "Your address hasn't changed? Your telephone number hasn't changed?"

Solemnity seemed called for, but Rebecca was happy. How could she not smile? "No."

The judge studied the papers by peering over the top of his glasses, as people of a certain age did. "You're Rebecca Stone?" He was just another anonymous man, in another anonymous room, wielding power.

"Yes, Your Honor." She felt ridiculous, calling him *Your Honor,* like a player in a bad television show, what a stupid, presumptuous epithet.

The judge signed a piece of paper, then another, then slid them across the table toward her. "Congratulations."

That was it. Jacob, her parents, her sisters, the nephew and nieces, Ian and Ivy were waiting in the room adjacent. Rebecca, Andrew in her arms, Christopher, Cheryl, and McDougal joined them there. Christine snapped photographs. She'd brought a Mylar balloon. *It's a boy,* it declared. But the boy had been among them for six months, of course. They shook hands with McDougal and went out for pancakes.

18

YOU GOT SO USED TO LIVING ANY WHICH WAY. LIFE'S CRUEL VICIS-
situdes couldn't interrupt life's real business: that was not a life.
There was much *need* and Rebecca was grateful for it. The day
didn't take a day, it contained Whitmaniacal multitudes: when
the baby woke at two, tongue clacking for some milk, when
Jacob woke at seven, ferocious for some cereal, when Christo-
pher woke at seven thirty, intent upon a cuppa, when Christopher
left at eight thirty, knotted and laced, when Jacob left at eight
thirty, groomed and grouchy, when Andrew napped at ten, joy-
ful then simply switched off, when Andrew woke at eleven,
starved and delirious, when Andrew napped at two, tearful and
resistant, when Andrew woke at four, refreshed and ridiculous,
when Jacob returned, restless and demanding, when the boys
ate at five, disgusting and dyspeptic, when they were bathed at
six, were read to, fell asleep, stirred or did not—every step in
between these was a day unto itself. Per this algebra, it wasn't
thirty days she was waiting out but thousands.

Still: Rebecca kept count. She counted like a woman try-
ing to master a dance. She counted like a penitent marking Our
Fathers. You heard stories, samizdat, maybe made up, about

what McDougal referred to as "interruption." Christopher told her of a couple of his acquaintance—or maybe it was an urban myth—who'd engaged a surrogate to carry a child. Upon delivering the baby, the surrogate declined to honor their contract, and the man and his wife discovered they had no legal recourse whatsoever and that, furthermore, he was responsible for the child, financially. *Why would you tell me this story?* Rebecca had wanted to know. Anyway, it came and went. Thirty days elapsed after what felt a decade, and Andrew Stone was his name, a formality that meant that Priscilla's name would be forever stricken from the record.

Now this was just their life, and Christopher fretted. "We should get some help." He was a blur, mornings, fastening his watch and knotting his tie, packing papers into his case, urging her to hurry with Jacob's shoelaces.

She was irked by this *we* but let it pass. "It's fine. You're taking Jacob today, yes?" He took Jacob to school, unless the ambassador needed him.

"I'm taking Jacob today." Christopher finished his toast. "You remember that tomorrow is that thing?"

She remembered but couldn't reach the specifics. There was often some *thing* and Rebecca often found herself making excuses. "Christopher."

"Look, just ask your mother to come." He knew the contours of this argument. "This one is important. It's the secretary himself. He'll want to meet you. All this socializing is the precursor—"

"—so I come and look pretty and sit and talk with the wives."

There was a sigh that he didn't fully articulate. "I can't control society—"

"If you know I'm not just another wife, why do you want me to—"

"Damn it, Rebecca." Christopher was angry. "There's a job, at the bank. I wouldn't ask if it weren't important."

She stacked dirty plates one atop the other. "A job? You have your dream job." This she remembered, at least. That to serve at the pleasure of the Crown was his dream come true, his Yale Younger Poets Prize. Andrew began to whine and Rebecca picked him up out of the mechanical swing.

"Dreams change. They have to." Christopher looked at her. "This is private sector money."

"We hardly need more money." Had he been keeping this from her or had she not been paying close enough attention?

Christopher was out of patience. "What would you know about that, Rebecca?"

What did she know of it? Very little, probably. This whole scenario (dirty dishes, fussing baby, the too-bright kitchen) was stupidly familiar. The thematic repetitions in her life were so uninteresting. "I'm just a wife, fine. I don't know about money, I don't know about anything. You go out into the world, I stay here."

"There is another mouth to feed, after all."

She held the wiggling complainant closer. "I think we can leave the baby out of it."

"I have little interest in a fight. I need to drop Jacob now. I'm just telling you that I want this job, at this bank. Bob says, *Public relations is diplomacy.* So you needn't frame it as me somehow betraying some old dream, some me you thought I was."

When they'd first met, they'd conspired. They'd be great, at their jobs, as people, as a couple. Rebecca had been but twenty-eight, but those promises were not the bluffs of youth, because Christopher had been of course already a grown man. It was the fever of early romance, in which everything seemed erotic and urgent, and everything seemed possible. "I'm not judging you." This felt important to establish. Christopher was the same man, more or less; to live was to change.

He was quiet. "I want this job. And you should want it for me."

"I'll ask my mother." She relented because that was how it went in a successful marriage.

"You know"—he had more to say—"something very sad happened, and then something very wonderful happened, out of that sadness, but you can't let it go. You wanted this, but you're still dissatisfied. You can't go back to—enjoying life, being that person you were."

This was fair. This was probably true. Rebecca had put the playpen in the kitchen, because that seemed to be where she spent most of her time. She bent over and put Andrew in it, sitting up, though he was still unsteady and would sometimes topple over, in slow motion, like a tree dying of natural causes. She smiled at him through the mesh of his prison. "I can't go back. To that life. You're right there. But I'm happy. Most of us in this family are very happy."

"You won't let the baby out of your sight. With Jacob, you were at work within—weeks. We made room for him in our lives. Now, our lives, they're unrecognizable."

"I need to be with him. It's different. You know why." Rebecca knew that Christopher wouldn't deny her anything when it came to Andrew, wouldn't put his foot down as he might with respect to Jacob: a bias to demonstrate that biology was no bias at all.

"It's not good for you. For me. We're happy but we could be happier. I'm going to get this job and that will change things. You need to make changes, as well. Hire some help. Find yourself again."

"I'm not ready to have someone new. Jacob has had a loss, too." The boy had asked. *Mommy, is Priscilla coming?* She hadn't told him that she was dead, though the books all said it was better to be honest. *Everything dies; trees as metaphor; no, Mommy and Daddy won't die for a long, long time.* Andrew had gone from being friend-who-came-to-stay to new baby brother, and Jacob accepted this. Children accept. It's adults who struggle.

Christopher looked away. "You do what you think is right. And you call your mother. For me. Tomorrow. One night."

How little he understood her, Rebecca thought. Christopher hadn't played what would have been his most persuasive card: poetry itself! The thing suffered without her (he could have said). *That* she would have liked to hear, *there* she would have agreed. She was a Younger Poet! James Merrill had said so. Her ego was monstrous, which was why her effacement of such was such an impressive feat. To spend the day grouping toys into like categories was an *accomplishment.* "I'll call her this afternoon," she said.

Christopher and Jacob drove off to Woodley Park Montessori, setting off just as the baby was yawning. Motherhood was in the timing, mother as not conductor but bureaucrat, the monster who makes the trains run on time.

19

AT THE MONTESSORI DROP-OFF/PICKUP THERE WERE TWO TYPES OF women (there were only women): the working moms and the mom moms. Rebecca cast her lot with the larger tribe and never discussed poetry. She didn't even bother brushing her hair. You're forgiven much when there's a baby on your hip. Among these women, Rebecca was a *legend*. Word of *what they had done* had spread, metastasized. This was a sort of fame and Rebecca thought of Diana, a midlength skirt, the red-headed prince at her hip. Everyone loved Diana and everyone admired Rebecca.

"I'll see you this afternoon. Have a great day!"

Jacob was uninterested. He ran away, and Rebecca and the baby walked back to the Volvo in chummy quiet as they did, now, mornings, because Christopher had gotten that job after all and was busy at the bank, a place she'd never been. But Rebecca had fulfilled her vow, put on something pretty and shook hands with the secretary. He was quite elderly but he was still handsome. The secretary had gripped Rebecca's hand tight and leaned in toward her ear. She couldn't remember what he had said. Christopher was proud: the man had known

Truman, Kennedy, Johnson, Carter, he told her. The man was a legend, and he'd tucked Christopher beneath his wing and there'd be lots of money to boot.

Rebecca drove. She couldn't help a little smugness, even if satisfaction was a mere siren call. Whenever Rebecca thought, *Job well done,* there was something: bronchitis, a field trip, Christopher schlepping up to New York, the time she thought Andrew had swallowed one of those curlicue gold Bs that held her earrings in place. You couldn't get accustomed to a rhythm that staccato but Rebecca gave herself over to it because sometimes it felt good to be punished and maybe some punishment was in order. How dare she feel joy like this after a sadness like that? But she glanced in the rearview and Andrew's eyes were closed and that was as it should be.

She turned the music down, and sang quietly. "'Maybe this time, I'll be lucky. Maybe this time, he'll stay.'" Her life was full of *he;* Jacob Andrew Christopher melded into a singular *he* that Rebecca was charged with satisfying or waiting for or worrying over or imploring to *stay.* Those early days, with Jacob, Rebecca had relived in every passive moment the experience of giving birth to him. She took scant recollections and sensory impressions and polished them into something resembling a memory but probably far from reality. She had Tchaikovsky, and masked attendants, the frustration of not knowing her own body, the reassurance of Priscilla's hand, the beautiful pulsing whorl of Jacob's soft head, the prickle of maternal feeling. She'd formed the whole thing into something effectively emotional but with no relationship to reality. It was like that Christmas commercial for freeze-dried coffee; it made you cry even if that coffee was disgusting. With Andrew, in these found moments, Rebecca thought of nothing in particular.

There was a duck pond, not far from the grocery, but pond, like poem, had an elastic and generous definition. It was a man-made puddle, and Rebecca suspected it had something to do with plumbing and the condominiums nearby. Some ducks had taken up residence there. Who knew where ducks came from, and how they chose a home for themselves. Mothers like Rebecca went there to throw balls of gummy bread into the water, so at the very least there was food.

Andrew was nine months old; what did he care about ducks? Some percentage of the things she did for the children were actually for her. The more clever rhythms in some of Seuss seemed strictly for Rebecca's benefit. The days were long and repetitive, too. She pulled into the little parking lot and sat for five minutes, ten minutes, fifteen minutes, twenty minutes. Rebecca let them slip by. She did not even fidget. Then he stirred, and Andrew was out of sorts, sweaty and confused. He wailed as she changed him. Thank God for the ducks, bless the ducks, Rebecca wanted to kiss each and every one of them. She was happy to look at a living thing that needed nothing from her.

She found a bench and gave him his bottle. Then he finished and recovered his equanimity. Whether or not he could see the birds, could recognize them as something akin to but different from himself, Rebecca couldn't know. His body shook, not that perpetual quiver of a child's body, but uncertainty, incompleteness. He was still so unformed. She wrapped her hands around his torso and he wobbled happily. "Duck," she said. "Duck." Then: "Duck!" A warning, a joke, she found it hilarious and laughed.

A brunette grinning so hard she looked idiotic pushed a stroller past Rebecca, hesitated, then asked if she could sit. Rebecca was accustomed to the smiles (the smiles concealed stares) and the half attempts at conversation. This was part of parenting, collegiality, but it was different with Andrew than it had been with Jacob. The only black people living in their neighborhood were some Nigerian millionaires who sent their daughters to school in Switzerland. Most people seemed to smile at Andrew the way they did the ducks.

"Of course." Rebecca pantomimed making room, though she took up little space.

The woman sat, went about her settling, lifting the baby from its stroller, coaxing the pacifier back into its mouth. "How old?"

The argot of mothers. Shorthand for *Can we be friends?* "He's nine months."

The woman lifted the arms of the baby on her lap, as though in triumph. "What a sweetheart. This is Michael. He's five months."

"Hi, Michael." This was the way such things were done; the mothers mere regents, vessels, unimportant, even though they were the ones conducting the conversation. "This is Andrew. I'm Rebecca." These casual chats never blossomed into friendship, so she rarely learned or retained the names of these women. Eventually everyone got back into their cars and went back to their lives.

"Caroline, hi." The woman sounded relieved. She pushed her modish sunglasses up her nose and smiled at the emerald-headed fowl that were tantalized and scandalized by the one morsel of bread Rebecca had tossed their way. They were unafraid, these birds: dogs, cars, mothers, toddlers. "He's yours?"

Rebecca had never mastered this kind of intramaternal talk, because it was a minefield: comparing milestones, spousal jobs, vacation destinations, zip codes, makes of automobile, postnatal weight. The mothers she met never had anything else to discuss; none of them seemed even to have jobs. Perhaps that was why she had no friends.

Rebecca had been happy to let Priscilla handle all this. Perhaps that's why she and Priscilla talked so much, conspiring over lunch, lingering after the five o'clock hour; a desire for a conversation about something real. Rebecca was unworried about coming up short—Jacob had walked early, talked early; Christopher had a great job; they lived in a fancy zip code; she drove a Volvo; she weighed the same as she had at sixteen—but she had no desire to discuss the question of Andrew's origin. Let strangers think her ovaries had failed her; she didn't want the baby who would one day be a boy to hear his mother discussing him as she might new drapes, an exotic ingredient, fashionable sunglasses: as a thing so lovely that you had to wonder about its acquisition. His story could not be easily summarized, but Rebecca didn't want to say even that.

"He's mine." This was what she always said, because it was what she wanted him to hear, and because it was true.

Caroline looked at her meaningfully, then turned her attention back to her baby, the pond. It seemed she understood the tone in Rebecca's voice but was unable to help herself. "Good for you." A pause. "My uncle was adopted."

Rebecca knew that people were unable to stop themselves remarking on Andrew. He did not need strangers to ratify his existence yet there was this desire on the part of people who knew neither baby nor mother to do just that. This had happened at one of those parties Christopher had implored her to attend. A wife with whom Rebecca had nothing in common save that they were both wives had clucked appreciatively. "It's so brave, what you've done." Rebecca wanted congratulations for the things that she *had* done. That fat, formless poem had won the Yale Younger Poets Prize. Instant, institutional approbation. Rebecca was a poet, even if she'd spent the last several months thinking about bottles and diapers. *That* was a matter to celebrate. Motherhood, at least Rebecca's instincts about it, was selfish. Becoming Andrew's mother was neither the least nor the most she could do; it was, simply, what she had done. A kind of madness, a moment that snowballed into a life, just like all life, if you think about it, sperm meets egg and there you go.

She looked out at the ducks. No particular response seemed warranted.

"It can't be easy." Caroline had more to say. "I mean, it's hard for me! And what you're doing is a *whole other thing*. The complications are so scary, I know. Withdrawal, they call it? Well, he looks so perfect. So healthy. He's so lucky!"

Rebecca lifted Andrew off her lap and to her chest, securing the buttons on the carrier. He weighed little on her lap but pulled at her back. The baby kicked his feet, either protest or instinct. Rebecca felt like she must say something but the words would not come now but would visit her later, the right riposte. That was her work, wasn't it, the search for the tidy turn of phrase, the most apt anapest. She did mumble something, some improvised *Have a good day* and *Enjoy* and *See you later* and *Take care*. Something utterly meaningless. Where the world, or Caroline, saw a crack baby, Rebecca only saw Andrew. Once, fetching Jacob from Woodley Park Montessori, a woman Rebecca barely knew held her by the wrist and pronounced her *a saint*. At the woman's touch she turned into something else, not stone, but dust; Rebecca dissolved. She wanted to be someone completely different from the person everyone seemed to think her. She drove to fetch Jacob, an hour too early, and the baby fell asleep in the car once more, which ruined the day's carefully worked out structure, one more reason to hate Caroline.

20

THE CONTRACT HAD BEEN MCDOUGAL'S IDEA. *NOTHING FORMAL*, HE said, as though formality weren't the essential quality of a contract. They shared a desire to come to something concrete, Rebecca and Cheryl. They worked it out: a face-to-face, once-a-month meeting, at which both Ivy and Andrew would be present, plus a weekly phone call, Wednesday evenings, per Cheryl's schedule at the hospital. This had been enshrined, it had entered the record, it was binding if unenforceable though Rebecca still dreamt, sometimes, of armed policemen entering the house on Wisconsin Drive and taking Andrew from her arms. Thus in September, they met by the elephant in the Natural History Museum. The babies were too babyish for it, content to be confined to their strollers, but it was nice for Jacob to have something to look at.

Rebecca arrived first, evincing her enthusiasm. Plus it put the onus on Cheryl. Would they kiss hello? They did not. Cheryl steered Ivy's stroller across the marble floor, waving a little, smiling a little. She'd lost all the weight of the baby, and seemed older, more polished, very pretty in her merino sweater, her ballet flats.

"Hi there!" Cheryl leaned over Andrew in his stroller, kissing him. She took Rebecca's hand and squeezed it. She placed a hand on Jacob's head, as though blessing him.

"Hi, Cheryl. You look just lovely."

"Hi, Cheryl." Jacob was doing this, increasingly. It wasn't parroting but mockery, Rebecca thought.

"*Auntie* Cheryl." Rebecca knew there had to be some kind of noun in play, some way for the children to internalize what was going on, even if it would be years before they understood it. They wandered through the exhibitions, ceding control to Jacob, who was delighted to lead the expedition. He ran ahead and Rebecca called after him, but the sound of her voice only floated up to the high ceilings. "How is everything?" Even in those wide halls, sparsely populated, it was a challenge, keeping their strollers perfectly in line. Rebecca fell behind, then Cheryl did.

"It's good. Work. Baby. You know what it's like." Cheryl laughed.

"That I do."

"There's a good day care, anyway. We've been looking for a while. But there's one, not far, not too expensive. I don't mind telling you—the day-care thing was killing me."

"I'm sure it was." Rebecca knew what it had entailed: Ian taking a regular Sunday so that he could be with Ivy one day a week, Cheryl turning to her mother-in-law and a neighbor for the rest.

"The hospital went to this new system. The schedule resets every ten days instead of every fourteen. It's supposed to make it easier to pay us, or something, I don't know. I'm sort of used to it now but the past couple of months have been—a lot of times, I had no idea what day it was."

"Sounds like motherhood to me." Rebecca had known all this. Those weekly phone calls had filled in most of the details. There was Cheryl's work and Ian's work and there was Ivy. But what could she do? Rebecca tried to imagine it, Ivy dropped at Wisconsin Drive every Wednesday. Rebecca, outnumbered again, the two babies who were in fact uncle and niece. It wouldn't kill her. She could have offered. She knew they'd looked at a day care in Bethesda, near Ian's work, but decided it was out of reach, financially. Rebecca could have supplemented that, could have put it within reach, could have paid for the whole thing, written a check covering the year and been done with it. Rebecca didn't know if Cheryl would refuse to allow it or graciously accept it. Ivy was Rebecca's son's niece. Cheryl was Rebecca's son's sister. That made her something to Rebecca, and what's money for?

"And how are you? How's Christopher?"

"He's fine. Busy." She had, in fact, no good sense of how Christopher was. That didn't seem like something worth getting into with Cheryl. She wasn't sure, indeed, how far she could go with Cheryl. Priscilla had been so inside of Rebecca's life, but her death had revealed that it had been a thing lopsided, unequal. Those months, as Priscilla's body grew resplendent with what would become Andrew, Rebecca hadn't even brought herself to *ask* who had helped Priscilla create the boy. With Cheryl, something similar seemed to pertain. What they were to each other and whatever its protocol was unclear. "Ian's doing well?"

"You should see him, Rebecca. He's always been someone who likes planning. He goes to the Safeway after work because it's on the way home. He packs me lunch, after I go to bed. I wake up and there's a tuna sandwich in the fridge, all wrapped up. Carrot sticks. Milano cookies." She laughed. "He's taken over the laundry. He's on it."

This was not a surprise, that Ian would be thoughtful. He and Christopher were men of different generations, different mothers, different countries. In Christopher's reckoning, the business of life was not his business; in Ian's view, he was as equal a partner as possible. To be fair: the times Christopher did help, toting the laundry basket upstairs, or picking up something for dinner, inevitably something went wrong. Generally, things were easier when Rebecca handled them herself. She tried to limit her sighs, her frowns, sometimes caught herself playing the martyr then had to confess that she didn't, in fact, mean it. "That's good."

They followed Jacob, propelled by a child's boundless enthusiasm. They looked on behalf of the babies, who could look, but who knew what they saw? They pointed at octopi and penguins, stumbled over the Latinate syllables of the dinosaurs' names, considered the depictions of early man, which required a leap of imagination to reckon with. And after forty minutes, Andrew was dozing, Ivy whimpering, and Jacob *starving*. They retreated to the cafeteria, almost empty, which gave the place an even more grim aspect than its institutional lighting already did.

"I don't know what we were thinking. A museum with two infants. I'm exhausted."

Cheryl's was a muted smile, touched with irony. "I like to pretend. That I'm still my old self."

"I got croissants, though I am skeptical about the quality of the croissants on offer at the cafeteria in the Natural History Museum." Rebecca placed the plastic tray on the table.

"I'm hungry, I'm hungry." Jacob bobbed in his seat, leaned across the table, those thick pneumatic sneakers knocking the chair, its metal legs sharp on the linoleum.

"Sit, sit." Rebecca ripped a pastry, and Jacob snatched the larger piece from her hand. He fell back onto his plastic seat and began to gnaw on it. She tried to put some firmness in it, in this *sit*, but so much of the time the words just came out of her, with no particular conviction and a worrying lack of patience. He was a baby, of course, but sometimes she wished logic would rule.

"Thank you." Cheryl had slipped an arm from her sweater and raised it over her shoulder, but rather than unkempt, she seemed glamorous. Ivy was at her breast, and Rebecca could see the subtle pulse of the child's skull, testament to the fact that she lived. "I'm hungry. I know it's early, but I am."

Rebecca put the paper cups of coffee on the table and moved the tray away. "Eat, please. I know what it's like, I remember, that feeling of—I would feel so depleted, sometimes, when I was feeding Jacob." Rebecca tore one of the pastries into several smaller pieces, as though Cheryl, too, were a toddler. "I know you must miss her so much."

"Yes." Cheryl reached for one of the pieces, chewed it thoughtfully.

"I'm sorry if I shouldn't bring it up." Rebecca waited. "But I think it's better, not to pretend?"

Cheryl looked down at the baby in her arms. "It's a funny feeling. I don't go around feeling sad all the time, or anything. I am happy. You know, because of Ivy. Because of Andrew."

Rebecca looked at the baby, asleep in his stroller, head flung to the side. He had a loud, nasal wheeze, Andrew; you could hear him even if you weren't attuned to him, as she was, as a mother would be. "But there's this whole other thing, too." Rebecca understood. "This happiness all wrapped up with sadness."

"I just wanted her to see Ivy. To know her. And Mom was so good with babies, you know?" Cheryl paused. "When I was still in school, we did this rotation, at Children's. There were these ladies, from the church, they'd come in every other day or so. We called them the Grandmas. Maybe they called themselves the Grandmas. I can't remember. We called them

Grandma, individually, but also, the Grandmas, collectively. Like, *Oh, ask one of the Grandmas* or *Grandma, can you take her?* They volunteered. There were a lot of kids there, kids who were abandoned, or in foster care, or just—kids no one came to visit. And you know, it's good, for the kids to be held, talked to, visited, even though they're babies, or sick, or asleep, or don't speak English."

"The human connection."

"But I think it's more than that, I have to say. I think there's something—an older person and a very young person. There's a kind of magic there. They're both right at the fringes of life. There's some sort of understanding. A common language, or like—they just *know* something about each other. And I mean really young. Like babies, maybe until they're two. And old people, like true grandmas, like a lady in her seventies. Some of them were. I think one of them might have been eighty, she must have been, she was so tiny and bent over, couldn't even stand upright. But she'd come and they'd sing or pray or whatever. And I think it did something. It didn't make a *difference*. If the baby had withdrawal symptoms, then praying wasn't going to stop its tremors. But there was something. Like a quiet, in the room. When these old ladies would be around. The whole big, noisy machine of the hospital felt a little more quiet."

"That's amazing." Rebecca sipped the coffee, which tasted quite awful.

"That's what I miss, sometimes. When I think of Ivy. And my mom. They didn't get the chance to do that. Have that kind of conversation or whatever it is, that connection that has nothing to do with me. That's just between them. And you know, she's a good baby, but that doesn't mean I couldn't use the help."

"Your mother did know how to handle a baby."

"I didn't know my grandma, you know. Grandma Shelly. Mom would talk about her only sometimes, and when she did, she always called her Grandma Shelly, which seems weird to me now, because I never saw the woman, as far as I can remember. Grandma Shelly seems like—such a specific name for a person who might as well have been imaginary. She didn't matter, in my life, at all. Then I saw these grandmas at the hospital, and it was like . . . A grandma can do magic. I get the point of a grandma. And I wish we had one. That's all."

Rebecca nodded. She knew enough to say nothing. She tore off more of the pastry for Jacob, who was busy with the dinosaur stickers he'd conned her into buying. Buying was always easier than not buying. It made him quiet, anyway.

"Excuse me." A man loomed over them. Rebecca hadn't noticed his approach, though the place was still mostly deserted. "I'm sorry. You can't. Do that here."

Cheryl looked up at the man and drew the muslin blanket down off her shoulder and over her breast, though it was already covered. "I'm sorry."

"What do you mean?" Rebecca looked at the man. He was in his fifties, which seemed to confer upon him the authority his polyester uniform did not.

"Ma'am, the ladies' room is just over there. Beyond that wall, down that hallway. We ask that you—do that, in there."

"I'm sorry." Cheryl slipped the baby from beneath the blanket. Ivy looked dazed, but did not protest.

"No. Don't apologize, Cheryl. Finish."

"She's finished. I think." Cheryl put the girl on her shoulder and rubbed her back. She pulled the blanket still closer around her, though she was quite hidden beneath it.

"Sir. Maybe a little privacy, please?" Rebecca stood and leaned over the table and reached for the baby. "Let me take her."

"Thank you." Cheryl wriggled back into her sleeve under the blanket.

"Well, there's privacy in the ladies' room, ma'am."

"Let me ask you. Do you eat in the bathroom?"

The man looked down at her. "It's just a policy."

"It's fine, Rebecca. I'm done, anyway." Cheryl seemed harried.

Rebecca was not finished. "Would you eat a hamburger in the bathroom? Put your plate on the toilet seat, sit down, chow down?"

"We've had customers complain, ma'am." The man seemed annoyed.

Rebecca laughed. "There's no one in here but us."

"I'm just telling you what the policy is." He shrugged.

"It's fine. We're all done, anyway." Cheryl began folding the blanket. "Thank you."

"Don't thank him!" Rebecca did not mean to scold but she did. She turned to the man. "The policy is silly. You wouldn't eat in the bathroom. But you want this child to? This is a museum of *natural history*. Nature! It's too good. The irony is too good."

"OK, ma'am. You have a good day." The man wandered away.

"I am having a good day." Rebecca smiled at Ivy, her damp lips, her slightly crossed eyes. "I am having a good day."

21

REBECCA WAS INVITED—THOUGH, WHAT'S THE VERB WHEN AN INVI-
tation cannot be declined?—to New Haven. The logistics
were anxiety inducing. Andrew was nearly one but stubbornly
still a baby. As he'd little interest in walking, he needed toting
from place to place. Jacob had been difficult, terrible threes not
twos, collapsing over the slightest of slights. The block tower
did not hold: tears. The page he most wanted to look at in his
truck book eluded him: screams. Rebecca found herself at such
times giving him the silent treatment. Once, after a tantrum,
he'd reached for his mother's arm and she'd recoiled.

It required a public relations push to prevail upon Judith.
Christine was out of the question, though the middle sister was
more amenable. She had a baby of her own! Judith and Steven
had all those bedrooms and only Jennifer, whom they dressed
like a living doll, in Laura Ashley dresses that hung below the
knee, and for whom they'd bought a horse. Rebecca knew Ju-
dith felt guilty: the twenty-thousand-dollar animal, the spare
Mercedes, their stubbornly white streets in a historically black
city. She volunteered with Planned Parenthood as means of
redress. Andrew was adorable and he was also a trump card.

Rebecca packed diapers and clothes and stuffed animals and dropped the boys at their aunt's home before proceeding to the train station.

Everything was just whim and luck, right? She just happened to have been rereading *Sandover*. Merrill, Merrill, merrily—he might like or understand or be amused by what she was up to, might he not? The pages and pages that had metastasized in the happy interval during which Priscilla was alive, the work that Priscilla's work had allowed. It was like the words and pages had grown independently of Rebecca; she had as hazy a recollection of that labor as she did of her labor. The body doesn't remember pain. Of course, Merrill was the judge for the series so why the hell not, and her instinct had been well founded. Surely he of all people would have relished the role of chance in the thing.

From the day she won the Younger Poets prize until the day Priscilla had been sent to the hospital, Rebecca felt invincible. Now, if Rebecca looked at the book's cover, she thought of Priscilla. A victory made into something else.

Rebecca sat on the train and thought about how unusual it was just to sit in the quiet. Andrew woke, most days, in a wonderful mood, in a joy that turned quickly into a powerful hunger, his *Mama* increasingly urgent, loud, though it never took her that long to get from her bed to his. His cries inevitably woke Jacob. Once, Jacob, stern, rubbing his eyes, his voice froggy, had stood in the hall, hair hilariously akimbo, and said, *Can't you make him be quiet?* He sounded like the man he'd one day be.

She couldn't make him be quiet: children are either quiet or they're not, and neither of hers were. The days were cacophonous: microwave beeping, radio chatting, Jacob barking, Andrew chattering, and often the television, too, because they'd beg for it and without the intercession of the television she'd never defecate again. There was yelling about the brushing of teeth and about whatever Andrew had done to bother his brother. There were screams as Rebecca worked the thick cream into Andrew's hair; the screams would be louder if she failed to do this and then picked at the tiny knots in his taut curls the following day. There were spilled cups of water and shitty diapers made worse when Andrew plopped down onto his rump. There were missing puzzle pieces and pages torn from books. There were stained T-shirts and crushed dreams ("I want *that other* Lego/GI Joe/Matchbox car"). There was the enmity that was fraternity, and it was a noisy business.

They had spent many hot afternoons in the backyard wading pool. Rebecca remembered, every time it came time to top the thing off, Priscilla's mouth on the little rubber nipple. She fell asleep and woke as the train neared Penn Station. What a blight. Rebecca walked the few blocks through town to Grand Central Terminal. She felt utterly alone and unremarked upon and this was a joy.

There were so many black people in New York, so different from Bethesda. Andrew was so like Priscilla—his face, his bearing, even as a baby—that it may as well have been the Immaculate Conception. There were times, seeing a black man, Rebecca would stare, study, consider: Was that him, was that the guy? Cheryl and Rebecca had studied the telephone bill and asked friends, though Priscilla did not have many. She was not active in a church, was not a part of any other group, was just another untethered American, bowling along alone and certain that was the way she liked it. This was vindicating; the realization that the intimacy Rebecca sometimes worried was her imagination was indeed quite real. Of course, Rebecca might simply have *asked* Priscilla, while she was still able. She never had. It was not her business, but now it was the unfinished business of Rebecca's and Andrew's lives.

They got nowhere. Rebecca knew the man could have been white, or Ecuadorian, or Bangladeshi. But black men were the only ones she scrutinized, because they were the boy's future. One day she'd be an old woman and a black man would come and kiss her cheeks and she would hold him to her breast and remember that he'd been her baby.

Rebecca caught sight of Grand Central. She thanked Mrs. Kennedy for saving the beautiful building. Her mother had taught Rebecca that, because Lorraine revered the president's widow. A person needed that, in the world: a guide or an incentive, like the mechanical rabbit a dog chases at the track. Maybe that's what Diana meant, Diana who had only just been once more mere miles from Rebecca, meeting with Barbara Bush to discuss AIDS. She'd worn a suit, was quite thin, her hair cut closer. She'd grown into a self-possessed elegance. She stood beside Mrs. Bush, hands demurely behind her back, shoulders still hunched to correct for her height, creating an impression of modesty. She was a woman of the new decade, powerful shoulders but radiant, unabashed, in pink. Rebecca wondered if James Merrill had AIDS. It was known or obvious that he was homosexual and hard to tell if the leanness of his face was age or something more nefarious. Rebecca had loved that poem about his nanny. *Having known grief and hardship, Mademoiselle / Knows little more.* She wanted to tell him about Priscilla, but barely knew where to begin.

Lorraine hadn't wanted to *be* Mrs. Kennedy—probably?—and Rebecca didn't want to *be* Diana, but they wanted to be modern and interesting and beautiful and maternal and care about historical buildings and AIDS patients. Rebecca wanted to hold James Merrill's hand, out of gratitude but to prove to herself that she was the woman she wanted to be, the sort of woman who could.

She barely got the chance. In New Haven, Rebecca shook

lots of hands and only barely touched Merrill on the shoulder. She was called upon to read and so she did, not in that stupid breathy way of poets who happen to be women. Rebecca *barked* as she did, sometimes (to always instant regret) at Jacob, when he was his most recalcitrant. There were so many people about and they took Rebecca for something that she was only sometimes sure she was. Either she was playing pretend on the playground or she was an impostor, there, in that beautiful library. One of the librarians showed her a Gutenberg bible.

The next morning the bed seemed very large, though it was not especially so. She lay in the quiet room and looked at the wall. She would call her sister, but knew the boys were fine, and knew Christopher was then, too, waking up, and he, too, was fine. There were four hours until anyone would need her. It was like she'd slipped into some alternate dimension, some state of biological repose. She'd read that caterpillars in the cocoon liquefy entirely before re-forming into butterflies. That was how she felt: a mass of liquid, a mush of cells, destined to become itself but not there quite yet.

Then she showered and put on an Armani skirt that was a year older than Jacob, but she didn't care whether it was still, strictly speaking, fashionable. She was a visiting poet, that bar was set quite low. She put on a white shirt and a black sweater. For Diana, dressing was diplomacy. For Rebecca, it was like a lover whose company she'd forgotten she'd enjoyed. People changed.

Rebecca looked in the mirror but did not really see. She'd been trained in these womanly arts at an early age—two older sisters—but while the art was to assess, it was not to see. The goal was to master the line, the flick, the dust, the lacquer, to shift eyes this way and that, to lift the lips thus, to squint, to scrutinize, to create a self, not consider the one that actually existed.

She visited a class, and though a Younger Poet officially Rebecca felt much older than the students: boys in plaid shirts, girls in heavy boots. They asked the usual, queries that said more about the petitioner than anything else. Rebecca offered answers, grew distracted, and yearned to be away from this classroom, like every other classroom. She missed home, the patch of unforgiving late-summer afternoon sun that warmed the pool water, the plastic cars underfoot, the undone dishes, the unanswered question of dinner, the junk mail, the occasional tables, the prints from the National Gallery, the books she hadn't looked at in a while. A year ago she'd have thought Yale University where she wanted to be, but there she was and it was devoid of whatever she had hoped to find there.

A journey in reverse is never the same. Connecticut seemed less verdant, Grand Central less what its name promised, the walk to Penn Station tinged with malice, every passerby a criminal. She got off the train and Baltimore was dark and unhappy. Judith's house seemed so big as to be garish. Jacob was weepy, Andrew sleepy. They both fussed in the car, then quieted, the two boys frowning out of the windows, damp eyes and sour smells. There was traffic, and they were not home until late, and Christopher hadn't left a light on for them. Rebecca microwaved oatmeal because she was too tired to think of anything more interesting, and didn't bathe them, because they were too tired.

Rebecca stood in the foyer and considered the abandoned overnight bags, the mail on the floor. She'd only just wanted to come back there and there she was and she wanted to be in some other place. She picked up the mail and put it on the table. She put the six abandoned shoes in their slots in the closet.

She put the dishes in the sink, running the water to loosen the plaster of cereal. She sat at the island, eating pretzels without enjoying them, and looking out of the window, though it was dark out and light within, so all she was doing was staring at her reflection without seeing herself. The hollow crunch echoed in her head. As a girl, she'd not understood that the food echoes in your own ears more loudly than it does in others'. Mortified, she'd tried to chew quietly.

She heard Christopher's car a little before eight, which seemed late and expected, and seemed like something she'd been waiting for and a surprise. She had filled the dishwasher and sat listening to the machine's reassuring gurgle.

"You're back."

She found that she could not smile. In that moment, as fleeting and terrible as the feeling she sometimes had about Jacob, she hated Christopher. Nine years ago, she hadn't even known the man, had never conceived of his existence, could have foreseen a life that had nothing whatever to do with him or indeed anyone like him. But here she was in a well-appointed kitchen with dirty floors and a thrumming dishwasher and bright overhead lights eating pretzels. "We're back."

"And how was it?"

His unlacing and stepping out of his Lobbs, tugging at the tie, slipping out of the jacket, moving the attaché from floor to table, dislodging the mail she'd just left there: all of it struck Rebecca as silly or too perfect or maddening or just more of the business of being a man. Rebecca wanted a drink, but there was nothing to drink. "It was fine. It was good. To be away, to be there. To celebrate and be celebrated. It was a reminder."

Christopher rummaged in the fridge. "That's good. The boys are good? No trouble? I'm sure your sister and her staff managed."

It was a routine, a joke they had, Judith and her Filipina

nanny, her personal trainer, the Latinos who tended the landscaping. "You might have left a light on for me."

Christopher's eyebrows danced with no joy. "Sorry?"

There was no anger, just clarity. "You might have. Left a light on. In the house. For me, coming home, with our baby, our son, the bags, you might have."

Christopher put his hands on her shoulders and squeezed them. "I'm sorry. I ran out this morning." He sat next to her and tried to catch her eye. "It has been a terrible day. I'm sorry. I wasn't thinking."

"What happened?" She had ceded enough of herself to him and the boys that she wanted, truly, to know.

Christopher smelled of old smoke and sweat, but this was not unappealing. "Something is . . . well, I'm a little worried, if you want the truth."

Christopher was given to understatement. He was unable to scold Jacob properly. Everything seemed distant and ironic when he said it. Rebecca knew that this was his way of saying that the evening had been worse for him than it had been for her. Indeed, hers had been strangely pleasant. Sometimes it was satisfying to be left alone. Rebecca remembered that she loved this man and touched him on the forearm. "Of course I want the truth."

"I had lunch with Dan Diamond today—remember him? He was at the Treasury, now he's on K Street. He was surprised that I had left the embassy for the bank. He said I should have called him first."

Rebecca had no mental image of this Dan, another of the many anonymous Dans in the world. "Why would you have done that?"

"Well, he's someone who knows things. And maybe he's right. He thinks—he's just repeating what he's heard, I should stress. This is just gossip. But he's heard talk of some funny business at the bank."

"Funny." Numbers made no sense to her, banking made even less.

"Of course, this is *how it always is*. Banks, enormous sums of money, it's not quite corruption but you know, it's easy, and tempting. Money begets money. So you can make a pile, just on the strength of momentarily possessing someone else's money."

"Isn't that—the actual definition of a bank?"

"Correct. Christ, don't we have anything to drink?"

Rebecca went into the dining room and brought back the gin. She poured some into a glass, added sparkling water. "There's no lime."

Christopher took the glass. "Getting tough on corruption is always popular, no matter who's president. That's why BCCI is under audit. But Dan says—what he's heard is that maybe BCCI and my bank aren't necessarily unrelated."

It had been on the radio, but those four initials meant nothing to Rebecca's life. "So what's he saying exactly?"

"Maybe I'm paranoid. I've heard those names. Abedi. Naqvi. The BCCI guys, the big ones, I've heard about them, at parties, around the office. I knew some of these guys, when I was at the embassy."

"So you're—worried." Why pretend understanding? When the boys went to bed late, they woke early, which meant she would, too.

Christopher finished the drink. "If BCCI is going to collapse, there will be a postmortem, and there will be people who ask whether we were in business with them."

Rebecca pictured a bank, some anonymous brick building, falling in on itself. The strange satisfaction of destruction. "Guilt by association."

"What if we are in business with them? We're an American bank. There are laws. There will be consequences."

How she wanted to say it: *I told you so.* "You loved working at the embassy. Maybe you just miss the foreign service. It was a noble cause."

"I just wanted to—" He exhaled. "I wanted something different. I wanted to be bigger, I suppose. Make money, do something."

"Why don't you go back?"

"It's not even been a year—besides, Thatcher has—days, weeks maybe. Hard to say who'll be there next, what will happen next."

"No one knows what's going to happen next." A folly, she wanted to point out, but she did not. This was a word that had lodged in her mind, a word on its way to a poem. "We'll be fine." This was the same conversation she'd had with Cheryl in the hospital cafeteria. This was her fundamental belief.

"There's less money than you might think."

"I don't care." This was a liberty. Rebecca had never once envisioned money as her future, even if to not think about money presumed the existence of some. "I'm not worried." But she was, because he so clearly was.

"If they've done something wrong, then so have I. Do you see?" He finished his drink. "I thought I might be important. Might make deals. Might help the bank raise its profile. I was supposed to come in and talk to the senators. To Kennedy, to Murkowski. I was supposed to help with deals."

"Maybe it's nothing."

"Maybe it is. I'm sorry I didn't tidy up. Leave a light on. I was distracted."

Christopher was so handsome. And he loved her. If he was thoughtless, sometimes, well, who was not? Rebecca had been ready for something else—a porcelain demitasse smashed in a moment of pique, a voice raised until one of the children stirred. Her breath felt heavy now, exhausted. Despite the hunger that now settled over her—pretzels were nothing—she knew she'd go upstairs, and Christopher would lie on top of her, his body lean and hard and fragrant, and push against her, and into her, and she would try to lose herself in it, and maybe would, for a time. Christopher would sweat, and then pull on his pajama pants and go and stand in the garage and smoke a Silk Cut and she would fall asleep and wake in five hours, still smelling of her sweat and his semen, and forget everything that had happened that day until some vague undetermined point in the future.

22

CHRISTINE, EVER DUTIFUL, KEPT CALLING. REBECCA RELENTED. There was a Halloween to-do on Christine and Tim's block in Silver Spring. Rebecca dressed Jacob as a cowboy and put the baby in a onesie decorated to look like a tuxedo. Christine dressed Michelle as a princess and didn't even bother with Michael. Of course, it hardly mattered, the two babies asleep in their strollers, the two toddlers looking mostly their usual selves in their warm jackets.

Conversation was almost impossible, the older children darting ahead and dangerously near the road, but fortunately they lost interest after ringing six doorbells and the entire company retreated. Tim had grilled hamburgers, even though it was then quite cold and unnervingly dark at only five thirty.

"Who wants salad?"

"Oh, give him some, Tim. Jacob, Uncle Tim has carrots and tomatoes." Rebecca cradled Andrew, held a bottle steady, sipped her wine, ate her salad, all at the same time.

"Anyway, this team—they presented the most startling study. Trauma, and g-u-n-s." Christine had taken to spelling even though Michelle was too young to pay attention to most of the adult conversation. "It's chilling."

"Is it?" Hearing her sister talk about work was a bit like hearing about a journey to a country she'd never even considered visiting, like Bhutan or Chad. But it was interesting, Christine's work, because it was about the world. "What specifically?"

"They need to expand the study. That's where we come in. The money. But essentially they're looking at incidences of anxiety and depression and hypertension and SIDS—a whole range of disease—and correlating it to g-u-n v-i-o-l-e-n-c-e. It's insane. People are d-y-i-n-g from being s-h-o-t but also from other things."

"The inner city?" It was a phrase you heard. They lived in the city! It was perfectly lovely.

"The long and the short of it is that the threat of g-u-n-f-i-r-e can actually make people crazy, eventually. Michelle, no more juice. Take a bite of your hamburger, please."

Rebecca watched her sister, a distorted reflection of herself, a cream-colored breast emerging from her sweater, an apricot-colored baby at her chest. "That's terrible."

Christine looked back, wide-eyed, intent, though anyone who studied epidemics for a living would be forgiven a tendency toward alarmism. "I just don't know what the world is coming to."

The world did not matter; there were two children and several pieces of candy. There were yells and spills and a general sense of mayhem. Even the babies seemed manic. Rebecca showed her sister the trick—that television was an opiate—and they left the elder cousins in its charge. Tim cleared the dishes and Christine spread a blanket on the dining room floor and let the baby flail about on his tummy while Andrew sat unsteady sentry, surrounded by plastic toys, the two companionable in their immobility.

"How are you doing?" Christine herself sprawled on her stomach with the two infants.

Her sister's edge of panic made Rebecca more resolute. "I'm fine." She said it like she didn't understand the question.

Christine exhaled, like she was psyching herself up. "Rebecca. Did you ever think that you might, possibly, be *depressed?*"

Rebecca laughed. "Overwhelmed, maybe. Tired, sure. But depressed? Like you mean clinical?"

"Postpartum."

"I thought it went without saying, Chris. Andrew's mine but he's not—mine."

"You don't have to have *given birth.*" Christine seemed to understand that she was the family's Cassandra. To correct for this, she aimed for even greater dramatic flourish. It was an odd tactic. She pushed her fingers into her unruly red hair. "I'm just asking. I worry."

"I'm not depressed." Rebecca felt defensive. "This is what I'm like!"

"It's been almost a year, Rebecca. You just don't seem like . . . you."

"This is who I am, now." Being with her sister made Rebecca more dramatic, by osmosis. But perhaps it was true, that this was who she was, now.

"You're a stay-at-home mother? Since when?"

"Since Priscilla died."

"It's more than that. You seem—you seem depleted, as well as enriched. And I don't mean tired, I know what tired looks like. Look at me."

Rebecca looked. Her sister did look paler than was normal, except for the skin around her eyes, tinted with sleep-lessness. This was the look of motherhood. But it was offset, or compensated for, by something else, a faint glow, a vague contentment. This was how Rebecca assumed she, too, looked. "Right. We're tired. We have babies. It's tiring."

"It's something else, Bec. It's like—you're punishing your-self."

"Should I be going to the spa?"

"Maybe you should be going back to work?"

"Because you did?"

"I did! I love my work. It's fucking horrible. Excuse me. F-u-c-k-i-n-g horrible. But it's also great. I go to meetings and my breasts leak all over my clothes, but I get to think and talk and be—I don't know. The person I was four years ago, the person I want to be ten years from now when our kids are teen-agers slamming their doors in our faces."

"I'm fine. I don't need anything other than—this."

"Look, I think you've done a great thing. An amaz-ing thing. We're all in awe. I know—I know they had some doubts, but I didn't. I think you've just become a mother again, just like I did, and it's great but you seem like you're having trouble, recovering your balance."

There it was again, that *great thing* that Rebecca had sup-posedly done. "You're kind to worry."

"What about hiring a nanny. Christ knows you can afford it. And you could go back to writing or just—live or catch up or feel like a human being again."

"I've never felt more like a human being." Rebecca wanted to lower her voice to its most serious timbre, lean toward her sister, and say, *Christopher is in trouble*. She did not. That was a matter for husbands and wives. "The money is not the point."

Christine was direct. "He'll know he's your baby, Rebecca. You don't have to change every diaper."

Rebecca smiled down at the three of them, Andrew now scooting about, Michael simply collapsed like a helpless turtle, her sister, rosy and satisfied. "You don't understand."

"You can't spend your life feeling guilty about your being white and his being black, about you being alive and her being dead."

That was not it! "I don't feel guilty. I feel responsible. I feel charged with . . . I don't know. Being alive, for him. For both of them."

Christine was no longer smiling. "You need to try something. Talk therapy. SSRIs. Meditation. This isn't helping anyone, or it's helping them but not you. You can't disappear into motherhood. It's not good for you. And I can see that's what you're doing. You've vanished." Christine was a doctor, and like every doctor she was an evangelist.

"What if this is who I am? Who I am now. Who I have become." Rebecca picked up her baby and changed the subject back to g-u-n-s. Then she packed up the children, their candy, the bags of stuff it was necessary to forever be packing up. But it lingered, what her sister had said, it infected her, and that night, though it was late, though she had things to do, Rebecca took out a pencil, a legal pad, and sat with them, just for a moment, not writing, just considering them, and wondering if it was true, what she had said to her sister, that she had never felt more like a human.

23

CHRISTMAS MUSIC WAS ODIOUS, CHRISTMAS WAS ODIOUS. FORCED jollity and mawkish sentiment. Rebecca wanted real feeling, something transcendent, but was given only this. A role to play: divine what the children wanted, buy buy buy, wrap it and pretend. Christopher spoke of *Father Christmas*, which she thought hilarious.

She played a compact disc, which still felt futuristic: Streisand. Rebecca sang along without embarrassment. These were the songs of her own youth, she had her mother's taste, as she had her mother's face. It was stirring and sentimental but having a child was freeing: you always had a tit out, and the niceties fell away.

Cheryl was coming over. Rebecca dressed in black but felt joy. Motherhood deformed your breast and then your vanity. As a girl, in her big sister's hand-me-down duds, then a college student, perfectly preppy, then a young woman dating Christopher, then a young wife, Rebecca had dressed the part: T-shirts with inscrutable slogans and old jeans, knees patched with old bandannas; mohair sweaters and silk-lined wool skirts; printed dresses of demure length, paisley silk scarves, gold earrings, necklaces with turquoise and amber and other semiprecious oddities, leather bags, cashmere cardigans, aviator sunglasses. It all sat unused, unless she felt like it: Louis Vuitton for a jaunt to the grocery store. The ruby earrings from Elizabeth that didn't look right on her, because she was a redhead, clipped to her ears (they were that big) and for no reason other than that she thought they'd make her feel beautiful for an afternoon. It was beauty for herself. Obviously, Andrew and Jacob cared little what she wore, and Christopher, too, often failed to comment.

Christmas was for family and family was now Cheryl. *We're a family now,* Ian had said to her, that day, over pancakes. They had good intentions, she and Cheryl. They had a vision, or Rebecca did: Andrew and Ivy costumed, Superman and Wonder Woman, cadging candy from the neighbors; Cheryl and Ian and Ivy, at the Thanksgiving table; birthday parties, Easter lunches, picnics at Rock Creek. There's vision, though, and reality. Cheryl a new mother, Rebecca a new mother, the complex dance of four adults, three kids. Only weeks ago, Cheryl and Ivy had come to the boys' joint birthday party. Cheryl held her brother while the assembled company sang and the candles wavered. This was approximate to seeing Priscilla hold Andrew, something that had, horribly, never happened. Ian had to work, because the weekends were the best days for the selling of cars. Rebecca missed him. She thought it hilarious that he was Andrew's brother-in-law. Whoever heard of a baby with a brother-in-law?

The doorbell sounded and Christopher called upstairs. "They're here."

That's what the doorbell was for, Rebecca thought. *To tell me that.*

"Hello!" Rebecca tried to sound enthusiastic but nonchalant—a sisterly visit an occasion at once special and ordinary. Words didn't capture such distinctly opposing feelings.

Cheryl leaned into the hug Rebecca offered. Hugs were better than kisses; kisses were insubstantial, showy. Hugs demonstrated connection, as they demanded connection. Hugs were a corrective, too, to Christopher's public school propriety. Hugs were American, boisterous, honest even when forced, which this one was, not that the affection between her and Cheryl was feigned. It was something else. A brokered peace.

"Hi, Rebecca." Cheryl had an unnerving way of using Rebecca's name, as though she were willing herself to memorize it, or as though she were using it ironically, the way teenagers might call parents by their Christian names to demonstrate independence.

Ian was in the car with Ivy, asleep in her car seat. The boys were napping, too, or Andrew was. Jacob was observing what they'd termed "quiet time," reading a comic book in his parents' bed. The house had a preternatural hush that was only eerie because Rebecca knew it would not last. Cheryl slipped out of her shoes and followed Rebecca into the kitchen. That they did not enter the sitting room—its armchairs with their Napoleonic bees, its blue-and-white drapery—was a measure of intimacy. A chicken was roasting, a lemon nestled inside. The room smelled as a home ought to.

"How are the boys?" Cheryl always asked about the both of them. Andrew and Jacob, in her estimation, were separate people but a single entity. Blood did not make this a family, everyone had to agree.

"So good." Rebecca broke the ends off the asparagus stalks and flung them into the sink. Could someone look at this mess, like the leaves at the bottom of a teacup, and divine the future? "Andrew is just intent on keeping up with his brother."

"We brought pies. They're in the trunk, Ian will bring them in when Ivy's up. Pecan, which was my mother's favorite." She looked at the clock on the oven. "She'll be awake soon, probably."

"I can't wait. Even though I've done nothing but eat for weeks. Thanksgiving. Birthday cupcakes. Christmas cookies. I get to this point every year, I just want to stop. One year, we should go away somewhere. All of us. Mexico. Just get away from the madness and go somewhere sunny."

"A resort. With a day-care drop-off. And a casino. And an open bar. Could I have some water, Rebecca?"

"Of course. How rude of me." Rebecca dried her hands on the tea towel. Her feeling toward Cheryl was maternal, though they were nearly the same age. She pressed a glass against the dispenser in the refrigerator door. Rebecca waited—always—for their conversation to transcend the quotidian, but this was so great an expectation. "It's so dry, the winter air. Murder on the skin. Poor Andrew's, especially."

"Thank you." Cheryl sipped the water. "You've tried shea butter? It's what we use. It's what Mom used."

"I've been using coconut oil." After Andrew's bath, she dipped her fingers in the glass jar, the wax going to nothing as she worked it over the baby's skin. After, he glowed beautifully and smelled like cake. "I'll have to try that."

"Sometimes . . ." Cheryl paused. "Black skin, it can require extra care. Especially in the winter."

"Skin is skin." Rebecca tried to sound reassuring.

"I'll bring you some," Cheryl said. "I probably have some, in the bag. I'll leave it."

What conversation ever achieved something beyond the exchange of updates, the confirmation of facts already in evidence? Conversation was time passing, syllables destined to be forgotten, intelligence with no purpose, divorced from the long game of life, an inconsequential thing. Conversations that actually were important almost never seemed so as they were unfolding; it came later, the understanding that a certain moment had been significant. "Cheryl."

"Yes?"

Anyway: What did Rebecca want? "You can get your own water. In my house. In this house. You should know that." Rebecca snapped an asparagus too near the top. There was only the tip left, but she threw it into the roasting pan.

"I'm sorry." Cheryl's eyes were, as everyone's, inscrutable.

"I need you to know that." Christine had not understood. Rebecca's disinterest was not depression. It was clarity. The trauma had been epiphany: so little mattered. She could not go back to being the same person that Christine and everyone else expected her to be. It wasn't so dramatic as to say that person had died with Priscilla—better to say that Rebecca learned something, from Priscilla's death, from Andrew's life, and she changed. But life lesson: people don't want one another to change.

"I know that." Cheryl was still smiling, faintly. There was something so stubborn about her. "I need you to know something, too."

Rebecca stopped. "What is it?"

"Skin is not skin."

"What do you mean?"

"I'm telling you about black skin. I'm telling you about shea butter. You could—you could listen to me."

Rebecca felt, absurdly, like crying. "I'm sorry. I just meant—you know, we're all human. We're all in this . . ."

"I know what you meant."

"I just thought . . . We're not pretending at something. We're doing it. Ian said, that day at the courthouse. He said, *We're a family now.*"

Cheryl laughed. "Fine, we're family. He's my *brother*. He's black. I'm black. I don't need you to tell me skin is skin, I need you to just listen for once." Then, more seriously. "It's not like it's some bad thing that we can't admit. He's black. It's a fact."

Rebecca looked down at the counter before her. "You think I don't listen?"

Cheryl smiled. "Sometimes you don't. You knew that."

"I didn't." Rebecca sniffled a little, wanted not to cry. "You're my son's sister. You come and go in this house as you like. You get your own water. You belong here."

"I'm your son's sister. I'm in your house and I'm telling you something."

"Sorry." Rebecca felt hot/silly/out of control, not a way anyone enjoyed feeling. She looked at the kitchen, at her wooden spoons, stained from use, at attention in the porcelain crock. Cheryl was a specter, an echo of her mother. How unhelpful, to wish one person was a different person. Priscilla was dead, and Rebecca was left with the woman's son and the woman's daughter and that was that. "You're right."

They were both quiet for a minute, two, three, five.

"The boys are going to be dying to open their presents. Are dying." Rebecca tried to sound cheerful. "Well, not Andrew, of course, but Jacob. He keeps picking them up and shaking them."

"What's the point in Christmas without presents? Not Christ, but don't tell Ian I said so. We went to church with his mom. She makes me call her Mama."

Rebecca knew how the Johnson women felt about God. She always rolled her eyes when people spoke of *God's plan*—as, weirdly, happened often. A white mom with a black kid made people think of a God, busily planning. Many want to believe in order. A well-enough-intentioned foolishness.

"How do you get along? You and . . . Her name? Nancy? Why can't I remember?"

"Leslie. Mama, though. But it's Leslie. We get along. There's Ivy. She gives you something to fuss over. Something to talk about." Cheryl leaned forward. "She thinks stones have power. Energy. She gave me this purple crystal. She wants me to put it on the dresser in Ivy's room. I don't even understand what it's supposed to do, but it doesn't sit right with me. It's not like it's voodoo or something. It's not scary. It's stupid."

"One of those." Rebecca didn't know quite what she meant. She tried to imagine Leslie, mother of Ian, churchgoing lady who liked magical rocks.

"You get it. Christopher has a mother. I met her. That year. At Jacob's birthday party. She was so thin. That's what I remember. She didn't say much."

"She said enough." Rebecca remembered that day. "But she's harmless, in the end. Or well-meaning. I'm sure Leslie and her crystals are the same. We all want good things for the people we care about. And like you said, the children, they're insulation. It's harder to give in to your annoyance when you have children. Or I'm so busy caring about them that I don't care so much about almost anyone else."

"Ian bought Jacob a remote-controlled car. I think he wants to play with it himself. You should have seen him at Toys "R" Us; he was like a boy again."

Cars were the only subject that held Jacob's interest. Ian's trade made him a hero. Jacob never questioned why Ian and Cheryl were associated with their family's most special occasions. He relished the attention. "He's going to love that. So much. I couldn't stop myself buying Ivy a doll. There's something about a little girl and a doll." Lorraine had maintained a halfhearted feminist stance against Barbie but was overruled by the time she'd had Christine. Rebecca had grown up in a house overrun with tiny plastic purses and shoes, Barbies modified by haircuts immediately regretted, slender plastic bodies spritzed, when she wasn't looking, with Lorraine's Chanel. Rebecca had wanted an American Girl for Ivy, but there were no black American Girls despite the preponderance of black American girls.

Upstairs, Andrew began to cry and Jacob called out for her almost simultaneously, urgent, that *Mommy* that traveled through walls and settled right on Rebecca's spine. She righted the boys' sleep-rumpled clothes as best she could, knowing there would be photographs. Christopher drifted into the general company from wherever he had been hiding—of late, he had been hiding—and Ivy and Ian came inside bearing pies and presents. Ivy sat on the floor by the fireplace and played; Andrew sat on the floor by the sofa and played. They mostly ignored each other, as a housecat does a guest. Jacob asked about opening gifts, or noisily impersonated a truck, or trotted between rooms in a futile search for something he couldn't articulate. Christopher sat with Cheryl and Ian, clasped a tumbler of Chivas, and peppered them with questions Rebecca could not make out from the next room.

Cheryl laid the table without asking Rebecca's leave. This seemed to be right. Rebecca turned the lights down, just a bit, and the scene was picturesque, the food appealing, even if the reality was messy, Jacob fiddling and spilling, Andrew fussing and yawning, Ivy wanting to be held, Christopher going for a refill, Ian going to change a diaper. Only Rebecca and Cheryl sat at the table the duration of the meal, ignoring or soothing the children, and intent on actually eating their food, because motherhood was mercenary and you needed sustenance to survive it.

24

REBECCA STILL CALLED ANDREW HER *BABY*, BUT HE BARELY WAS ANY-
more. He was old enough to start at Woodley Park Montessori
in only weeks. Jacob would enter first grade at Sidwell. Re-
becca would be granted her days and was unsure what they'd
hold as she'd already gone to the trouble of learning to write
at night. That had cost her: no dinner with her husband, no
nights by the television. But so what? Those nights were not
silent—the boys in their beds, breathing, stirring. The school
day would bring impenetrable quiet to the house on Wisconsin
Drive; she used to wish for that most fervently and now she
feared it.

But that was the future and this was the now. She'd drawn
the curtains to keep the August sun at bay, and dressed the
boys only in their shorts, and turned up the air-conditioning,
and gave them yogurt with frozen blueberries for breakfast.
(Purple yogurt calcified on the table.) Andrew had pooped in
his diaper but Rebecca hadn't changed him yet, because he was
standing contentedly behind the curtains she'd just drawn, no
doubt getting purple yogurt everywhere. Rebecca was happy
as long as he was happy. Jacob was watching the ninja turtles.

Rebecca was not thinking beyond the shitty diaper to the day they were about to have. The key was not to do this for too long. The boys would get impatient and she would get flustered and then she would have to improvise and improvisation mostly failed. She sipped her iced tea. Judith had a pool, but that meant a drive long enough that both of the boys would get crabby. Rebecca was tallying pros and cons so feverishly that she was not wholly conscious of hearing the garage door engage, slide up, the mechanical shudder it gave when it had done its work, nor was she conscious of the engine being turned off, or the door opening. Christopher came into the kitchen.

Rebecca felt in flagrante delicto; all she was doing was thinking, and thinking didn't *look like* anything, or more to the point: it looked like nothing. "Christopher." This was unusual but the boys barely seemed to notice, diverted by the television.

Christopher put his bag on the floor.

He was on the verge of saying something, so Rebecca said nothing, just looked at him, though she did, absurdly, stand, as though royalty had entered.

He held up a finger, pointing at the ceiling. "I just need twelve minutes. Twelve minutes. And I know it's half ten in the morning, but I'm having a drink." Christopher took down a glass. He looked at once wild and placid.

"OK." Rebecca did not know what else was called for.

"I'm going to have a cigarette, too." He had waged his war. The gum, the transdermal patch, acupuncture. This was a cessation of hostilities.

Why hector? She could only nod. "We were going to go to Judith's. I thought maybe, a swim? I was just about to call her."

"Call that girl. The one next door, what's her name?"

"Stephanie?" She was the rather dim Nebraskan cousin of the McKinneys at the end of the cul-de-sac. She was staying with her aunt and uncle until she started at Catholic University in the fall and had sat for them a couple of times. Rebecca was suspicious of her, because who would go to Catholic University if not someone with suspect opinions?

"Tell her to come. We can pay double if she comes now." Christopher filled the glass with Chivas. "For Christ's sake, it smells like shit in here."

It took more than twelve minutes, naturally, but Rebecca cleaned Andrew, pulled shirts over both the boys' heads, filled thermoses with iced water, and pressed forty dollars into Stephanie's hands. She said to try the public pool or a movie. Rebecca barely cared, in that moment, choosing to trust Stephanie, not picturing, as she did in her worst moments, a car accident, one of those drownings in two inches of water people were always warning about. Sometimes you had to believe that all would be well.

Christopher was sitting at the backyard table, suit and tie despite the heat. There were two cigarette butts bent and bruised, the teak of the table smudged black. Rebecca sat. She had known him for one-quarter of her life. She knew enough to not say anything. She sipped her tea.

"This morning the secretary and Bob resigned."

She thought to wait. But he waited too long—hung fire, and she yearned for the fire. *Let it burn. Tell me.* Rebecca waited.

"I heard it from the receptionist." Christopher lifted the glass but did not drink. He put it back down. "They didn't bother to tell me to my face. Then, I saw Bob—he was walking out, just walking away from the whole thing. He looked me in the eye and told me I could refer any inquiries to Hill and Knowlton. Just like that. *Any inquiries, Chris, it's Hill and Knowlton.*"

The Chris not Christopher, she knew, was insult to injury. "So you were right to suspect something bad."

"Hill and Knowlton are publicists, the ones you call when the shit hits. Damage control."

"Bob is an asshole." Rebecca had come to hate him. They'd spent the Fourth of July together at the Congressional Country Club, a grandiose name for a place that had nothing to do anymore with Congress and its particular delusions of grandeur. You did sometimes see a member who was a member, anonymous men, pallid in golf clothes. The fireworks had gone off and the babies had started crying. His wife had leaned her beautiful head toward Rebecca's and said, *I don't know how we do it*. It was supposed to be sisterly, but Rebecca had enough sisters. "He called you Chris?"

He sighed. "I gave them my time. My reputation. Now, where do I go from here? As you can see, I decided the answer was to go home."

"They're jerks. And, evidently, crooks." She felt vindicated, like her personal distaste had a moral dimension. "Obviously, you didn't do anything wrong." She knew this mattered. Christopher believed in the system. They'd once walked hand in hand spinning wishes for the future: she'd imagined some future president would ask her to bless his administration by reading in front of the crowd, he'd imagined he'd do *good* on behalf of the world. Now here they were, just another couple in the suburbs.

"I just did my job, which, you know, was to lie, apparently."

Money was boring, money was idiotic, money was abstract in a manner that was even more irritating than poetry. Rebecca had shitty diapers and summer days. "Well, not to get all Marxist about it, it is a bank. So I'm not sure what you'd expect."

"What to expect." Christopher frowned at his glass, twirled it to rattle the ice. "A few months back. Morgenthau, the district attorney in New York, the one who took down BCCI, his name came up, and I said, *Oh, should we be worried?* and they said, *It's a front in the Intifada. Morgenthau is after the Arabs, not the Americans.* Laughter. Like the district attorney was a pesky younger brother."

This was like poetry; the spaces in the conversation, the gaps, were where the information was. It was what *you* made of it. Maybe everything in the world was subjective. "So they're racist as well as corrupt."

Christopher laughed. "Maybe so."

"I'm sure it's not so bad." She hesitated because it sounded quite bad, actually; if he was telling her, it had to be.

Christopher lit a cigarette theatrically, but it was a gesture impossible to execute without some flair. He exhaled noisily. "It's plenty bad. This is what's out there, you know, in the world. Bad. You wouldn't know, though."

Not really a question, but an assessment, the candor of drunk at eleven in the morning. She sat up. "I wouldn't?"

"You know your poetry, yes. But you don't know much about how the world actually works."

"Do tell."

"I'd like to switch places, sometimes, you know that? Think about poetry, poetry about nothing. Your poems, they pretend to be about Ovid but they're all just about poetry itself. It must be nice, I think. Not to think about the way things are, in the world."

She crossed her arms in front of her. She knew his anger was for being made to look a fool. He'd been proven to be not important enough to be told the truth. "Maybe I know what's out there, in the world, as you say. And maybe I'm happier doing what it is I do."

"Last year, Bob comes to my office." Christopher broke the cigarette on the table. The tip smoldered. *"I need you to take this meeting.* What is there to say but yes? *He's no one,* he says. *He was at the LSE, so were you. He'll come in, you can talk about the bank. It's thirty minutes. I need you to do it, he's someone's cousin. Someone's cousin,* I say. *Gaddafi,* he says. He laughs. Then goes white. *Someone's cousin,* he says. *It's nothing. Do this for me and the secretary. A personal favor.*"

Christopher usually spoke in euphemism. Their marriage was small talk. It was like a party. Maybe Christopher's life was like a party. She was not used to hearing stories from work or maybe she was not used to paying attention. "So maybe you're the one, then. The one who can't see what's right in front of you."

"Gaddafi. He said it, and he'd said too much, and we both had to pretend it hadn't happened. I sat in my office with this chap. He wanted to meet the higher-ups, but I couldn't introduce this *person* to the former secretary of defense."

Rebecca had never truly cared that the man had once been the secretary of defense. That did not seem so important, nor so difficult.

"It's always *someone's cousin. Someone's cousin* wanted an invitation to be wherever Diana was going to be," Christopher said. "Now *someone's cousin* wanting to meet some powerful men. But who is that someone? And how many steps away from someone criminal do you need to be in order not to be a criminal yourself?"

"What did you expect? That you could work in the embassy, work in a bank, and the things that were being done—by the government, by the bankers—those things wouldn't affect you somehow?"

Christopher leaned back and surveyed the yard. "Was it naive to think so? That I could be a man near power, a man with some power of his own, and that power would be used for the greater good?"

"We've done what we wanted, mostly. We've made this life."

Christopher laughed. "I've made this, for us. This money. And you just don't care, do you, how it's happened."

She could not recall being so mad at anyone, ever before, not even Isaiah, love of her youth, the day he'd sat her on his face, pulled apart her ass with his soft hands and sighed and said, *The ugliest part of you is the most beautiful to me.* "I don't see what our lives have to do with—"

"Let's say they were working with the Libyans. I don't know whether they were banking for Gaddafi, but I know which of the three of us sat in an office with the man's nephew, making small talk."

"Small talk. You did as you were asked."

"Not much of a moral defense. Doing as you're asked." Christopher seemed calmer. "Anyway, to discover that the whole thing was some sort of illusion, that maybe they were up to no good. I feel insane."

"I hate him." It was satisfying to say this. "I hate her, too. But I hate him more. He said to me, you know, at that dinner, for whoever it was, he said to me, *We think it's just beautiful what you're doing.* Just beautiful. *You're going to give that child a beautiful life.* What the fuck does he know about beautiful lives. You don't get a medal for loving a black person." Her mind went to Stephanie, Catholic Stephanie, whom she did not know at all, and she hoped she'd not driven off the road.

"I guess I thought everything would be different."

"But it's not so bad. The way things turned out. We have each other, we have our sons, we have this life."

"This is *criminal,* you realize. Maybe it's insider trading. Hell, maybe it's treason. I knew—I knew they were no good, but I suppose I imagined that I was."

He was a good man, he was her husband, distressed and sweating in his suit. "We're good people." It had never occurred to her that they were anything but.

Christopher stood and took off his jacket. "Every fucking asshole I've met in this city is a lawyer and I cannot think of a single one I can call." He tossed the jacket onto the table, covering the now empty tumbler, the cigarette butts. "You're the one of us who has it better, Rebecca. To stay here, at home, with the boys. That's real. That's good. There's nothing good out there in the world, is there?"

She pushed back in her chair and stood. "Come inside. Change out of your clothes. Take a shower. We'll discuss what comes next."

Christopher kissed her, softly, gently, then more roughly, his tongue touching hers. "I'm tired of discussing what comes next," he said.

25

WITH THE BOYS OFF AT SCHOOL, REBECCA WAS FREE AT LAST, YET
she *missed* them. Motherhood was idiotic. She put a television
in her office to replicate their constant chatter, and there was
John Major among the MPs, the lot murmuring discontentedly,
in keeping with the long national tradition of crabbiness. How
could work hold her interest given this?

"Madam Speaker, the House will wish to know that the de-
cision to separate has no constitutional implications. The suc-
cession to the throne is unaffected by it. The children of the
prince and princess retain their position in the line of succes-
sion. And there is no reason why the Princess of Wales should
not be crowned queen in due course."

Diana's *due course:* impeccable clothes, those beautiful sons,
that irreducible quality that was part glamour, part grace, part
show, part pomp, part something impossible to define that was
hers alone, maybe the weight of the hopes and fantasies of ev-
ery woman (they were all women) who was forever looking
at the princess. Diana was unique in the world. In her weaker
moments, Rebecca still thought of herself that way: as unique.
Most moments, she knew better.

"Madam Speaker, I know there will be great sadness at this news. But I know also that as they continue with their royal duties and with bringing up their children, the prince and princess will have the full support, understanding, and affection of this house and of this country." *And me!* Rebecca wanted to add. What did Diana need of Charles, anyway? Fish and bicycles!

Rebecca set aside whatever portent was in it. Her due course was work and because it had been a job well done, she didn't mind giving in to the television's seductions. She had it right there: the evidence. *The New Yorker,* folded open to the page (page! in its entirety!) given over to Rebecca Stone.

It had been months in the making, months of rations, energy a finite resource (only so much zooplankton had rotted into petrol) and Rebecca neglecting the laundry, relaxing the rules re: daily baths, avoiding even the marital bed. A poem was the fruit of something near paranoia, and it was time-consuming. She had earned this, a day in her office, television turned up loud, distracted and reliving her own success.

The poem truly began in January 1982, an icy Wednesday worth remembering, a sky purpled with clouds, a plane that crashed into the Potomac. Air Florida flight 90 had lifted but failed, skimmed over a bridge and acceded to gravity. This was Icarus, the impossibility of flight, the way we try to lift up but always fall down, or so it seemed to her at first. A poem was one matter and another and a third, fourth, fifth; the poem was a theory toward their bond, less a map than a guess. What did she know? At least, at last, she had a subject. Tragedy had given her that (Priscilla had given her that, too): something to write *about.* She wrote—about how we try to live but end up dying, about the kind of cold that causes floes to form, about the drivers on the Fourteenth Street Bridge unaware of death sweeping down from above. And, yes, only she would see it, but she wrote about how, the day after that plane had crashed, she'd met Christopher for the first time. The plane was the thing, it was plain. Maybe a poem was a map and it led somewhere quite stupid.

Rebecca turned off the television and took out the new *Vogue*. She'd earned that, no? Rebecca had sent her papers off to Alice Quinn. It was that woman who called the whole lot *Folly* (what greater folly than to feel invincible?) and published it. Rebecca had earned some easy entertainment and was annoyed when the telephone intruded upon this.

"Rebecca, it's Cheryl. I'm sorry to call, but I need a favor."

"Of course." It didn't matter what it was. Rebecca had been waiting for this opportunity, that student always first to raise her hand. "Is everything OK?"

Everything was fine. Ivy was ill, suddenly—this happened, a condition of being three almost four, your natural joy could switch without warning to tears and vomiting—and Cheryl had gone onto her weekly double shift and Ian was at work.

"It's not a problem." Rebecca was already putting on her shoes. "Don't say another word. I'll call you when we're home. Ian can come whenever he can come."

Ivy's day care was in the basement of Good Shepherd, but tolerably nondenominational, and was inexpensive, too. Rebecca went to the main office.

"I'm here to pick up Ivy Barber."

The doughy woman at the desk raised her eyebrows. She put the cap on her pen and frowned. "I see. Are you on her blue card?"

"I'm not sure what a blue card is. Can I see Ivy? Is she feeling OK?" There had been vomit, Cheryl said. It was her trade, so she was not overly worried, but she was a mother. Rebecca knew about vomit's violence, the rack of a small body. A child's pain is terrible in a way that an adult's is not. It was her responsibility to hug the girl, plus she'd brought along some of Andrew's clothes in case she was dirty.

"Ma'am, I cannot let you see one of our students unless I verify that you are on the *blue card*." The tone of every tyrant everywhere. Forget the absolute: tiny tastes of power corrupt, too.

Rebecca's default mode was genial. Flies and honey. Her dad had taught her about math and sports, but society had taught her that. Put on lipstick and everyone will love you. Then she had Jacob and discovered something else: she could be fierce. "Please look at the card, then, if that is so important. There's a sick child waiting for me."

The woman thumbed through a little recipe box filled with index cards. They were, indeed, blue. "Barber, Barber," she said to herself.

"It begins with B." Rebecca jingled the car keys in her hand.

She moistened a fingertip with her tongue and flicked and flicked.

Rebecca had always found this licking of clerical fingers disgusting. She listened for the sounds of children but those were curiously absent or perhaps she couldn't pick them out over the ambient hum of her own annoyance.

"Barber. Your name again?"

"It's Rebecca Stone. I'm Ivy's . . . aunt." Rebecca faltered. Near enough the truth.

"I'm sorry, miss, but you're not on the card." The woman was triumphant.

"It's Mrs. Stone." Rebecca summoned the power of the patriarchy. "It must be an oversight. Cheryl is at work. The child is sick. She called me. So here I am."

"Well, the school is authorized only to release a child to the people specified here in writing. It's the school's policy."

This is not a school, Rebecca did not say. "I am her aunt."

The woman pondered this. "This is the school's policy."

At Woodley Park Montessori, even those who didn't know Rebecca knew by sight the white woman who came to fetch the black boy. There were two other black children there, with black mothers. Once, another of the mothers had mistakenly thought one of those other children, a boy named Marcus, was Rebecca's son. They pretended that this was no matter, but it was. She wondered what would happen if she dispatched Cheryl to fetch Andrew. Cheryl could declaim her kinship and be believed: he looked just like her.

"You'll have to call Cheryl. Immediately. Ivy needs to go home with me now." Why was she not on this all-important blue card? Was there meaning in this as there was meaning in everything?

"I'm afraid that's against our policy. We require written authorization. A copy of the designated person's ID must be kept on file. I'm afraid there's nothing we can do now. I don't know who you are. I need the child's parents."

This was a woman who believed: Satanists running day cares, music urging teens to commit suicide, LSD in the Halloween candy. Rebecca took a breath. "I am Rebecca Stone. I'm her aunt. I've just told you that. So you do know who I am. Is there someone else I can speak to?" Had Cheryl not written down Rebecca's name and telephone number for a reason, or had Cheryl simply forgotten, for that moment, that her family was as large as it was?

"I don't see how you can be her aunt. And I'm afraid the director is in a meeting. At any rate, this is the policy and it's not going to change. For the safety of our children."

"You don't see?" Rebecca knew what this meant. "Cheryl telephoned me. And asked me to come. Cheryl is my family.

Ivy is my family. I don't need you to see. I need you to take me to where Ivy is right now, or let me speak to someone who can *see*."

"Ma'am, I'll have to ask you to lower your voice. This is a school. This is a safe space."

"This is the basement of a Catholic church. I need to speak to the director now."

The woman frowned, but it was a triumphant frown. She left Rebecca in the shabby office that smelled of pine-scented disinfectant. Everything about the space—the construction paper collages Scotch-taped to the cinder-block walls, the worn upholstery on the chairs meant for parents who were waiting—communicated what sort of place this was. A place for children was the one place in which a woman like Rebecca could be assured of her authority.

The formless gormless woman returned, another woman with her. This woman wore a purple turtleneck and eyeglasses on a chain. These gave her a kindly aspect. Rebecca could imagine this woman reading a story to a bunch of children seated in a semicircle. But this woman, crucially, was black. She could be made to understand, or she could be overruled.

"Can I help you?"

Rebecca ignored the first woman altogether. She extended a hand. "I'm Rebecca Stone. I'm here to pick up Ivy Barber. She's been taken ill. It seems that Cheryl hasn't listed me as one of the people authorized to pick her up. But I can assure you it's an oversight."

"Well, as you're aware it's the policy . . ."

"Ah, what's the use in policy if we can't think? I'm Cheryl's brother's mother. Cheryl's brother's adoptive mother. I've known Ivy since the day she was born. You can call Cheryl to confirm this, of course. You know, she works double shifts midweek at Foggy Bottom. Ivy's father works in Bethesda. He's tied up until six. The child is sick, and I am here to fetch her."

The woman looked at Rebecca. "It's just that we have this policy in place."

"Look. I'm clearly not a criminal. Please, call Cheryl, call Ian, but it would be lovely if you could do it quickly so I can take the girl home."

The woman took the blue card from her underling's hand and picked up the telephone.

Rebecca listened as she asked for Cheryl, because of course, in such an instance, you'd call the child's mother. Their conversation was brief.

"I'm sorry." She replaced the receiver. "Do come with me. Ivy's waiting in the teachers' lounge."

Rebecca took the girl home. She bathed her and put her in Andrew's pajamas and turned on a cartoon. Ivy fell asleep on the sofa, warm with fever, and Rebecca carried her to Andrew's bed, surrounded her with stuffed animals so she'd feel reassured when she woke. Christopher came home and Rebecca sent him to pick up the boys, so she wouldn't have to rouse Ivy.

She let the boys watch television because it was impossible, otherwise, to get them to play quietly. Ivy woke, vomited once more, and Rebecca changed her clothes again, washed her face and her mouth. She was flush, her beautiful skin aglow, her perfect hair mussed. Rebecca carried Ivy downstairs to where her uncle and Jacob—what was Jacob to her, there was no word—were eating their dinner. Rebecca made Ivy a piece of toast and held her warm body on her lap while the children talked about whatever children talk about. Ivy managed only a couple of bites, but chuckled more than once at the boys' prattle, and Rebecca knew, in that way a mother knows, that the sickness that had overrun her would have run past her by that time the next day.

Ian rang the doorbell at six thirty. Like any father would, he hurried past Rebecca to his child, scooped her up off the sofa, pressed his chin against her forehead. "Hi, baby. How are you feeling?"

"She'll be fine." You couldn't not smile: Jacob and Andrew huddled under a blanket on the floor, Ivy's damp face peeking out from another blanket.

"Rebecca, you're a lifesaver."

"It's nothing. Leave her for a minute. Come, sit."

Ian covered the girl back up and followed her into the kitchen. "I rushed over. What a stupid day. It's a busy time of year. Christmas presents and bargain hunters. I'm sorry, otherwise I would have been over earlier."

"Ian, please. There's nothing to be sorry about. You know I love Ivy."

Ian washed his hands at the kitchen sink. "I do know that."

"I'm happy to help. And it was basically nothing. She slept most of the day. Kids get that way, don't they, when they're sick. It's scary the first time it happens. You're so used to them being full of energy, it's weird when they want to just lie there and do nothing. But I'm an old hand. So, don't worry about Ivy, I'm almost certain that she's going to be back to herself by tomorrow."

"We don't have much experience with it, I guess. She's been pretty healthy. We're lucky. It's different now that she can talk. So different from when they're just babies and are so helpless and you feel insane."

"When the baby is sick, you feel like a crazy person. When they're bigger and they're sick, you just feel sad because they're so pathetic." Rebecca laughed. "She did throw up a lot, but she kept some toast down. And some juice. And she doesn't feel as warm. I have a feeling she just needs to wait this out."

"You're the best, Rebecca. I'd have called my mother, but you know, she's in Upper Marlboro, it's a drive, and the school made it sound like an emergency."

Rebecca shook her head. "Don't thank me again. It's what we do. Why don't you eat something? The kids are happy with their show. I don't want to think about you going home and eating a sandwich over the kitchen sink."

"Men cook, Rebecca. I'm known far and wide for my lasagna."

"You're not going to go home and put your sick child to bed and make a lasagna. I'll join you, actually. Some nights, I like to have dinner with the kids, even though it's so early. I like the togetherness, but if you want to know the truth, the thing I like best is that after the kids are bathed and put to bed, there's nothing left that I need to do. I can just do whatever I like." She sliced into the meatloaf, an unappealingly shaped thing, but it was good, she knew, because she was the one who'd dutifully chopped all those mushrooms, who'd pulverized the parsley and basil. She was the one who'd steamed cauliflower and smashed it through the ricer until the boys would eat it without complaint. She was the one who'd poured little plastic cups of milk, and toasted bread for Ivy, and cleared the table, and wiped it of crumbs, and gone upstairs to fetch blankets, and put the cassette into the video player. Christopher was at his desk, in their bedroom. It was amazing what you could choose not to know.

She put the plates on the table. "Turkey meatloaf. Spinach. Cauliflower in disguise as mashed potatoes. Do you want a glass of wine, Ian?"

"OK, this does look better than what I was going to have. No wine, thanks."

Rebecca sat across from him. The fixture over the kitchen table was unforgiving. You looked like you were being interrogated. Rebecca had wished for a dimmer switch for years. Even in the unflattering light, Ian looked his handsome, open self. A salesman's confidence, that instant warmth. He was not unlike Christopher; they both sold things for a living and had, accordingly, developed that ease with people, that utter belief in what it was they were selling, not cars, not banks, but faith in the promise of luxury, technology, wealth, power. The things that protect.

"This is delicious. Rebecca. Do you cook like this every night?"

"It depends. Sometimes I need the distraction. It's like the opposite of my work, because it's so real. It's a relief. Ivy was napping and I figured, I'll make a nice meal, that way I can hear her if she calls, and I'm using the time productively. Some days are like that, I want the distraction, or I want to have to think about cracking eggs or something, instead of, you know. Whatever."

"That's how I feel about the Orioles, I guess. But cooking has a practical application. My watching baseball doesn't do anything for anyone. But we all need our escapes. I like my job, don't get me wrong. But you know, you can only have the same conversation so many times a day."

"You must talk to some real characters."

"Divorcing men. The occasional spoiled teenager, but it's mostly divorcing men who need what I have to offer."

Rebecca sipped the wine she'd poured. She remembered, as was impossible not to, other meals, glasses of wine, at that table, with Christopher, with Priscilla. Those were over now. Diana and Charles were separating and Rebecca understood but could never admit to anyone else that this meant that she and Christopher would, too. Admitting you can see what fate has in store exposes you to mockery as much as believing in the curative powers of crystals.

"It's so cute, don't you think?" Ian gestured toward the den with his knife. "The three of them. Together like that. There's something about it I love to see."

"Looking at a child is like looking at the future. Sometimes I see past the moment, I see the boys playing, and the scene gets sort of frozen, and I feel so good about the future. It's a passing thought. But it's so powerful. I see the men they'll be. I see. I don't know. I see everything."

"I know what you mean, I think. Ivy lifts me out of time. But I get nervous. I worry about . . . everything. Boys. College tuition. My little girl making her way in the world."

"But you saw them." Rebecca smiled. She wondered what that bright light did to her face as she did, knew she was transformed, aged, made into something else by a trick. "How can you look at our children and not feel better about everything?"

They finished eating, and Ian did the washing, then he carried Ivy to the car and drove off into the night.

26

ANDREW HAD CRIED THE FIRST DAY REBECCA LEFT HIM AT MONTES-
sori. It broke her heart because he was so fat and darling, small
fingers sticky with nervous sweat. Now, he barely bade Re-
becca farewell. That morning he had kicked off his shoes and
run into his teacher's bosomy embrace. Of course you wanted
the children to have a happiness independent of you. Rebecca
got back into the Volvo and drove to her parents' house in
Greenbelt.

She'd long stopped thinking of the split-level as having
anything to do with her life, but pulling into the driveway had
that feeling of familiarity. Rebecca knocked but it was conces-
sion to formality, last-minute warning; she opened the door,
which was unlocked, of course.

"Becky! Have you had breakfast?" Doctor Greg Brooks
was gifted at dadhood. He'd changed diapers and prepared
bottles, not much done at that time in history. He'd zipped his
girls into jackets and escorted them to the air and space mu-
seum, where he pointed out the *Spirit of St. Louis* but told them
all about Amelia Earhart. He brushed hair and learned a ser-
viceable braid and made each one feel pretty without compli-

menting their looks but by applauding their ingenuity. He only rarely slipped and called her *Becky*.

"I've had breakfast. We've been up for hours. I'd have a coffee, though. Hi, Dad."

"Hi yourself." He led her into the kitchen. "You all to myself, not a grandchild in sight?"

She shrugged. "I just thought it would be nice."

"You know I adore the boys, the whole gang but—it's hard to *talk*."

Rebecca recognized the mug, the inverted comma of a rainbow, once white porcelain gone vanilla from years of use. "That's an understatement. Thanks. How is everything, Dad?"

He had taken his retirement, having served with distinction, a dentist-cum-actuary for the federal government. Greg Brooks had been born during the Roosevelt administration, and raised his daughters to believe in science as a public good, art a worthwhile endeavor. "It's fine. I'm volunteering, I told you? Conversational English. We're just supposed to sit and converse."

"But you're doing more?" Rebecca knew him. She noticed the rooms were quiet, not even sports radio, which she had come to expect. "I know you're doing more than just conversing."

"Well, this woman—can you imagine going to Vietnam not knowing a word of their language? And figuring out how to enroll your kids in school? How to take the bus?"

"I can't." She never got it all done and had little idea how other women did, leaving aside the question of a foreign tongue.

"You remember Dr. Kline, he's still practicing—I took her to see him. She's got three kids, he saw all of them. They'd not been to a dentist, never, not once."

Rebecca hated thinking about teeth, but she liked thinking about her father playing the hero in his own small ways. He was a good man: what a great thing, to be able to say that. "Dad. That's so great. I bet you're their most popular volunteer."

He shrugged. "Well, I don't know about that. But it's nice, you get to be an old man and you stop feeling useful."

"Come on, Dad." She and her sisters had prearranged this round robin as a way to exercise their filial duty efficiently. At the same time, Rebecca needed him, just as she had when she'd turned up on their doorstep, near thirty, highly educated but heartbroken, well versed in literature but little else.

"Help me understand." Her father's eyes gleamed with mischief. "Are you checking up on me or am I checking up on you, I can't tell."

The coffee was bitter but warming. She shrugged.

"You've never needed much checking up on, though, have you?"

"I've had my moments."

He'd forgiven/forgotten them. "You're a great keeper of secrets, Rebecca. Of course, I've read your poems. I show them to everyone. You'd find it horribly embarrassing, I'm sure."

She shook her head.

"I guess it's all there," he continued. "I remember that day the plane crashed. You and I were together, we sat and watched it on the television news." He paused. "I was surprised to read about it again, all these years later. It clearly—it *meant* something to you. And I was there. I feel touched, somehow. Don't tell me if I'm wrong to feel that way. I enjoy it, this feeling. Like I'm a part of your work."

If she'd been a chef, she could talk about flavor. If she'd been a painter, she could talk about color. If she'd been a lawyer, rhetoric; a doctor, the body's systems; a physicist, the enshrined laws the entire universe obeyed. Rebecca felt she had to keep her work mostly to herself. "It was a terrible crash. That day, it was so cold, and those pictures—they were so terrible. A man running across the ice and throwing himself into the water, trying to save someone who had survived. I can't imagine, surviving a plane falling from the sky. Or anything, I guess, surviving anything."

"The television has done something to us. To human beings. We can see so much, but maybe we weren't made to see this much. Maybe it's too much."

She was grateful that he'd taken the particular memory and made it philosophy. "I guess not." That period, near a year, Rebecca had tarried in the house of her youth, unable to make a start in life. Poetry had felt like a vice, and she had sneaked off to the library, Saturdays, to photocopy her work (five cents a sheet), to clip self-addressed, stamped envelopes to the sheaf of papers still warm from the machine that she mailed off to the addresses she found in the library's pristine copy of *Writer's Markets*. She'd collected rejections, tiny slivers of mimeographed paper, that smeary purple ink, boilerplate apologias, those envelopes returning home insistently as salmon. It seemed not so long ago. She'd survived.

"So, something is the matter." Her father peeled an orange. The room smelled of it. "You'll tell me or you won't."

Rebecca felt a twinge of guilt, a desire not to tattle. "I don't know."

Her father chewed. "Marriage is—not easy."

"It's been bad. Dad, it's been—" At the end of the previous summer, Christopher had tendered his resignation, and eight days later his mother had died alone in her Kensington duplex: a cardiac event, a slip, snapped bones, the ultimate failure altogether of the heart. Elizabeth had been eighty. This had quite near broken his heart. So months had slipped by in this discomfiting détente.

"Well, of course, he's had a hard time." Her father knew it all. Morgenthau had secured indictments against the secretary and Bob, who, it turned out, left the bank with about six million dollars each. Christopher spent his days taking meetings, atoning while asserting his fundamental honesty. "He's found a job?"

Rebecca shook her head. "There's money, from his mother. But there's something else."

"A man's job is his place in the world. Especially a man like Christopher. I would be the same, I think. I spent thirty-two years at my job, as you know. It mattered to me, what I did, every day. That gave my life shape. That and you girls, of course. Your mother. But the job, it mattered. It's his pride. It's his center. It's like your poetry."

"So I should be—understanding."

"Your work, your book, they matter to you."

"They do." She stood and refilled her coffee, just for something to do. This was like talking to a therapist insofar as Rebecca felt trapped.

"You're my child, my youngest. Naturally, I want only what's best for you. And there are my grandchildren; I want what's best for them."

"I feel like—" She might as well say it aloud. "I feel like it's my fault, his unhappiness. Like it began the day I woke up and realized that I could never let Andrew go. That I decided what our family life was going to be and that changed everything." Maybe there was a finite amount of love in her and Rebecca had exhausted that supply.

Her father was thoughtful. "But of course, the one has nothing to do with the other. Christopher found himself in a bad spot, which had nothing to do with him and nothing to do with you. It was bad luck."

She knew about bad luck. "But ever since then."

"Andrew is a blessing. You can't think about what happened in any other terms. He's your son. And Christopher's, too." He thought for a moment. "I know your sister had her reservations. I know your mother had her reservations. But I told her, *Rebecca makes good decisions!* And I stand by it."

"We barely talk." Mornings, after dropping Andrew, Rebecca went home and Christopher went out. It was like she'd opened a window and chased out a moth. And Rebecca didn't rue it; she sat down at her desk and she wrote. "Sometimes I don't know what to say to him. Sometimes I imagine not saying anything to him, ever again, and what worries me is that I am able to imagine it. And it's not even something I fear. Not for me, not for the boys. Lots of families divorce. It's commonplace. It's almost—nothing."

"It's not nothing." He shook his head emphatically, gathered the citrus peel into his palm. "But there are certainly worse things."

"I feel like I'm supposed to do something. Like we're both waiting for something to happen."

"Aren't we always, in life, waiting for something to happen?"

Rebecca didn't want philosophy; she wanted to be told how to proceed. She'd known it, so clearly, when it had to do with Andrew; now that it had to do with herself, she was at a loss. "I guess so."

"You could try counseling. It's valuable, I think. Like taking the car in to be tuned. Responsible."

Christine and Tim did that, she knew, but Rebecca had always judged that a weakness. But as strange a purgatory as this was, she didn't want to be *without* Christopher. Without him, she would be lonely, but of course, with him, she was lonely. "I don't know what I want, Dad. Maybe it's not important."

Her father stood and as he did, she realized, to her dismay, that his stance was shaky. He walked to the trash can and dropped in the discards from his fruit. He was an old man, her father, and she was not a girl, and though he was wise, he had nothing to offer her, because maybe no one did. She remembered with such clarity other, earlier days, in that same kitchen, with her father, who the years had transformed when she was not paying attention. That poem, it had taken up a whole page, but it had also taken up all those months, and there was something unfair in that exchange. Rebecca had a sudden desire, to take her father away, out of that house. To go to Tastee Diner and order pancakes and conjure other, earlier visits to Tastee Diner to eat pancakes, to slip out of time into some kind of enchantment, and not look back, as Orpheus did, to be sure the spell would never be broken and that things would always be just as they were, however unhappy they might seem.

27

EASTER WASN'T SACRED BUT IT WAS SPECIAL. SHE AND CHERYL HAD decided it would be thus, that Christopher's absence wasn't to be an impediment and it wasn't: it was barely remarked upon, because conversation could only progress so far with so many children about. They sat, Ian, Cheryl, Rebecca, the three kicking, fidgeting kids, and the meal that had taken Rebecca hours to prepare was finished in a matter of minutes, but that was how it always worked.

"We can talk about it." Cheryl placed the stack of soiled cake plates on the counter, breaking the silence Rebecca hadn't even known she was invested in maintaining. "I'm just saying. Not trying to push."

There was no point in pretending she didn't understand what was meant. "Where are the kids?"

"They're watching television. Ian's got it under control." Cheryl's face was nothing more than empathy. She was so full of that particular quality you'd call her *beautiful* even if her face didn't have the mysterious mathematical harmony that lands some women on magazine covers. It was in the sound of her voice, the straightness of her spine, almost in her scent, and *beautiful* seemed the best word for it.

Rebecca switched off the faucet, tugged at the rubber gloves.

"Maybe a glass of something." Cheryl poured what was left of the chardonnay. "I think—I think maybe it's just what you need."

Rebecca took the glass. She sat on one of the tall stools. Already, for no reason, she could feel herself wanting to cry. "It's nothing, Cheryl." This was feeble she knew, even as she said it.

Cheryl's mouth was lopsided, disapproval and doubt. "So, Christopher's in Denver. For work?"

"He is!" She felt it was important that she hadn't actually been dishonest. Christopher had taken a position at the National Transportation Safety Board in March. *There's a whole structure of diplomacy that exists between the government and our corporate citizens,* he had explained, excited. The work renewed him. "They have a field office there."

Cheryl had not poured her own glass of wine. "It's funny timing, I guess."

"It's been coming, Cheryl. You can see that."

"Have you guys—"

Christopher had come home, that first day, suited and smiling, then after dinner had sighed and begun with something along the lines of *We should talk.* He mentioned unhappiness, he mentioned the children. He mentioned that this was all quite normal, in this day and age. "A separation." That was the noun they'd used. "We've talked about what it'll look like. What it will involve."

Cheryl looked struck. "Rebecca, I am sorry." She waited. "I can't say that I'm surprised. Maybe it's even been a long time coming. Maybe there's some relief in that. But that doesn't make it—it's still sad."

That night, after that conversation, they'd found each other in bed, which was sort of predictable, wasn't it, the embarrassing and fleeting consolation of orgasm. "I don't know, you deal, right? You don't have time, for sadness, not that much."

"Sure, life must go on, I get that, but . . ." Cheryl looked doubtful. "It's just us, talking, you don't have to put up a brave front."

"I am fine. I swear." She meant it, the tears some kind of side effect, a measure just of heightened feeling. She was inured to Christopher's unhappiness, and absent that was left surprised that she didn't have quite as large a measure of the stuff. "Is that terrible?"

"What happened?" Cheryl leaned back against the counter, her head framed by the cabinets. She looked taller. She was intent, she wanted them to get to something.

"It wasn't one of those big dramatic things. It was just—you're one kind of person, years pass, you have a kid, you become a different kind of person. Then you look around and you're not the one your husband fell in love with and maybe he's not the person you fell in love with and it's just like—what are we doing here?"

"I guess in the ideal situation you'd both change, together. In the same ways, or complementary ways. But what about you, Rebecca? Do you still—is this what you want?"

What could she say: that thus far, what happened to Diana happened to Rebecca, so she'd known, on some level, that it was coming? Diana was Rebecca's big sister, role model, example, she was everywoman, cautionary tale, fate personified. "It makes sense, I guess. He's less than happy. His work. His world. Maybe I haven't been the best, at paying attention. At being a wife, the kind of wife a man like Christopher needs."

"Well, that's a two-way street. Has he been what you need?"

"What if I don't—" It was so cruel to hear it aloud. "What

if I don't need him? What if. I'm happy, in other ways. The boys, my work. My life. It's selfish but I'm happy, and I don't have it in me, maybe, to make him happy.

"Fair." Cheryl nodded. "From the outside, from where I sit, he has it all. You both do. He always seemed to be so delighted in you. And you, too, in him. I know you can't tell from the outside, I know it's not that simple. But it's sad. You should allow yourself to be sad about it."

"I guess I just feel like we're dodging the real bullet here. Like we're not forcing ourselves to get to that point where we *hate*. I don't know. You probably don't understand."

"What makes you say that?"

"You, Ian. It's so perfect. Not a fairy tale, those fairy-tale marriages are bullshit. But like—a meeting of the minds."

"Well, we have our problems, too, Rebecca."

"You do?" This was a surprise.

"We're normal people. I don't see why you'd find that weird."

"It's just surprising."

"All people have problems."

"But what—"

Cheryl looked up at the ceiling as though the answer were written there. "He wanted another. Wants. Another child."

"But you don't."

"He's one of seven. He's used to it. The chaos, the noise, industrial-size dinners."

"But you don't—"

Cheryl was quiet. It was a silence with something stoic in it. "You can understand why."

Rebecca waited. "I guess I think of you two as having the best marriage. That kind of perfect marriage. Did you watch *The Cosby Show*, Cheryl? You must have."

She laughed. "Must I have? I watched it, sure."

"Did you see the last episode? A year ago, I guess?" She was not guessing; she remembered. That trial in L.A. had ended, those policemen exonerated though everyone had seen them hit hit hit hit hit hit hit that man. They needed a little comedy.

"Maybe." Cheryl was noncommittal.

"It was during the riots." Rebecca had a point to make. A year on, a riot still didn't seem like something that could happen *there*. It was the kind of thing that happened in places where there wasn't enough food. Here there was enough food; Rebecca threw plenty of it in the garbage. "It was the last episode, which was too bad. I enjoyed that show." Also: Andrew needed that model of being black, Bill Cosby and his silly faces, his beautiful wife in her smart clothes. *This is the man I want you to be,* Rebecca was telling him. *I want you to be Bill Cosby.*

"I remember the riots. I think that's what we mostly watched. CNN."

"So it was the last episode, of this show, this groundbreaking show." She felt ridiculous, talking about television. "And the last scene, it was so lovely. Cosby and his wife, dancing. That show, it was such a fairy tale about romance. Like you could have four kids and still be . . . in love."

"They had five kids."

"Anyway, they dance, and the lights come up, and they just dance off into the audience. They run out and you see the whole thing—it's all pretend. The house is just a set. The books are just props. It's just fake."

Cheryl laughed. "Rebecca. It's a television show. Of course it's fake."

Rebecca was hurt. "I know that! But maybe it's good, to remember that, that happily ever after is for television shows. Real romance, real marriage—life has so many little disappointments, all these paths you never thought you'd take."

Cheryl lifted the stack of dirty dishes and set them into the sink. "You're dodging the question, I think, Rebecca."

"Am I?"

Cheryl shrugged. "It's OK if you don't want to talk."

"I just don't know what to say is all. If I had an easy answer, some simple summary of why it's not working, why it's time to—I know we took a vow. I get that."

"I know life is more complicated than arbitrary vows."

"I'll probably feel sad, later. Truly sad."

"Probably."

"Christopher—when he gets back from this trip, I think we're going to sit the boys down and explain it to them." She had no sense of how that might play out.

"I'm sure that won't be fun. But it's got to be done."

Rebecca pushed aside the glass of wine. "I don't feel like anything's ending, if that's what you want to hear. I feel like it's changing, and maybe it's a change for the better."

"You really are an optimist, aren't you, Rebecca?" Cheryl looked at her with either amazement or pity.

PART THREE

28

NEW YORK WAS HOT AND FETID. IT HAD BEEN CHRISTOPHER'S IDEA,
New York: when they'd put it to a vote (that or Ocean City),
the boys had sided with their father, as they were moved by
some general feeling toward him, perhaps pity. Rebecca had
thought it might be nice to sit on the beach. But the kids of
broken homes deserved family vacations, too.

Rebecca didn't even chafe at the small stuff that usually
drove one crazy in a divorce. She could sit through a meal
without wondering why Christopher chewed so loudly. It was
good she didn't hate him; Jacob was Christopher, again. Of
course, they had to believe that biology didn't matter, but it
sort of did. Rebecca watched: the way Jacob scratched his head
when he was bored was Christopher; the way Andrew loved
tart things (marmalade pickles sardines olives) was her. It was
DNA versus *monkey see*, though you couldn't say *monkey*, no
matter how much affection you put into it, if the baby was
black. Younger Jacob had worn a pair of soft pajamas embla-
zoned with monkeys. Rather than hand these down, Rebecca
had thrown them into the garbage.

Three hotel rooms were a not inconsiderable expense, but nonnegotiable. Jacob smelled, as boys that age did, some admixture of sweat and hormonal by-product (she did the laundry; she knew precisely what stage of development he'd reached), while Andrew would want to share a bed with her and she'd wake up with the boy's feet in her face, or his hand clutching that part of her bicep that he loved to clutch. This had to be a vacation for *her*, too.

They had done the Statue of Liberty and snapped a photo of the kids in front of the bull on Wall Street. They ate a fancy lunch at Windows on the World, but the view (it wasn't natural, to be so high) frightened Rebecca. They went to look at the old ships at the Seaport, they walked in SoHo and Rebecca was vigilant about her purse. They went to the Met and Jacob was begrudgingly fascinated by the mummies; they went to the Museum of Natural History and Andrew was worried that the people in the dioramas were real. They took a yellow taxi, bought hot dogs on the street, ordered frozen hot chocolate at Serendipity, rode the subway, ate at the Oyster Bar, and stared at the backward zodiac on the ceiling of Grand Central and Rebecca remembered the late Mrs. Onassis and, again, blessed her. If you didn't know otherwise, you'd have taken them for a happy family with one black kid. The truth was stranger still.

The brokenness of the family unit made parental cooperation simpler: Rebecca was going to have a coffee with her editor at *The New Yorker*, but she and Christopher were accustomed to handing off duties. Still, Christopher was flummoxed when Rebecca told him the boys would not be interested in the Guggenheim (no reflection on Meret Oppenheim) and suggested a carriage ride in Central Park, FAO Schwarz, dim sum in Chinatown, that kind of thing. She didn't want to waste energy worrying about them; she wanted to worry about herself.

A part of Rebecca hoped the woman would invite her to the Algonquin (wouldn't that have been perfect?), but Alice Quinn suggested they meet at the Bryant Park Hotel. Rebecca entered the dark lobby, running through the list of possible topics of conversation she'd come up with the night before.

"Rebecca Stone?"

"That's me!" Rebecca had studied this one particular gesture of Diana's—she couldn't afford couture, but she could *learn* something—that entailed dropping the chin and raising the eyes. It made you look (well, it made Diana look), appropriately, regal. "That's me." She said it once more, revising, removing the exclamation mark.

"I'm so happy we could meet." Alice was a mannish, small woman, with a nice smile. She looked like the sort of woman who took a class in pottery, owned a large cat or a small dog, had a well-worn *Moosewood* at home. She smelled of soap and had wrinkles at her eyes. "Sit, sit."

Rebecca was disappointed by the hotel's simplicity. She'd imagined something elegantly fussy. There was little grandeur and there were lots of tourists coming and going. But she was a tourist, too.

"You live in Maryland. What's that like?"

Rebecca had that desire to impress that she would on being interviewed for a job, or when chatting with Terry Gross. "It's a nice enough place to be from. A place that's no particular place. No defining characteristic. Not even much in the way of a cuisine, if you think beyond crabs. I never eat crabs. I mean, I don't sit at a table and hit them with a mallet and rip them apart. It seems savage to me. Or like eating spiders, which is quite horrifying." She sipped her Darjeeling. She was talking too much.

"I grew up in Connecticut. There's a similar lack of . . . specificity to the place. I used to wish so badly that I was from somewhere interesting. Of course, the older I get, the more I find my definition of interesting changes. I suppose I thought it would give me, you know, something to write about, something to have to feel about."

"Right." Rebecca put her cup in the saucer too forcefully, so fully did she agree. "Maryland aspires to be Washington, D.C., but that, too, is a place that's not actually a place. Potemkin. All those white façades and that suggestion of authority. It's sometimes moving but often very silly. Nothing I'm interested in *writing* about."

"You know, I've worked with Walcott. And I remember, specifically with him, thinking that the place, that had to have made this huge difference. You can hear it, I think, in the work. But of course, it's silly to be jealous of a *place*. You don't accrue more material, simply being from a specific place. It doesn't make the work come any more easily. I suppose envy is always useless. Of course, St. Lucia must be quite beautiful."

"My husband is from London. My ex-husband. But I remember feeling that, the first time he took me. I spent all afternoon at Sir John Soane's and I couldn't imagine a more beautiful place in the world. There was nothing like that, there is nothing like that, in this country."

"But you have the Smithsonian, of course." Alice's tone had changed from conversational to prosecutorial. "And you're teaching at Hopkins now, aren't you? Isn't Baltimore where the Walters Museum is?"

Rebecca had wanted to tell a joke, about Connecticut and Katharine Hepburn's odd way of speaking. Now it was too late. "Yes. The Smithsonian. And the Walters. I try to go, when I can. I have two small children." This had nothing to do with anything.

"Ah yes, you mentioned once. There was something, in

Folly, about the fingers at the breast." The woman did not even hesitate; she recited the line in question.

Rebecca had never had her work quoted back to her. Alice's recall was astonishing, flattering even if she had just reread the thing at her desk as preparation for their meeting. "Yes. We changed *breast* to *duct.*" Rebecca knew the words because they were her own. "I can't believe you remembered that. You must read so much."

"It's very memorable." She pushed her empty teacup forward. "I thought of Ted Hughes, if you don't mind that."

Rebecca did not mind. She loved Hughes's hard sounds and dark ideas, had wanted forever to be regarded as what she regarded him as: muscular, insistent, proud, unapologetic, deft. The woman across the table from her knew a Nobel laureate well enough to bring him up in casual conversation. This woman knew the lines that Rebecca had written, had taken those lines and improved them and given them her most prestigious seal of approval. Rebecca was a poet in a midtown hotel lobby on a muggy afternoon. In most ways, Rebecca had not ended up the person she had planned on being. Not in this. She had always seen herself right here, with an important woman—and wasn't she an important one, too—making conversation about art. "How kind of you to say."

"How old are your children?"

Oh, but not this. They had gone from Walcott and Hughes to this? Rebecca didn't care, at that moment, where in the world they were, what they were doing, if Andrew was tired, if Jacob was moody, if Christopher was suckling on Nicorette and trying not to lose his temper, if their lunch turned out to be too expensive, if they got turned around on the subway, if a pickpocket relieved Jacob of his wallet. She didn't want to be that kind of mother, the one who can't stop talking about her children, can't stop thinking about them. Surely there had to be another kind of mother for Rebecca to be. "They're seven and four." But no, this was not right. "Oh. I'm sorry. They're ten and seven. Hm. That's funny. It just came out of me, like that, so quickly. Time's passage. I wonder if in some corner of my mind that was the ideal age, that's where I have them fixed, at seven and four. Seven and four. I wish I were into numerology. There might be something there."

"Maybe so."

Rebecca panicked. "Speaking of seven and four. Eleven. When I was a girl, probably eleven, now that I think about it, I had a strong feeling about the number eleven. It started because one day I found a dime and a penny. Not so noteworthy, right, but then the next week, again, I found another dime and another penny. Eleven cents, twice in a row. I started testing myself. I'd look at the clock, just glance at it, and it seemed like it was almost always eleven minutes past the hour. We had this digital clock in my science classroom, that counted down the seconds, too, and once I did this and it was at eleven past the hour and eleven seconds. What did it mean? It drove me crazy." Rebecca wanted Alice to think her interesting but she was babbling.

"Either everything means something, or nothing does." She nodded her head as though the matter was settled.

Rebecca did not know what to say. "Isn't that how the mind works, though? It shows its own bias toward organizing experience. Toward teasing out something, some moral, some lesson. It's all got to be *for* something. Or else otherwise everything is so frustratingly random."

"You're talking about God, then?" Alice had a small smile. "Is this something you're working on?"

They were back to the question of her work but if Rebecca had failed to impress Alice Quinn, she was still impressed with herself. As if to prove a point, she glanced at her wristwatch and it was—well, of course, it would be, it had to be: eleven past three. She didn't point this out. It was interesting to no one but her own eleven-year-old self. "I'm working on something else. It's nice to be old enough to know the starts are false. I can turn my back on them. I can push myself past them."

"Well, that's what editors are for, too, Rebecca. Don't forget that. I do hope you'll send us something new when you have it. It was such a pleasure to work with you on *Folly*. And such a joy to see it in the pages."

This had the air of leave-taking. Rebecca let the woman pay the bill and embraced her tentatively on the sidewalk. She hurried away as though she had some place pressing to be. She stopped behind a parked van and watched the small woman disappear into the cityscape.

Rebecca found her ex-husband and her sons lingering in the hotel lobby, the Grand Hyatt aiming for grandeur, with cascading fountains and an impossibly high ceiling. Jacob was sprawled on a leather sofa, and his legs seemed so long. Christopher looked exasperated. Only Andrew seemed happy to see her, hugging her tight at the waist. She placed a hand on top of his hair, so thick and curly that sometimes, after his bath, she'd discover that his scalp was still dry, untouched by the water she'd poured over the top of him. "Mommy."

Christopher had disregarded her advice and taken the boys to the United Nations. Andrew was diverted by counting the flags, but Jacob had been bored, and they were all irritated. "I'm here," she said. "Mommy's here."

The next day was hotter still. Maybe it was the tall buildings, holding the wet air close. They'd chosen New York thinking it would have so much to offer, but they mostly just wanted to go swimming, and there was nowhere to go swimming. The woman at reception advised them to try a playground on the East River. There, she promised, were fountains to play in.

Rebecca sat on a bench beside Christopher and they watched their sons, slender as sylphs, screaming and splashing among clever concrete animals, seals and whales spewing water that Rebecca was sure was dirty. "Don't drink it! Close your mouth!" Rebecca reclined in the sun. Sometimes this was nice, punishing heat on the skin. The playground was crowded, the relief of all that water. Rebecca tracked the movements of her boys through the scrum of bodies, bodies of every shape and color, but they were hers, so it was always easy to pick them out, Jacob's long torso, the girlish pink nipples, the prominent stalk of his throat, the balloon of Andrew's tummy, joyous and round in contrast to his thin arms. The look on the younger boy's face was joy; so, too, on his brother's. The older boy had set aside the pretense of disinterest. He was running with abandon. He lifted his brother onto his back and she worried about Andrew's grip on Jacob's wet shoulders. It was one of the best feelings possible to have, wasn't it, to watch two children at play, or maybe it was only thus when they were your children, and you had this evidence of their bond, and it was so profound it was impossible not to imagine it lingering, persisting, that someday you'd be dead but they'd have this, one boy's hands clinging to his brother's back, a metaphor, but real.

"That's better, then." Christopher's sigh was a long exhale.

Rebecca knew that he breathed thus to simulate smoking. She let it pass. "It's nice to just sit. This is supposed to be a vacation for us, too."

"You should have seen the kids' faces on the UN tour." Enough time had passed for the insult to mellow into something else. Christopher laughed. "Poor lads."

"They spend so much time trying to be grown up, or Jacob does, and Andrew tries to imitate him because that's what little brothers do. Then you take them to a playground and they run around like this and you see they're just boys. I want to tell Jacob, but he doesn't understand, or he doesn't care. Growing up isn't some great privilege. It's awful. How much better to run around half naked than to have tea with an editor or see how international diplomacy is made."

"Or not made." Christopher enjoyed bringing the subject back to the things he cared about. His job required diplomacy (what job did not?), but he missed the proximity to power. Now, he mostly did paperwork.

"You miss it still? The embassy, the bank?" To sit and have a conversation proved something about who she told herself she was. It was so silly to make a life (a human being) with another person, then divorce and be unable to speak to them. There had been no betrayal, just a change. Maybe she was lonely.

"The world is run by people whose names most of us never learn. They know the people whose names we do know. I used to be one of those people, didn't I? The nameless."

This was Christopher's philosophy. "You do important work, still, Christopher. Your children will admire you, when they're older."

"I'm a middleman. I convince lawyers from Boeing to be forthright with lawyers from the Department of Transportation. Just another person in the suburbs of Washington, D.C., who spends his days talking to lawyers."

"By that metric, I'm a housewife who occasionally publishes a page or so."

"You're *respected*, though, aren't you, now? I'm a casualty of someone else's corruption."

"It still bothers you?" Rebecca didn't understand why. "You're an honorable man, people know that."

He corrected his posture, squinted from the sunlight. "I

don't begrudge the secretary getting off. He's an old man. No matter how many millions you end up with, you're going to die. But Bob—he's a crook."

"They are. You're not."

"I told you, once, how someone's cousin came and sat in my office and made small talk."

She barely remembered that morning's breakfast, yesterday's meeting with Alice. "You told me."

"I guess that's what I've learned. Maybe the only thing. That everything is connected. The Indian Ocean ends up in the Mississippi River, eventually."

"Maybe you should be the poet in the family."

"If Gaddafi was enriched by BCCI, and my bank was BCCI—it's a syllogism. The Libyan state's greatest achievement was, of course, Lockerbie. I just don't know what this says about me, you know?"

Rebecca didn't want to think about Lockerbie on a sunny day at the playground. Violence had no place in the American idyll. "You feel guilt by association. It's not like we got rich."

Christopher's house in Rockville was nice enough, but a government salary only went so far. Rebecca had taken the job at Johns Hopkins because she was flattered to be offered it and also because she needed to, hellish commute notwithstanding. They sent both boys to public school now. They were just middle class enough to be able to joke about their poverty. "True enough. Six million dollars, they earned? Six million dollars."

"We're better off." Rebecca washed her hands of it. "If you had—done something, made dirty money. Think how you'd feel then."

"Quite so." He was thoughtful. "I feel something, even so. Disappointment. Some sense that life doesn't turn out as you plan."

"That's why." Rebecca had wanted to say this to him for a

long time. She knew that people organized their lives around symbols they'd invested with meaning. They had to. Life was too scary otherwise. "That's why the NTSB. You want to feel like you're doing something, when people fall from the sky. Like you're helping to figure out why. But sometimes people do terrible things and we are not to blame."

"Or the list of people who are to blame is so long that we're surprised to find ourselves on it." Christopher looked at her. "Anyway, I took the job because it was the only offer. I sit in conference rooms. I make telephone calls. I'm a chaperone. A father. If I wanted to atone, I'd have joined the Peace Corps."

Rebecca didn't believe this. It was too convenient. But it was interesting to learn that Christopher saw himself as nothing more than a father. Perhaps no one felt like they'd accomplished anything or perhaps that was the only interesting thing to accomplish in life. Who thought about investment banking or cardiology or selling real estate or animal husbandry on their deathbed? "You're hard on yourself, Christopher."

"That may be." He looked at her again, more intently. "They did a bad thing, whatever the jury says. But you know that I did not."

"Of course, Christopher. Look at us. How many divorced couples take their children on vacation and have a good time? I'm having a good time."

"I am, too. Who'd have thought?"

There was music, loud, that grew louder: the Jackson Five. A family across the park, with tablecloths, large aluminum containers of food, a big portable stereo. Rebecca knew this song well, but everyone did, their songs were a part of the American way of life; you knew the words and had no recollection of having learned them. She loved this song's plaintive longing, which was so romantic it had to be at least somewhat sexual. It was strange to think of a preteen Michael Jackson singing with such passion. Of course, he had that kind of voice, a gift from God or an otherworldly accident. Rebecca played those Jackson Five songs at home, because she thought it useful for her son to hear America's son, and understand, *Oh, we are both black*. Andrew was her angel and what was Michael Jackson but a manifestation of the divine? True, he had ceased being recognizably black, but Rebecca tried to ignore that. Andrew, with his perfect Afro, the spread of his nose, his dancing eyes, was like the little boy that Michael Jackson had been, back when he'd been a little boy electrified by joy and singing with the passion of a grown-up woman that he must not be *left*, that he'd be there to *comfort you,* so *glad* that he'd found you. Across the park, some children were dancing.

"I know this song!" Andrew threw his wet body onto Rebecca's lap, but she welcomed it, the relief that his body always was. "I love this playground."

Rebecca pulled him close, up onto her, which was not as easy to do now as it once had been. He was heavy, and she was out of practice. Toting a baby around is a regimen, one she'd long abandoned. Her muscles had gone slack as her milk had dried. Or maybe she was just older. She had barely marked her forty-first birthday. Her sister Christine had brought over an ice cream cake and the boys presented her with construction paper cards. "You're so big." She thrilled at his cold, wet ear on her cheek.

"Do we have any snacks?" From where she sat, Jacob seemed impossibly tall, so thin his irrepressible hunger made sense. His skin was pale as the inside of an apple, a potato. "I'm starving."

"No one's starving." Christopher ground down on his gum. "We can go for a pretzel. Then head back to change for dinner. We can go to Little Italy. They've got those restaurants where you order a pork chop and then a plate of spaghetti that's the size of a hubcap. That should be enough to fill even you, Jacob."

"I love you." Andrew said it, the words that were well trod, internalized, then leapt off her lap as quickly as he'd lighted there. That was life: perpetual motion. How she thrilled in these unguarded confessions, the sort of thing that Jacob (not even a teenager yet!) was unable to muster any longer. A chubby wet child confessing his love. The unremitting heat of the sun. Even the hunger, because she was hungry, too, just from watching them play. These were all welcome, because they made her feel like a human being. Exist in the moment, she had urged herself, so many days and weeks when the moment seemed most miserable. But there was this, in the moment, too: occasional, exquisite joy.

Christopher seemed to note Andrew's words. Or maybe he smiled at Rebecca for no reason at all. That night, they went to dinner and there was indeed so much pasta that even Jacob could not finish it. They walked, afterward, stopped for ice cream, took a taxi back to the Grand Hyatt even though they'd spent more money on this trip than they should have. They were happy, and there was some correlation, not that money could buy happiness but that happiness was sometimes achieved when you'd invested. Dinner was more than a hundred dollars. Never mind.

Rebecca was blissfully alone in the frigid hotel room, slipping out of her sticky shoes, unbinding herself from her damp bra, when Christopher knocked at the door. There had been some premonition, chemical, bodily, that he might do this. "Rebecca. It's me."

It had been three years. Her last birthday, Rebecca had wondered, briefly, idly, whether there would ever be another man. She could bring herself to happiness but she could not reach that particular kind of completion, however temporary, whatever apparatus she employed. She didn't mind admitting that she'd thought of it. Christopher was still a handsome man.

She buttoned the shirt back up over her bare breasts and padded over the cheap carpet to the hotel room door. It was not lust, on his face. A TWA flight bound for Paris had exploded off the coast of Long Island. The office, knowing he was local, had left a message with the concierge, asking him to go. What could he do? He packed his bags and went. Rebecca explained to the boys the next morning, vague and reluctant over the details. A child should not know that a plane sometimes faltered. She took them to a diner for scrambled eggs and home fries, and they drove away from the city, its preposterously tall buildings lingering in her rearview mirror for a surprisingly long time, eventually, to her relief, giving way to blue skies.

29

REBECCA WAS BARELY LISTENING TO CHRISTOPHER. IT WAS ONE OF the liberating things about being divorced from him. He could talk and it didn't implicate her. She sliced the cake—lemon, to conjure spring—and handed plates to her left. Cheryl placed forks on the plates and passed them to her left. Slice, plate, slice, plate, seven times over. Rebecca didn't object when Andrew and Ivy pleaded to take their cake into the den. They wanted to watch television, or maybe they wanted to be alone, the natural alliance of children versus adults. They were the plates from Elizabeth, fragile, irreplaceable, but Rebecca didn't care.

"If it's OK with Auntie Cheryl, it's OK with me. Just be careful not to spill."

Cheryl nodded her assent, and Ivy and Andrew pushed out of their chairs and, plates balanced carefully, left the room.

"Not too loud!" The boys needed constant reminding about this; they turned the volume too high, reaching Rebecca wherever she was in the house.

"That was delicious, Rebecca." Ian was attentive to sounding appreciative. "I would say I'm stuffed but I am not too stuffed for this."

"I hope you like the cake. This in-between season, not quite winter but not quite not winter. I never know. Lemon seemed like it might be the flavor of spring."

Ian tasted the cake. "Oh it's good."

"Does anybody want tea? Coffee? Rebecca, I might, if it's OK?" Cheryl looked around the room.

"Of course. I might have some tea, if you're making some." Cheryl had assumed command of Rebecca's rooms. It had taken eight years but it had taken. When Rebecca had moved the children to the local school, she'd listed Cheryl and Ian both on the mandated blue card.

Christopher wanted tea, and Ian said he'd have some, and Cheryl stepped through the swinging door.

"Can I have another piece?" Jacob hadn't finished his first, though the last bites of it were even then in his mouth.

Rebecca sighed but was flattered. Who were these domestic arts for, anyway? She sliced another wedge and he handed her his plate. He was nearly as tall as Christopher, and his feet were enormous. His Adam's apple bobbed around almost independent of his long body. The last time she'd seen him undressed, she noted the thatch of hair beneath his arms. He was still the baby she'd once held, the one who, when weaned, grabbed at her breast so angrily, like it was a citrus he meant to juice, like a stressed executive with a rubber ball, that she'd worked that into a poem. "Seconds for Jacob."

Ian cleared his throat. "Jacob, why don't you go and sit with the kids."

"I'm still eating my cake." The majority of the things he said came out as a complaint. This was particularly plaintive. Jacob wanted to be with the adults.

"Go on." Ian winked. "Keep an eye on the little ones. Make sure they don't spill."

"But . . ." Jacob's whine was maddening.

Rebecca sensed that Ian meant to say something. Also: she felt strongly that Ian and Cheryl were to be obeyed. Two years earlier, when Rebecca and Christopher's divorce gave them occasion to revise the documents that governed their lives, they had amended their will, to cede to Ian and Cheryl, in the now even less likely event of their simultaneous deaths, custody of Jacob and Andrew. It was better to be prepared, who knew that better than their family?

"Go on, then." Christopher, like every part-time father, counted on being obeyed.

Jacob muttered something, and abandoned the table and the adults, the plate so small in his large hands.

"Such a teenager, already. Advanced in his attitude, I think." Rebecca was apologetic.

"Never mind." Ian was hard to rattle. "We were all there, weren't we? When I think about what I put my mother through."

"It's hard to believe when they're small. Like Ivy. She's still so sweet. It's hard to picture that someday she'll roll her eyes at everything you and Cheryl say. But it's coming."

"You don't see her at home." Ian laughed and his laugh had music in it. "She's on her best behavior here, but believe me, I get plenty of eye rolling."

"I thought they were sugar and spice and everything nice."

Christopher sounded drunk. Perhaps he was. Should she let him drive home? Make some strong tea? What was her responsibility, and would she be able to meet it? "You want some more cake?" He hadn't even eaten his first piece. She thought if he ate more it would sober him up.

"She has her moments." Ian was impatient. He'd sent the boy away for a reason. "Listen, there's something I need to tell you."

There were few more effective ways to change a room's atmosphere than such a pronouncement. Suddenly, the cake seemed soggy and uninteresting, the lights too bright, Cheryl's absence notable. What was taking her so long? "Is something the matter?"

"Everything's fine. It's fine." Ian's wide eyes narrowed when he smiled but also when he was being serious. "I shouldn't have said it like that. It sounds like I'm making a big speech. Everything is fine," he said again. "Rebecca. Christopher. You know we think the world of you. Of. What you've done. For Andrew. For us. For Cheryl's mom."

"You're not getting a divorce. You're not moving away."

Ian laughed. "Nothing like that. See, it's all come out so different than I wanted. I'm just trying to. Clarify. That before I say anything, you need to understand that Cheryl and I, you know. We think the world of you."

"I know that." She'd come, over time, to assume so. It was odd to have love declared. It made the thing seem suspect. Christopher was nodding slowly and looking toward the window. He was not given to direct exchanges. He had to be drunk to navigate a complicated conversation. The day they'd finally admitted that they needed to divorce, they'd shared a bottle of wine.

Cheryl came in. She'd found the tray, the teacups, the sugar bowl, she'd known it all. She filled the cups and handed them around. The room was quiet as befitted this ceremony.

"I see you're talking." Cheryl was in on this, too.

"I wish we were. What's the matter?" Rebecca panicked. The television was blaring, but she didn't want to leave and scold the children.

"There's no problem. I just . . ." Ian was at a loss.

"We need to tell you something. About something. Three weeks ago, Ian was on his way home from the dealership. It wasn't so late. Eight? Late enough that rush hour was over."

"There was no traffic." Ian watched his wife.

"Now that night, he was bringing home one of the new cars. They do that sometimes, the salesmen. Give them a run. Get to know how it feels."

"The series three. A beautiful one, jet black, black interior. A special choice but there's someone out there who'll love it."

"So he's driving home, a little late. In this brand-new black BMW. You can tell where this is going."

"I can't." Christopher must have been eager, to pipe in thus. "What's happened?"

"There are certain things you need to know, Rebecca. Christopher. Certain things you need to understand. If you're going to raise a black son." Ian's words were not unkind. "All little black boys need to hear this from their mom or dad at some point. If Jacob were black, you'd have had this talk already."

"What talk?"

"They pulled him over, Rebecca. The police." Cheryl crossed her arms.

"Which is fine. I'm used to it. It's a nice car—"

"But more than that—"

"A brand-new car, with dealer plates—"

"They made him get out and lie on the ground—"

"It was dark—"

"He was wearing a suit. A Brooks Brothers suit. Like he does every day at work—"

"It was cold. There was still salt on the pavement. Stained my tie. The dry cleaner says there's no getting that out. I had to throw it away."

"They called another car, and another. Three cars. One

man, in a suit, on his way home, lying on the icy pavement. Six policemen. Cars rushing by."

"Not so many. Downtown Bethesda, eight at night. Maybe some people heading to the movies. A restaurant."

"Guns drawn. Shouting—"

"She wasn't there—"

"You said there was shouting. I'm telling the story—"

"There was some—"

"Screaming at him, *Get on the ground, boy, show us your hands, boy. Boy,* that's the thing. He's thirty-five years old. We know what that *boy* is."

"This was different."

"I can't stop imagining it. You try. Imagine it. Flashlights. Sirens. And Ian. He's been at work the whole day. It's freezing. He's lying on the street. What else are you going to do in that situation?"

"But I don't understand." Sometimes the truth was the best. Rebecca did not understand.

"You don't understand. That's why we're telling it." Cheryl's eyes were tired but fierce. "That's his point. You don't understand. Ian wanted to tell you. To prepare you for the talk you need to have—"

"I wanted you to know." Ian was clearer now. "Maybe I shouldn't have."

"Go on, Ian. Please." Rebecca pushed her plate away. She wanted to get up, move around the table, sit by the man, hold his hand. That was her instinct.

"I don't remember, is the thing. One second, I'm driving home. Thinking about dinner, I'm so hungry. Thinking about how I need to go to the dentist. Thinking about how I want to take off my tie and kiss Ivy good night and shower. Feel warm again. It's so cold and so dark. This time of year, I'm so ready for the clock to change. Spring forward. Then these lights, red lights, blue lights, and I know it's for me, for this black BMW. I'm not speeding, by the way."

"He's not *speeding*. That's not the point."

"So I do what you do. Pull over. Hazards on. Car off. Hands on the wheel."

"But this is ridiculous." Christopher scoffed. "What about *just cause*? I've never heard of anything like this."

Cheryl laughed. Not even meanly, but genuinely. "You've never heard of anything like this, Christopher, that's why we're telling you."

"Then the shouting. But I couldn't make it out. And I didn't know what to do. I'd already done everything I could think to do. I'd turned off the car, had my hands on the wheel. Hearing this voice, yelling at me, and I know I'm going to need to do something, I know I'm being told to do something. I just don't know what it is."

"He can't hear well. I don't know if you knew that. But he can't."

"I can't hear well, it's true. Been that way since I was a kid."

"Not that it's the point."

"So I open the door. I figure that's it. They want me to open the door."

"What would you do?" Cheryl looked at Rebecca. "What do you do?"

"What can you do?" Rebecca didn't know. "I would have opened the door."

"I opened the door, and they're still shouting."

"Screaming at him. In the middle of downtown Bethesda. Five blocks from the dealership. Restaurants. Pedestrians. This beautiful place that we live in."

"*Get down, get down.* I barely understand, but I know to get down."

"He needs to get down."

"I sort of throw myself out of the car. On my knees. I don't know what else to do. But I figure. On my knees. They'll understand."

"On his knees." Cheryl was whispering.

"On my knees."

Like a prayer, Rebecca thought. *Or like a beggar.*

"On the knees of his Brooks Brothers suit on Old Georgetown Road. Like a—I was going to say a *criminal,* but that's something else, isn't it. Like an *animal.*"

"They said, *Hands on your head.* I put my hands on my head. They said, *Down motherfucker.* I lay down. On the road. They said, *He has a gun,* and I prayed that they saw I didn't have a gun. It was the keys. I had the keys in my hand. Just an instinct. I don't know. The keys, they're in my hand."

"Like a criminal." Cheryl stared at Christopher. "But less than. You worked with criminals, didn't you, Christopher? That's a criminal. Your old bosses are criminals. My husband is not a criminal."

"Innocent until proven guilty." Christopher took a bite of his cake. "The world out there. It's gone mad. Planes fall from the sky. The people with power abuse it." He still sounded drunk. "Please. Finish the story."

"I lay there on Old Georgetown Road. The road itself was right up under my cheek. Dirt on my suit."

"You know why that matters?" Cheryl was calm. "Respectable. It's the thing they wanted us to be. His mom. My mom. You wear nice clothes, people will know you're a nice person. You dress like the person you are. But of course, that doesn't actually make a damn bit of difference."

"It's not like I was . . ." Ian searched. "In jeans? A sweatshirt? My suit. Be calm. I told myself. Nothing less calming than telling yourself to be calm. I breathed deep. I thought of Cheryl. I thought of Ivy. I thought of Andrew. I thought of you.

I thought of the people I love and thought, well, I'm not going to die on Old Georgetown Road on a Thursday night in February. I'm not going to do that."

"You thought of us."

"I thought of you, Rebecca. Of course I did. I thought of my family."

"That's what he wanted to tell you."

"What happened?" Christopher was rapt.

"Nothing." Ian coughed. He looked embarrassed. "I put my hands on my head. My face on the road. I waited. I counted. It took forever. Ten minutes. Minutes and minutes. Hundreds and hundreds of seconds. I kept counting. It was like when Ivy was born. And the nurse said, *Count with me. Count. Keep counting like your life depends on it. Make Mom breathe*, Mom, meaning Cheryl, get her to breathe. That's what I did. I did that."

This was still inside of Rebecca's body, this counting, this breathing. Jacob would be twelve in the fall. A dozen years since she'd been in that room, outnumbered and afraid, breathed as her body tore asunder and the baby who became the near man in the next room, the one watching cartoons with his brother and his brother's niece, entered the world. Had she ever lain down in the road? Rebecca knew that she had not. *Why don't we do it in the road?* That song had made her blush, as a girl.

"So he needed to tell you. You can see why. All little boys want to be police officers when they grow up. Some little boys need to be told why that's not the best option."

"I can't quite—this is terrible." Christopher was reaching for something better to offer.

"Obviously nothing happened. You're here telling us this story. You didn't do anything wrong!" Rebecca felt hysterical.

"He did something wrong." Cheryl was determined. "He was who he is. That's wrong."

"That's not it." Ian put a hand on his wife's forearm. "But I lay there. On the road. Then they came over. One of the cops. He said, *Get up*. He said, *Go home*. He said, *Don't speed*. He said, *That's it*."

"What do you mean that's it?" No gesture seemed right. Rebecca wanted to throw something at the handsome wallpaper that Joyce Cohen had recommended.

"I got up off the road. The one car drove away, then the other, then the last. They got back into their cars and drove away. I was still holding on to my keys. The keys they thought were a gun. I got back into the car. I was all wet and dirty. I sat in the car, I turned it on, I drove home."

"They must have thought you were someone else. They must have been looking for a black BMW and your black BMW drove by and they thought, well, they thought it was the car they were looking for."

"Rebecca." Cheryl was shaking her head. She bit into the cake. "Rebecca."

"She doesn't know, Cheryl. They don't know. They didn't need to know. But now you do need to know. This is what happens, Rebecca. It happens when you're a black man, it's going to happen to your black son. And you need to know that it's coming. That's what I wanted to tell you."

Rebecca looked at them. She felt at once calm and enraged. "Christopher. Will you tell them to turn the television down? I can't hear myself think."

"You see why I sent Jacob out of the room." Ian was still apologetic. "But he should hear it, too. He's to be his brother's keeper, right?"

Christopher left the room.

"I don't know what to say." Rebecca wanted to cry. "You're a good man."

"That I am." He still knew it, she could tell, the way he said it. Ian knew this, would never forget it.

"It doesn't matter how good you are, Rebecca. A black man is still a black man." Cheryl drank her tea, calmed. "He came home. He didn't want his dinner anymore."

"But this was a mistake. A terrible mistake. Ian, I'm so sorry. I don't know what to say." She had already said that.

"Andrew's going to be nine. But he'll be twelve. Sixteen. Twenty-one. He needs to be told the things he needs to know." Ian was gentle. "Black kids don't get to be kids much longer than twelve, really. I don't mean to be presumptuous, you understand, Rebecca. I have so much respect. You're wonderful parents. You love Andrew. But I hope you'll tell him this story. Or I hope you'll let me. I think he needs to hear this from me."

"A living, breathing black man. Just the thing they're always saying we don't have in our families." Cheryl was triumphant. "A kind, smart black man who wants to help."

"Cheryl."

"No, it's fine, Ian. Cheryl is right. They do say that. Bush said it. Clinton has probably said it. I'm sure you're right. We're very lucky to have you, of course. It takes a village. Isn't that Mrs. Clinton's book? If you'll help me with this, help Christopher and me with this, well, that's very kind of you. But don't you think"—Rebecca thought—"it's getting better? It's going to be different. You were born before man walked on the moon. Andrew was born in 1988. A lot has changed."

"They say that things are changing. It looks the same to me." Cheryl began stacking the plates.

"Please, leave that. Cheryl. When the time is right. Of course, I will trust you to talk to Andrew about . . . about the things he needs to know. There are things that you know. A black man. Things that you know that I can never know. But I want you to keep your mind open, your heart. Things will change. The life Andrew's going to have, it's not going to be the way your life was. Not the way Priscilla's life was." This was a risk, talking about Priscilla in this way, but it felt right. The woman was dead, dead too young, yes, but she represented the old, the past, the *once upon a time*. They had transcended that stuff. Bill Clinton was the first black president! Rebecca had given Andrew—and Jacob, too, both of them—Bill Cosby, and Michael Jackson, and Michael Jordan, and Thurgood Marshall, and Oprah Winfrey. They had a picture book about Martin Luther King.

"You don't know, do you, Rebecca, what my mother's life was like?"

"Cheryl." Ian was trying to keep the peace, but the peace had been broken, or was no longer needed.

"No, it's fine, Ian. Maybe you're right. Maybe I don't. Maybe I never did. But, Cheryl, you know that Priscilla mattered to me. To our family. She was part of our family." Rebecca's words caught in her throat. "Then she made us a family. You did, too. You made us into a family. And now it's too late. We are a family. It's binding. It's irrevocable."

"My husband comes in here and tells you the truth. You need to listen." Cheryl was sharp.

This—a real rebuke—had never happened. Rebecca accepted it. "I am listening. I'm sorry, Cheryl. I am listening. Ian, I cannot believe this happened to you. I am so sorry that it did. Let me talk to Christopher. He's still so young, Andrew. He's my baby. But yes, of course, we'll tell him this. You can. When the time is right."

Cheryl and Rebecca gathered up the dishes, ferried them into the kitchen, while the fathers and the children watched television. Andrew and Ivy were both yawning, and even Jacob looked tired, that profound exhaustion of adolescence, asleep until noon. They said their good-byes at the door, as they always did, as though they could not bear for the evening to end. Maybe Rebecca couldn't. There still seemed to be something she needed to do. She embraced Ian as she always did, but this time, this night, she kissed him, on the ear, on the temple, on the forehead, because it seemed warranted.

The tea or the conversation had proved sobering. Christopher drove home and Rebecca couldn't sleep not because she was worried about him but because she was too hot and too cold, distracted, unhappy. She remembered a night in London, years ago, Andrew still a baby, in diapers. He'd wept miserably, and Rebecca had gone to comfort him, shushing him, imploring him not to wake his grandma.

"Where's Jacob? Where's Jacob?" The boy had been crying but was still mostly asleep, weeping for his brother.

"He's right here, honey. He's right here." The older boy was asleep in a tangle of sheets they'd improvised on the bedroom floor. He snored, oblivious. "Jacob is right here with you."

She couldn't imagine loving someone so much that you mourned their absence even in their presence. What anyone thinks about is a mystery but what a child thinks is an especially poignant one. Had he been dreaming, that baby Andrew, weeping over being left behind, forgotten? Was this not reasonable? Didn't he, more than anyone, know about being left behind? Rebecca's heart, jet-lagged and foggy, broke. All she ever wanted was for her children to be happy. Despite what Ian and Cheryl said, she was certain they would be. Andrew, his natural equanimity, his sweetness, his beauty, which was near regal, he had such dignity for a boy of eight: Andrew would be a man welcomed by the world. Everyone would see what she saw, she was sure of it.

30

SHE WAS MOSTLY ACCUSTOMED TO DAYS ALONE. THE DAYS WERE never so long. She forced the boys to brush teeth and wash faces. She made toast or oatmeal. She had her work and then her work. The former was reading student poems, never so good but never so bad, either. It was department meetings or the office hours during which tearful and self-absorbed young writers would turn up under the guise of wanting to chat when what it was they sought was transformation. *Teach me,* they said, but all they wanted to be taught was how to be Rebecca. That she could not instruct them on. They were too young to appreciate the luck and chance that goes into making a person. She was forty-two years old and it was impossible to summarize for them what it had taken for her to transform from weeping undergraduate to poetess in black pants. She tried to take the *poet* out of it, reminded them of their responsibility, to sing of arms, and the man. And besides that, she wrote, constantly.

Summer was hers. Rebecca had thought rapid change a condition of infancy but people are at essence mercurial. Jacob was moody to the point of silence and nights he tarried, shuffled from bedroom to kitchen, down to the den, refusing to sleep, though it was sleep he seemed to need most. The dark exhaustion collected under his eyes, especially Saturdays and Sundays, when he woke early(ish) to mow the neighbors' lawns for a bit of spending money. Rebecca was shocked, pulling into the driveway, seeing the boy, stripped to his shorts, pushing the bright green mower over the slope of the McKinneys' front yard, his shoulders locked, his arms muscled, his body lean and aerodynamic and wholly changed, his hair absurdly set with a palmful of gel, newfound vanity. She'd thought of the mother in a favorite storybook she'd read and reread the boys, years before, who, having become separated from her daughter, cries, "Where oh where is my child?" Where was he?

For now, he was away from her, they both were. Labor Day was Christopher's, because she'd labored enough. He'd invited her along, a long weekend in Delaware. It sounded like traffic and heat. She invoked her work and was left to it. Rebecca woke at seven on Saturday, because she was thus conditioned, but slept until eight on Sunday, because she'd stayed up late the night before, drinking wine and watching television with the *Norton Anthology* open on her lap, mostly ignored. Ah, well.

She took a cold shower because the morning was hot. She played the music she wanted to listen to, too loudly, free from her sons' scorn. *All the people turn to hear her sad refrain, and catch the cry of pain that's in her song.* She couldn't nail the notes like Liza. She remembered how Christopher, teaching Jacob his ABCs, had said "zed" instead of "z," and she laughed aloud. She turned on the television while she was making another cup of tea, and the television informed her that Diana, Princess of Wales, was dead.

Rebecca let her wet hair go dry. She felt a sadness that obviated tears. Her own father had died two years earlier and she'd cried, pathetically, noisily, sobs with absolutely no dignity to them. Lorraine had not approved. Rebecca saw her mother roll her eyes, not that she wasn't bereaved, but her model was decorum on the level of Jackie Kennedy, stoic faces and funereal black. Rebecca didn't know what was the better luck: to have a bad parent you're ever trying to outperform or a good one to whom you can never hope to catch up. She knew it wasn't a footrace but an odyssey. Sometimes she felt sure of her step, confident in the pace, others, she didn't want to run at all. Rebecca had sat at the table in the kitchen of her girlhood home and wept noisily. Even the children had found it unsettling.

On the television, they went over and over it. Diana was in Paris with her new paramour, they had left the Ritz, they had been pursued, there had been an accident, they were trailed by photographers and it was said they kept photographing her as she lay dying in the wreckage of the car. There was closed-circuit footage of Diana, dour, leaving the Ritz. She wore a black blazer and white pants. She looked as ever she did, though if you knew these to be her last moments, you couldn't help see in her posture, her mien, the sense of her own doom. The irony. Diana was the huntress and her namesake nothing but prey.

Rebecca made that cup of tea, had a drink of water, but drifted back to the sofa and the television. Why didn't Christopher call? Surely he knew. This was like a death in the family. Or maybe it wasn't. Maybe Christopher never knew or understood that Rebecca had this feeling about the princess she'd never seen. Maybe he thought it was an interest in pretty clothes and hollow glamour, something she should have long outgrown. Maybe Rebecca had kept this a secret, played this close, or maybe it was obvious and there was no one who truly knew what she cared about.

She had guarded her new work—that was the way—but

the title she'd been using (though often that flourish came last) was "Diana." The poem or poems had been months of work, but years of thinking. Rebecca hunted the woman for her own purposes. That the woman was *dead* now was astonishing, but perhaps Rebecca ought to have predicted it. She, Rebecca, was complicit, had helped use the poor woman up. She was a parasite, or a bird of prey. She'd done the same thing to Priscilla, turned her into a subject, an idea, the genesis of a poem, the moral of the story. Poets sang the past to help understand the future. This seemed idiotically predictable, Diana's death, because in Rebecca's life, good news and terrible news were always intertwined. She had gained the happiness central to her existence because Priscilla had died. Rebecca had a happy enough life, but she never got very far from this kind of thing, never far enough, death, as with Diana, stalked us all.

The things Rebecca sat in her office thinking about likely had no ramification in the world. This was the thing she could never explain to her students, who considered verse tangential to the endeavor of being *poets*. It was the whole point, though, and it was pointless! It was never oracular, except by accident. It was describing, fruitless describing, notes on the present to some future generation who'd consider them a gloss on the past, and barely interesting at that. "Diana" the poem was a lark, a whim, as everything Rebecca had ever done. Diana the person was something real.

Of course, history would repeat. One of Diana's perfect sons would grow up and marry a beautiful woman with lovely clothes and an inviting smile. Kennedy's son had grown up, marrying that beautiful girl who looked like an animate statue, like Galatea, indeed, an ideal made flesh. Maybe he'd be president, and his wife would lead a tour of their White House. That Carolyn, she was a version of Diana, as Diana was a version of Jackie, as she was a version of someone else, and Rebecca herself was part of this genealogy, at least in her mind, which put her approximate to beauty, consequence, grace. She was a woman. Death was a betrayal, never mind its being a certainty.

Rebecca kept watching but there was nothing to report but horrible particulars. The woman was dead and the story, one story, was wholly over. She'd have a new ending to her poem.

"I can't believe this."

"I can't believe it myself." Diana had a voice as beautiful as her face, that soft Englishness, an accent that spoke to breeding, to authority, to comportment. It was how Christopher spoke, too, even after all his years in the United States, and it was something Rebecca loved without understanding why. Diana was sitting in the armchair by the window. She was still in her black blazer and white pants, which were quite spotless.

"I guess—you did good things. That must be a consolation, right?"

"I don't feel very consoled." Diana had a girl's laugh, but there was a bitter flourish in it. "There is a vanity to charity. You do something good because it makes you feel good. It's not all that different from buying an expensive dress, is it?"

Rebecca weighed this. "Of course it is. You did good things!"

Diana shrugged. "It made me feel important."

"You are important!" Rebecca leaned forward. "You embraced that man with AIDS."

Diana's eyes twinkled. "It was all bigger than me. I was in over my head. Do you think less of me, knowing it?"

"So few of us ever get to change anything. But you did."

Diana walked to the window. The summer afternoon was bright. "Did I, truly? Aren't things rather—the same?"

Rebecca shook her head. "You're being unfair. It's—"

"I did walk on the landmines. You remember? I wore that vest. The mask over my face."

"I remember."

"That place. Girls and boys, their arms, their legs had been blown right off their bodies. These rounded knobs where their limbs should have been. You think it would be tough, like a bone, but it's soft, the scar tissue. Soft as a newborn. There was a girl, I couldn't hold her hand as she didn't have one. I touched the end of her arm, it was just a bit of flesh, the size of an apple. You had to cry."

"You used your gift. The cameras saw what you saw."

Diana shrugged. "I was terrified. But I was very good at pretending."

"I think, if you pretend, sometimes it comes true. If you pretend hard enough."

"So you've pretended?" Diana turned to look at Rebecca. "You've pretended yourself to wherever it is you are now."

"Sometimes I think that I have."

"Is it something to be ashamed of? Something you're proud of?"

"I don't know."

"It's not so terrible. We all pretend. I had a fairy-tale wedding in a ridiculous dress."

"I have my work. But my sons, they are real."

"They're a comfort. My first, you know—he's to be the king of England, but I couldn't believe it when he lost his milk teeth. When he learned to write. When he'd sing me a song."

"My husband, he says that what happens out there in the world is what matters, but he also says that what happens out there in the world is mostly horrible. Immoral. Maybe evil. So maybe I hide, here, at home. Your boys are princes. Actual princes. But so are mine. They're what matters the most to me."

"Our children are special even if they're not. Yes, mine are princes. I'm a princess, but that didn't matter, in the end. I'm still dead."

"Cars still crash." Rebecca began to cry. "They're away, now, my family. My sons, my ex-husband. The traffic is terrible, these long weekends, so many drunk drivers. Sometimes I torture myself, imagining what kind of a life I could have without them. None. If they died in a car accident, I would have to kill myself. What if that's what this is, that you dying is just an omen?"

"I'm more than just an omen." Diana turned back to the window again. "I'm a real person."

Rebecca was quiet. "I'm sorry."

Diana shrugged. "I'm no one, to anyone. You didn't know me at all."

"I do that. I'm sorry. I—tell stories, to myself, about people. I imagine or I lie. Priscilla, I tell myself I knew her but what if I didn't, what if I'm deluding myself, what then?"

"She's the other mother. The black boy's mother."

Rebecca looked at the framed picture on the table, Andrew's school photo, his chubby cheeks, his hilarious missing teeth. "I'm his mother. And she's his mother. It's complicated."

"Sounds simple." Diana sat. She smoothed out her smart white pants. "Maybe, you might consider, none of us knows anyone, not really, not at all."

"I used to think I was doing her proud, raising her son. But this isn't what she wanted—what she wanted was to live, to have the life that she had, with her daughter, and her son, and it would have had nothing to do with me."

"No one's life has anything whatsoever to do with yours. You think you know everything about me. My divorce was announced in Parliament. But you don't know anything, and neither do those MPs."

"I adored her. I love her. How could I not—she gave me my son, my life."

"You adore me." Diana crossed her legs and studied Rebecca. Her eyes were very blue.

"I do. I did." She hesitated. "I want to be like you. I want to be good."

What if Rebecca had been wrong, all this time—what if Diana was a spoiled, empty-headed creature, given everything, asked for nothing, besides two sons, whom she delivered? What if she touched the hand of the man with AIDS then wept in the washroom, scrubbing herself with hot water and soap? What if she had been a cruel wife and a rude daughter-in-law, what if she had been a pretty brat in nice dresses?

"God, it's hot in here." Diana fanned herself lazily with a hand, frowned.

"I don't know anyone, do I? Not even myself."

"You do." Diana walked behind the sofa and put her hand on Rebecca's shoulder. A bit of grace. A regal gesture. She squeezed it lightly. Rebecca still felt it, the pressure of Diana's hand on her shoulder, but she didn't look up, just continued staring at the television until it was quite late in the day.

31

SO, DIANA WAS FINISHED, BUT SO WAS "DIANA." REBECCA PRINTED the four pages of it and sent it off to Alice Quinn. They whittled away at it. It turned out to be multiple poems, and the magazine published one and then the other, and in due course there was a letter from Knopf and a modest check and a book with a Titian on the cover. There was the short list for the biggest award—she didn't win, but it was enough, in the end, to be at a dinner with Charlie Williams and Louise Glück. Hopkins was pleased enough to offer her a sabbatical though it wasn't, technically, her turn. A reporter from the *Post* came to visit Rebecca in her office on campus, and Andrew was delighted to see his mother in the newspaper.

"You know you're set now." Karen and Rebecca shared an office, a dusty, forgotten place near the handicapped restroom that was imbued with some secondhand chic whenever Karen was in attendance. Karen always wore the same Tony Duquette necklace, with a gemstone the size of a cockroach. It had been a gift from her loving husband, Mohammed, an Iraqi oddball whom Rebecca had met at various departmental functions. Other than that: black pants, black turtlenecks, a black coat, a black pashmina. Karen was precisely the kind of person she seemed to be, the type with a loud laugh, interesting earrings, heavy perfume, quick to write a check if the purpose was noble and to tell a meandering anecdote with no particular point.

"Oh, I don't know about that." Rebecca shifted the papers around on her desk, a pantomime of work. She did know, of course, that she was *set*. She'd come back from the ceremony in New York feeling like a superhero, able to leap tall buildings, and known the world over. Not a celebrity, what poet is, but *celebrated*, which was actually far better. When the admissions office revised the college's promotional material, her name would appear in bold type, her nomination would be mentioned. Would-be poets would track down her books, *Galatea* and *Diana*, and arrive in Rebecca's classroom having formed opinions about how she handled line breaks and allusion.

"I do." Karen lit a cigarette, though this was technically against the rules, perching by the window that could only be forced open a couple of inches, admitting the chilly November air but doing nothing to mitigate the scent of her slender brown Mores. "It's damn lucky, is all. The tenure committee loves a star."

Rebecca was accustomed to the woman's rudeness, which she disguised as forthrightness. Karen wrote brittle, minimalist short stories about divorce and death, with bleak final sentences where stage direction substituted for denouement, as if casting eyes at a mirror approached catharsis. *Harper's* and the *Atlantic* had liked a couple of them well enough, but it drove Karen mad with jealousy that Rebecca had been offered first refusal by *The New Yorker*. What artist didn't have their madness? Rebecca liked having someone to sit and chuckle with, someone who understood. "Books of poems sell fifty copies and they're considered a hit. Finish your novel. Anyway, you already have tenure."

Karen stubbed the cigarette out, impatient. "True, true. You know. I want to stay in the dean's good graces." Karen was adept, far more than Rebecca, at the business of being a writer, which in the academy entailed lots of receptions with wine of dubious vintage, handshakes, and air kisses with the administrators' wives. She didn't have children, herself, so there was plenty of spare time.

"You're the master of good graces, Karen."

"Perhaps I should be more difficult. That's one way to assert your artistic worth, I think. Act like a complete pill. People just assume it's because you're terribly smart."

"Maybe." That hadn't been Rebecca's way, of course. She served on the committees no one wanted to. She did all that she could. She had taken the job principally because it was on offer. To get paid, as a poet—what a hustle. But she now rather liked it, even the needier students, the sheer amount she was always charged with reading, the long drives back and forth. The boys were old enough to be left alone and, besides, it was nice to be wanted. "It seems to work for Stephen, anyway."

Karen's laugh was smoky and loud. Stephen was their much-hated, deeply entrenched colleague. He wrote poems about fishing. "That fucker. Seriously, though, you're so famous, are we still going to share an office? I would be lonely without you. I would have no one to read the worse sentences aloud to."

"You're awful. I'm not going anywhere. You overestimate the speed at which this university operates. You overestimate everything. People care now, but let's discuss in April when I'm back to being the only person in the department who knows how to refill the copier."

"I know how to do that. I just have no interest in doing it. Listen. I told you about Bilal? We need to get that going. I want you two to meet."

Karen brought up this Bilal once every ten days or so. He was a Lebanese banker who was friends with Karen and her husband, and she was eager to play matchmaker. "You know this time of year. It's a quagmire."

"What, precisely, do you mean by that?"

"Thanksgiving. The boys' birthdays."

"Your National Book Award."

"Nomination."

"Well, he's very handsome."

For the most part, Rebecca thought herself too busy to be lonely. Lonely seemed a luxury, an indulgence. She had her sons, her students, her work; to mourn that she did not have (what was the word? romance?) a man seemed silly. There was not a person alive who had everything they wanted, and so much that she had once hoped for was now hers. The silence of the house, the couple of afternoons weekly she was there and the boys were not, that long-elusive silence: given that, how could she ask for more? What good was *handsome,* anyway? It was so odd, if you interrogated it for even a moment, this desire for physical beauty. It had nothing to do with anything but guided most of our more important decisions. "It is a busy time. This time of year. I know we've—well, I wonder if maybe in January—"

"Christ, Rebecca. You do not know how to look out for number one."

"I do, I'm only—"

"It would be good for your *poetry* is the thing. To get fucked, well and good. He has green eyes. Beautiful, like a cat, only sexual. And you should see his hands. Rebecca. Big, thick fingers. They're capable hands, you can tell just by looking at them. That, right there, is my muse."

"You and Mailer."

"I'll take it."

"It's just a bad time. It truly is. I'm not just saying that to say it. Let's talk in the winter, after the holidays. We can set something up."

Rebecca thought of this Bilal, whom she'd never seen, as she drove home, tried to imagine his—or anyone's—capable fingers on her, tried to decide where it was she most wanted those fingers to land. Years ago, Christopher had taken her to see Kissin at the Kennedy Center, and though the music was lovely, the blur of his fingers had transported her. What must it be like, to have hands that could actually do something? What would it be like if those hands belonged to someone who didn't look like she did, didn't look like Christopher did, didn't look like Isaiah had, but someone who looked like how Moham-med looked, someone with a name so foreign, someone from a country so far away?

She could drive with less urgency, now. Jacob would be twelve in only a week; was old enough to be trusted, but not so old to be reckless. He could walk home from school, and he was there in time to meet his brother's bus. The boys whose bottoms she'd spent years dutifully wiping were now self-sufficient, or enough to be able to get their own glasses of milk, unwrap a banana, turn on the television, pretend at doing their homework. They wouldn't burn down the house or get into the liquor cabinet. This was such a marvel that Rebecca stopped at the Giant on the way home, bought milk and cereal because they always needed milk and cereal.

She could hear the screaming from the garage, even over the noise of the automatic door. It was urgent enough that the milk and the cereal were forgotten, for the moment, as were the many student pages waiting for her benediction. She hurried into the kitchen where Andrew was weeping and enraged.

"What on earth?"

"Leave me alone!" Tears poured from Andrew's eyes, as he was still young enough to cry with fervor. His nostrils flared, and though he was still her *baby*, he looked quite surprisingly like a man. Even his voice, strained, had a masculine huskiness to it.

"You stupid idiot. You little brat." Jacob was vengeful. He stood on the far side of the kitchen island, angular and agitated, his cheeks pink and his hair mussed. "You're always messing my stuff up. Always. And I'm *sick of it*." On this last, he, too, screamed, and it was girlish, but he was so angry he didn't seem to notice.

"What is going on here?"

"You're so stupid, Jacob. You are so stupid." Andrew choked. At last he seemed to notice that she was home. "Mom."

"Baby, what—"

"Oh, great." Jacob was still screaming. "*Baby, baby*. He is a baby. A stupid baby. A—fucking baby." He hesitated on this, the worst possible word. He was still testing the limits of his own vocabulary. Rebecca remembered, suddenly, that though it had been Jacob's favorite meal at five/six/seven, he'd often struggled to remember the word *carbonara*.

"Jacob!" It felt silly but important to scold for this particular profanity. She didn't care, really, but you were meant to, as a mother. "Watch it."

"Yeah, take his side, take the baby's side, your baby."

"No one is taking anyone's side. Please stop screaming and tell me—"

"Mommy, Jacob *hit* me—"

"Jacob—"

"Mom, it's not *fair*. He does it on purpose."

"I do not—"

"Will everyone please calm down, and lower their voices, and talk like human beings?"

"Mommy." Andrew gave in to his tears, threw his body against hers. It still felt good, this, and it was so much rarer now, that she was on some level pleased for the tears, the scene, the emotion, because it returned her baby to her.

"Great, now your baby is going to act like a baby and you're going to yell at *me*." Jacob was still enraged and spat this last word, and strangely, he, too, seemed on the verge of tears. Rebecca couldn't remember the last time she'd seen her oldest son weep.

"No one is yelling. Well, you're yelling."

"Because you do anything for Andrew and nothing for me. Because he's always the baby and I'm always not. Because you love him more. And he's not even a part of our family."

"Jacob!" This was too far, at last, worse than his *fucking*, the worst possible thing. This threat had been there, from the beginning, and now, here it was. She genuinely did not know how to proceed.

"He's always doing this. I'm *online*, Mom. And he picks up the phone and he breaks the connection and he thinks it's *funny*."

Andrew wept on Rebecca's stomach, and she pulled him nearer. His body's ambient heat was remarkable. He was so alive, Andrew. She hoped that in his tears, in his emotion, he had not heard what his brother said. "I'm sure that's not the case."

"You're sure. You *always* take his side." Jacob was holding the cordless telephone in his hand, and he threw it to the black-and-white tile of the floor. "*Always!*" He hesitated, perhaps regretting the drama of the gesture. Then he turned, slowly, and stomped through the foyer and up the stairs.

Rebecca held a paper towel under the running faucet, dabbed at Andrew's wet eyes and sticky nose. She ran her hand over his hair until the sobs subsided, sat him on one of the tall stools at the island. She told him to tell her the whole story, but she couldn't listen to his evasions, his attempts at recall, his transparent play for her sympathy. He knew her too well, and the story didn't matter much, your typical brotherly scuffle, meaningless in the long run. Unless it was meaningful, and someday Andrew would recount this to a therapist in a book-lined office, how his brother declared that he did not *belong*. Was Jacob right—did she always take Andrew's side? And if she did, was it because he was younger or was there some other reason? And if there was some other reason, was that so wrong, truly? There was no guidebook; there was no *What to Expect*. She had to go upstairs and talk to Jacob, that was clear, but he needed to calm himself, regain himself. The boys would have forgotten this by the morning, but her throat was dry and she wished for Christopher, for someone else to turn to for validation or advice or at the very least someone with whom to have a glass of wine. Andrew continued to sniffle, miserably, for a few minutes, then he ate some of the leftovers she had designated for dinner.

When the younger boy had been fed, had his bath, was in his bed, Rebecca knocked tentatively at Jacob's door. He was deep in the shame of emotion, she knew, so she told him only to be sure to eat something for dinner, to not stay up too late on the computer. She went to bed herself, for whatever reason so exhausted that she quite forgot that she'd left the gallon of milk in the front seat of her car.

32

EVERY SCHOOL SMELLED THE SAME. WHAT WAS IT? BODIES, PRO-
cessed food, feet, sweat, and that peculiar scent of a child's
neck, multiplied, intensified. Rebecca shifted and the wooden
seat creaked beneath her. It was too small but not uncomfort-
able. Christopher ought to have been there, too, but there was
a meeting "on the ground" in Seattle and what could be done?
The note in Andrew's backpack was addressed to Mr. and Mrs.
Stone. Why bother changing her name back at this point in her
life?

To the kids, their teacher was Ms. Melissa, but in truth she
was Mrs. Gould. This left Rebecca uncertain how to address
the woman, so she tiptoed around it as you might a word you
weren't sure how to pronounce.

"I'm glad you were able to come in."

The teacher perched on the edge of her desk, in a stud-
ied, we're-all-friends-here way. Rebecca was not fooled. She
crossed her arms against her chest. "Of course. I'm always
available when it concerns my children."

"I do have some concerns, in fact. So it's good you've
come."

Did you ever shake it, this fear of authority? The school itself made Rebecca nervous. The other parents' casual prosperity, all that talk of the stock market and renovations. It was a public school, but theirs was a tony zip code. Rebecca knew how well off her family was, so it was ridiculous to be so bothered; she knew she was a success so it was ludicrous not to feel like one. Amid these mothers, mothers in Mercedes station wagons loaded down with tennis rackets, mothers in minivans plotting playdates, mothers in smart running clothes, mothers lingering in the parking lot because there was nowhere all that pressing to be, Rebecca felt like an impostor ever on the verge of being unmasked. Surely some of them were attorneys; surely some of them were painters. Rebecca didn't covet their car phones or their personal trainers, she just wanted to be back at her desk. "Well, let's talk about it."

"Well, Andrew just had a birthday, correct? So he's on the young end. Most of our fourth graders start the year already nine, at least that's how it's seemed to work in this class. So that could explain some of it."

"It?"

"I've noticed, I don't know if you're aware—a kind of maturity gap. It's to be expected. As I said, I know he's actually, literally, a bit younger than many of his peers."

"He's nine. November 27, he was nine." To Rebecca he seemed at once wholly grown and still her baby. He no longer wanted to be kissed good-bye if there were any other children about.

"Of course. Andrew has a big brother at home, yes? I don't know if you'll remember how he was, at Andrew's age. Of course, every child is different. They all grow up in their own ways."

"Yes."

"And surely Andrew is quite different from his brother."

"Sure." Rebecca's maternal skills were finely enough honed that she could hear such statements for what they were. Once, one of her colleagues at Hopkins had expressed surprise over Rita Dove's Pulitzer. *They had to give it to her.* He'd chuckled meaningfully. Eventually, people reveal themselves. You had only to pay attention. What could she say, in that moment, to that man. *My son is black?* Nonsense.

"He's not where I had hoped he'd be, Mrs. Stone."

"He was having some trouble. We've been working on the math. I've got a reading tutor, she comes Tuesdays and Thursdays."

"I'm not sure the trouble is academic. Though I'm glad to hear you're mindful of that. The extra help can only help. In many cases, when there's been a trauma, at home, it makes sense that there's . . . a delay in achievement. But it's not insurmountable."

"A trauma?" Ms. Melissa or Mrs. Gould was young, or maybe she wasn't. Rebecca studied the woman's unassuming navy dress, her cheap sweater. Rebecca had lost her ability to determine how old other women were. She didn't know anymore how old she thought of herself as being. She was in middle age, was what she knew, that's what they called it, once you slipped over forty, and she hoped it were true, that she'd be there until eighty-six, with her sons and her unfinished work. "Our divorce is ancient history. We're all in a happy rhythm with it." She didn't say: *We get along! We go on vacations together! I sometimes have fantasies about going to bed with Christopher!*

"Oftentimes, the children of adoption face some particular struggles, academically. I can recommend a book. Then, compounded by the question of his race. Racial difference."

"I don't need a book. I live it. I'm not sure that I understand what we're talking about." The children of adoption, like he was a breed of dog. That was another thing: *adopt* as a verb shouldn't refer to pets. The question of his race? There was no question! Look at him!

"The issue seems to be mostly behavioral. Andrew disrupts. He talks. Well-meaning, not backtalk, but he can't control himself. He needs to learn, better, how to understand the dynamics of a group. That sometimes it's not his turn to talk."

"I see." It was true. Andrew, he was a great talker. Rebecca found it horribly charming. Maybe they had been permissive, ever hanging on his words. Or maybe he was like his father and this was a complication of nature/nurture. There was no way to know, of course. It wasn't as though Andrew was an experiment and Jacob the control group. They were her sons and Ms. Melissa or Mrs. Gould was full of shit. "He is a talker. I love that about him."

"I'm afraid we've been at the point, more than once, when Andrew was truly disrupting the class. I've had to have him pull his desk into the hallway so that the group can focus."

They send me to eat in the kitchen / when company comes. "You have him what?"

"Group conversation is one of our fundamental techniques. We feel it's good preparation for high school and of course for college. But we need the children to respect the dynamics of the group."

"Yes. The dynamics of the group are important."

"Andrew can just be very disruptive."

"Spirited."

"Yes, that, as well."

"I'm just trying to put a positive gloss on it, you see. Engaged. Curious. Enthusiastic. Perhaps he has a lot to say. Perhaps he has something to add."

"There's something else."

Rebecca nodded.

"I feel that some of his behavior to the girls in the class is. Troubling. A little."

"This is the first I'm hearing of this." Andrew, holding hands with Ivy, the niece who was nearer his sister. Two years ago, he had mastered tying his shoelaces and Rebecca had found the two of them in the foyer, Andrew kneeling before the girl, patiently tying and retying until the fit was just right. Years before that, one of her favorite photographs, Andrew offering the girl his apple, the yellow fruit in his fist, the girl on her tiptoes, leaning forward, to bite into it, Adam tempting Eve for a change.

"It's nothing so terrible."

"You brought it up."

"I'm very attuned to where my students are."

"I am similarly attuned."

"I am fairly certain Andrew was . . . Well, one of our students, she's just started *developing*. And Andrew seemed to be. Staring. At her breasts."

"They say it's hormones in the milk. Does the cafeteria serve organic milk? It doesn't matter. It's in the water. People flush their pharmaceuticals down the toilet and it corrupts the drinking water."

"Mrs. Stone?"

"You're telling me that a nine-year-old boy looked at a nine-year-old girl and that's why you make him drag his desk into the hallway to sit alone?" Andrew, her Andrew, thinking about a girl? Well, it was bound to happen, but it was a small heartbreak.

"I think we're getting the issues confused."

"I don't feel confused in the least."

"Perhaps I should ask the headmaster to join us."

"I don't think that's necessary."

"I want to be sure that you understand. Andrew is a wonderful boy. I just wish that he could learn to . . . restrain his enthusiasm."

Rebecca smiled. "I should think that an enthusiastic student would be the thing you most wanted."

"Well, there's enthusiastic and there's disruptive."

"And which is it?"

"I thought I had made myself clear."

"I teach, you know. At Johns Hopkins. They brought me in as a guest writer. I took root. I know what it's like, sitting in a semicircle of chairs, trying to foster a conversation. I know there are some people who won't shut up and some people who won't pipe up."

"I didn't realize."

"You should. You know who talks in my seminars? The men. They won't shut up, Ms. Melissa. Or Mrs. Gould. The men, they won't shut up. Sometimes I just want to say, please, for the love of God, shut up, shut the fuck up. But you see, they're men and their teachers, their Ms. Melissas and Mrs. Goulds, told them that it was *great* when they contributed. They were excited that they were enthusiastic."

The teacher fidgeted.

"But of course, they were all little boys who looked like Conor and Kevin and Asher and Liam. They were little boys who looked like my Jacob. They weren't little boys who looked like my Andrew."

"I'm not sure we're understanding each other."

Rebecca laughed. "I am. Quite sure."

This was a kind of anger she couldn't hold. It wriggled from her grasp, it wanted to be free. Rebecca freed it. It was cold, but she drove home with the windows open, the wind like a slapping hand hoping to revive her. Nothing seemed to matter even if everything did. She tried to remember the Hughes, couldn't summon the final line, but she thought someday they'd see how wonderful her son was, and be ashamed. Maybe she'd send him back to Sidwell. There wasn't quite money, but she could borrow from Judith. Christopher wouldn't like that but it was a possibility.

At home, peace reigned, temporarily. Jacob was shut up in his room, at the computer. Andrew was watching television.

"Let's turn that off now." Rebecca was making a circuit of the rooms, sorting the mail, righting the pillows, trying to dispel the disarray that followed in the wake of her sons. "Come. Let's make dinner together."

Andrew sighed, as only a nine-year-old boy can, bearing the weight of the world. Then, warmed to the idea, he skipped into the kitchen behind her. "What's for dinner?"

"A fine question." She studied the contents of the refrigerator.

"I know. Let's have breakfast for dinner." Jacob had joined them. He was especially attuned to mother and youngest, she thought, forever sensing collusion.

"That's an idea."

"I want bacon."

"I want bacon, too."

"The good news is that we have some." She removed the slender envelope from the refrigerator. "Though you know what we could do? Instead of breakfast for dinner? Carbonara, which is basically the same thing. Bacon and eggs. Only with pasta instead of toast."

"Yes. That." Jacob nodded seriously.

"Oh yeah, I want that." Andrew wanted only what his big brother wanted.

She put the boys to work. Andrew filled the large pot with water but couldn't maneuver it; his brother helped. Andrew poured salt into the cold water. Jacob wielded the knife over the garlic. Andrew ran the rock of cheese along the grater, but Rebecca finished the job. A certain harmony prevailed. It was rare enough that Rebecca was afraid of spoiling it. But this kind of busy work had the effect of a certain kind of gas: you could get the truth out of them, while their minds were mostly elsewhere. So she asked, the maternal questions it was her duty, her right, her responsibility, to ask: about homework, about friends, about soccer, about whatever it was Jacob found to do on the computer.

She tried so hard to remember the details, the names of all the players in their lives. It was harder and harder to do this, maybe age or maybe distraction. She would ask herself which had come first, Elvis's death or the accident at Three Mile Island, and have to think long and hard but be unable to answer with any certainty. Her work required her mind and there was only so much mind to give over.

"We need a vegetable. Some kind of vegetable."

"Spinach!" Andrew liked spinach.

He pulled the brick of it from the freezer and Jacob unwrapped it and dumped the whole thing into the boiling water. The boys moved around each other in practiced steps, having spent their whole lives sharing this room. This felt like something, the extraordinariness of an ordinary Wednesday. It felt like the thing she had always wanted. Oh, she complained: the picking up, the errands, the folding and washing, the ferrying here and there, but that was so stupid, wasn't it, so predictable, just patter. You were expected to lament the minor debasements of motherhood because what else was there to make conversation about, or how could conversation communicate that learning to tease milk out of your own nipple was outweighed, ultimately, by watching one son help the other open a package of spinach?

Andrew laid the table without even being asked to. Rebecca opened a bottle of wine, because it felt like wine was warranted, like there was something to celebrate. They ate dinner and talked about whatever it was families talked about.

33

SHE KEPT THE BLACK BANANAS IN THE FREEZER, WHICH WASN'T
even thrift but simply common sense: the boys ate that much.
They rattled around behind the ice cream, ungainly parenthe-
ses that fit nowhere. You had to exercise care: opening the door
often upset them, so the black bruised fruit fell to the floor, and
sometimes on your foot, which hurt like hell. They were so
cold to the touch they were hard to handle, but Rebecca tugged
at the resistant skins to get at the mealy flesh, which fell into the
silver bowl like excrement, no way around that metaphor. Dust
thou art, et cetera.

Baking had become bête noire; banana bread her compro-
mise. To be a mother was to bake. Cupcakes, cookies, fund-
raising sales, classroom celebrations, the soccer team, oh, the
mathematics of it all, the ⅓ tsps., Rebecca had ceased to find
diverting. The most base alchemy and besides, the kids didn't
care, but the parents did. If you showed up with Rice Krispies
treats your peers looked askance. Did you not *love* enough?
Anyway, this recipe was so simple she could do it in her head: a
half stick of butter, melted in the microwave, sugar, four of the
bananas, flour, a teaspoon of baking soda, salt, the magic egg,

chocolate chips if she didn't care, blueberries or raisins if she did. This day, she didn't care, or cared more, celebration was in order, so chocolate chips, why not. She sprinkled sugar in the buttered pan, so the bread would have a crust of the stuff. This was how much she loved her children, how much she loved herself.

The phone had rung in February, Jim Willis on the line from Ohio to inform Rebecca that she'd won 1999's Ruth Jameson Award. So she'd gone from being Younger to this. She'd happily exchange youth for one of poetry's richest prizes, endowed by the estate of that dotty dowager. Jameson had died with a town house full of stuff. Her Chagalls had been liqui-dated for the New York City Ballet. Her correspondence (oh, but she'd known *everyone*) endowed a seat at the University of Chicago. Her early-twentieth-century dolls had reaped more than a million dollars and that was set aside for this particular purse, an investment in a poet who might prove to someday be truly great. Jameson's money—her father's, truly—was like the tufts of dandelions, blown across the country, thousands and thousands of small rewards for people like Rebecca. Now she wouldn't need to ask Judith for money to send Andrew off to a new school.

So, naturally: a party. A party for herself, an excuse to gather them all under one roof, the people she loved in this world, and to eat banana bread and have them say that the thing she'd been doing, shut up in that little office, or off at Johns Hopkins, was worthwhile. That she was their mother, sister, daughter, former spouse, friend, incidental family, and that she was a success. Rebecca had invited Cheryl and Ian first, picturing a simple celebratory dinner, but Cheryl, upon hearing her reasons, had assumed control of the operation.

"We'll make a party of it, Rebecca. Your sisters. Your mother. Christopher?"

"Yes," she told Cheryl. A family from Jacob's class was going through divorce as mutually assured destruction. Poor bespectacled Brandon, it was impossible to tell what was adolescence and what was battle scar. Rebecca felt proud that they'd done this so well.

"Who else?"

"We should have Karen," Rebecca said. Yes, she was odd, and could be difficult, but it wasn't until meeting Karen that Rebecca had understood her own loneliness. There were the occasional three-dollar coffees at the Starbucks near the grocery store with Jessica, a mother from Jacob's soccer team, the linger-in-the-foyer conversations with Courtney, whose son Liam was in class with Andrew. But those weren't friends, merely colleagues in the business of motherhood.

Rebecca was taking the banana bread out of the oven when the doorbell rang.

"I hope you're ready to celebrate." Cheryl kissed her on the cheek and pushed past her into the foyer. "It smells so good."

"I made a banana bread."

"I told you to leave everything to me." Cheryl fixed Rebecca with a look of maternal disapproval. "And you're not dressed."

She went upstairs like a penitent teenager, put on the green dress she'd been saving for this occasion. She lingered over her preparations, her potions, hearing the doorbell ring and the house fill with voices, familiar but distorted by the distance. She emerged, feeling faintly ridiculous, like it was a surprise party and she was meant to feign shock.

"There she is. The woman of the hour." Christopher was in the kitchen with Cheryl, putting olives into a little bowl.

"You look lovely." Lorraine touched Rebecca on the shoulder and in that instant, it fell away, temporarily, the years of maternal disapproval. Once her mother had corrected her gait, encouraged her to do better in algebra, needled her for being less popular than her sisters. Now it was decades later and such things were forgotten.

"Thank you." Rebecca nodded, knew that she did look lovely, in that particular bright green. She looked at the room, all that industry: Cheryl filling the bucket with ice, Judith stacking napkins on top of plates. "Everyone is here."

They sat at the dining table. Christine told a story from their childhood, one of those anecdotes worn smooth as a rock by the sea: when Rebecca, nine, on a visit to their father's mother, had put salt instead of sugar into her tea, and politely sipped it anyway. No one could remember just how their father had realized the girl's mistake, or they all remembered it differently, as happens, with history.

Uncle Tim took the cousins (they lumped Ivy into this category as well, naturally) into the backyard to play. Jacob shook off his sullenness and kicked a soccer ball with his cousin Jennifer. Andrew demonstrated his remote control car (from Santa, he pretended, though they knew better by now) for his cousin Michelle. Ivy and Michael were in the tree house, conspiring. Steven talked to Christopher about investments. Karen talked to Christine about her upcoming trip to Damascus. Lorraine talked to Cheryl about the blueberry crumble cake she'd brought (Lorraine wanted the recipe). Rebecca sat beside Ian and was silent.

"You're quiet." He stirred his coffee.

"Taking it in, I guess."

"It's all for you. Must feel nice."

"I was thinking it feels nice, the whole family together without its being Christmas. No gifts. No particular obligation or reason."

"But there is a reason. Isn't there? You're the reason."

"Nominally. But it becomes bigger, doesn't it. When I see Andrew and Ivy and Jennifer and Jacob and Michelle and Michael—well, you feel nice, don't you, or better about the state of the universe, seeing all the children at play. Seeing that they can still play like children even if they spend so much time trying to be adults."

"Ivy wants to wear makeup. Makeup. She's barely ten."

"That's how it is, in the classroom. The girls talking about who their boyfriend is going to be, the boys all stumbling on the playground like apes."

"I'm not ready for makeup. She's not ready for makeup."

"She's perfect as is." Rebecca knew, though, makeup was alluring and it was fun. She'd be that aunt, the permissive one, slipping Ivy cast-off clip-on earrings, nearly empty bottles of fragrance, a pot of lip gloss. Not to undermine Cheryl and Ian's authority but to cement her own position. "We've got to talk birds and bees with Andrew. I'm outsourcing that one to Christopher."

Ian shook his head. "That I don't envy you. But it's coming, for all of us."

Later, Karen stopped Rebecca in the hall, offering a farewell. "I should run. Thanks for having me. Your family is lovely. And I might as well tell you what I would want to hear, which is that I'm jealous as hell."

Rebecca laughed. "Just finish your damn book already." Karen had been talking about a novel since they'd met, talked about it the way you might an illicit lover or a persistent dental problem.

Karen dropped her voice lower. "Look, you keep putting me off about Bilal but I'm telling you, you're making a huge mistake. He's very curious to meet you, we saw him just last weekend."

"I don't know, Karen." This joke felt old now. Rebecca wondered how happy Karen and Mohammed's marriage was. That was what this seemed to be about.

"Just think about it. He's not coming back."

"Christopher?" Rebecca shook her head. "I don't want him back."

"He's here. At your party. But not in your life."

"He's in my life. In a fashion. And that's fine. And Bilal, fine, I'll be in Ohio next week, but after that, I'm here, I'm yours." Rebecca wanted everything. She wanted to be celebrated and she wanted not to be bothered. She wanted to be with her children and she wanted to be with her work. She wanted to be married and she wanted to be divorced. She wanted a man to want her and to fuck her and she wanted to be allowed to sleep in the center of the bed, all four pillows around her, a bulwark against the night. She wanted it all, and all was something impossible to possess.

"Perfect. You'll be high on all that money, all that prestige."

"I don't know about that. But why not blow some of it on a nice dinner out?"

"Honestly, the Jamesons—what they've done to this planet. Birth deformities in developing nations. It's just money laundering disguised as largesse."

"I'll take what I can get. I'll give a hundred dollars to UNICEF." Rebecca had earned it. It was best to just make the thing into a joke.

"I guess it's the nature of children to rebel. Ruth Jameson spending her daddy's fortune on poetry. Anyway. Finally. I'm going to call Bilal, we'll make a plan."

Rebecca tried to picture Bilal, but could imagine only the man who had died with Diana in that tunnel in Paris. "I'll talk to you soon."

The company dwindled, but the party's essence was somehow intact. They sat in the kitchen, eventually, Rebecca and Cheryl and Lorraine. Christopher and Ian were elsewhere, discussing whatever men discussed, and the children had, of course, turned on the television.

"Ivy's so tall. So thin, too, like she'd been carrying baby fat and I didn't even realize." Rebecca filled her wineglass, because they'd all moved on to wine.

"She speaks like an adult. With such authority. And she's—ten?" Lorraine was sitting at the island, picking at the remains of the cheese.

"Only just." Cheryl nodded. "It's true. I am in for it. Little miss. She should be a lawyer, she's always negotiating everything."

"How's your mother-in-law, Cheryl? I remember hearing she wasn't well." Lorraine put the cheese knife down to underscore her concern.

"She's not. She's not terrible, thankfully, but you can see that it's the end. I know what it looks like." Cheryl shrugged. "She's an old woman, she's had a long life."

Rebecca knew Ian was the youngest of seven. She was amazed by that sort of fecundity: two kids often felt overwhelming, seven near lunacy. She knew that Ian was doted upon, especially adored. She tsked to show that she was listening along.

"I'm sorry to hear it." Lorraine did sound sorry, as few did when using that word.

"Ian thinks . . . Well, you know him—he thinks he can do something, but what can we do? She lives an hour away. He's got work, I've got work, Ivy's got school. We can't stop our lives and sit by her bedside for six months. It's just life, but life is like that sometimes."

"You see worse, at work, sure." Lorraine was resigned.

"I hope I don't sound heartless. I don't mean to. She's the closest thing I've got to a mother, myself."

Rebecca knew this, had forgotten it. It stung. "You have me."

Cheryl paused. "You're not my mother. You're Andrew's."

Rebecca faltered. "But you do—have me."

"That I do."

"And me!" Lorraine laughed and it lightened the mood.

"I'm sorry for Ian. I'm sorry for you." Rebecca was rushing, maybe drunk. "I'm sorry about your mother. You know that, but it's worth saying, even ten years later. It's unfair. I got the best possible end of the deal. I got Andrew. I got the happiest thing in my life. My entire life depends your mother's death. It's terrible."

"No. It's not terrible." Cheryl exhaled. "It's a happy ending."

"It all changes, even though you think it never will." Rebecca touched her mother's wrist, giving in to some larger feeling. "I agonized over feeding Jacob, breastfeeding him. It was the hardest thing I had ever tried to do, to make some part of my body do something it had never done before. It was like trying to wiggle my ears. I used to worry he would starve. Now he's this beast who drinks a gallon of milk every two days."

"My mother taught you that. I remember her talking. You were so nervous."

"I was." It was reassuring, somehow, to know that Priscilla had talked about her.

"She said it was easy to do, once someone showed you. She showed you."

Rebecca remembered a day, raw with emotion, that a maudlin song on the radio had moved her to tears. "There's the family you make, and the family you're born into." She had not detailed for Cheryl the conversations she'd had with

Priscilla. She ought to do that, while she still remembered. It would be a chance, at last, for Rebecca to give Cheryl something, information about the mother now gone. Most likely she already knew it all, but it would feel good to try.

Lorraine cleared her throat. "My granddaughter Jennifer? Judith lets her get away with murder. Absolute murder. Kids get away with anything these days. Parents let them."

They gossiped a little, not unkindly, about Rebecca's sisters and their permissive parenting: the way Christine let Michael carry around that video game player, the way Judith spent a fortune monthly on Jennifer's horse. It made Rebecca feel like the good daughter, and she enjoyed it. But Rebecca still thought about Priscilla, and the way Cheryl seemed happily reconciled to the line between life and death. To Rebecca, this made the whole present seem as tenuous as it was. But these were not celebratory thoughts and she pushed them away.

They drank more wine and talked about Lewinsky and global warming and they talked about the Internet and they talked about other occasions on which they'd met and talked about other things, long-settled elections, the death of Princess Diana. It was one of those moments Rebecca could sense the very revolution of the earth beneath her feet, its endless, determined, spinning. The sounds of conversation merged into a noise that she'd miss, hours from then, when it was gone, when they'd all gone home, when the boys were in bed, when she padded around the house in her wool socks, eating leftover cake because there were still so much cake to be eaten, missing the people who were no longer there, and remembering that she'd missed them even as they'd all been together, in one room, around one table, talking about the future.

34

A CONTRACT WAS FOREVER, BUT ONCE MONTHLY, WHICH SEEMED SO much when the babies' life spans were measured in those units, proved to be not enough: Ivy and Andrew adored each other. It was another note in their endless improvisation. Ian's dealership was quite near their house, so he could bring her over in the morning and Rebecca could run her home later, though sometimes Ivy would stay all day, at their table for pancakes, for grilled cheese, for spaghetti, hours of her and Andrew's shrieks and chuckles. Special treks—the zoo, the aquarium, children were diverted by animals because children and animals were very near the same thing—Andrew would always want to ask Ivy along, and Rebecca readily relented. As angst descended upon Jacob, Rebecca was happy to have a companion for Andrew, and Ivy was always so happy.

Rebecca rang the doorbell and could hear the frantic footfalls through the town house's insubstantial door.

"You're here! Hurry." Ivy pulled Andrew into the house. He stepped out of his sneakers and followed her back up the stairs.

"OK, bye, kids. Hello!" The house was so modest, but always seemed big, because the Barbers had so little furniture. They had enough, of course: just what was needed. There was less to look at than at her home.

"You're here." Cheryl emerged from the kitchen, dressed for a workout. "I was finishing my Tae Bo. Come on in. Where's Andrew?"

"Pressing business." Rebecca closed the door and set Andrew's sneakers side by side on the tile.

"You want some coffee?"

"Sure." Rebecca followed her into the spotless kitchen. Cheryl was thorough. Rebecca sat at the island and Cheryl poured. "Thanks."

"You're welcome." Cheryl shook her head at the sound of a shriek from above. "Those two."

"I wish Jacob could still do that. Get lost in play. He's so secretive. On the Internet, I suppose."

"I know I just did my workout, but I want something sweet."

"Let's go to Starbucks! We'll throw the kids in the car, get a chocolate croissant."

"No, I shouldn't. I'll have a grapefruit." Cheryl made a face. "Join me?"

"Sure."

Cheryl sliced the fruit, dropped each half into a bowl. She set out a knife and a spoon for Rebecca. "Maybe I'll put a little sugar on mine. Just a pinch."

Rebecca sliced into the fruit. "You look great."

"Got to *feel* great, though."

"That's hard to argue with. Are you still thinking of Disney World? For spring break?"

"I don't know. It might wait—now we're talking about the

fall break. You know the kids have another one in fall, right? Keeping on top of that schedule is enough to drive a person actually insane."

"It's going to be rough when Jacob starts high school. Two different schedules. They're almost the same, but not quite the same."

"Well, you know. We can help out. We always love to have Andrew here."

"You're sweet. Thank you. We'll see what develops." She tasted the fruit. "I'll take some sugar, too. I was thinking—we should do something special for Mother's Day! It was so fun, last Saturday. Or was it two Saturdays? Having everyone together. I know it was a celebration for me, so I'm a monster. But still. I would love to do that again. So much more fun than brunch at Clyde's or wherever. It'll be warm by then, we can do it in the yard even."

"It's an idea." Cheryl finished her fruit and set the bowl down.

"You throw a great party! Come on, put a little enthusiasm in it."

Cheryl laughed. "You'll pardon my lack of enthusiasm, Rebecca. Maybe, just this once?"

"What's wrong?"

Cheryl shook her head. "You know—Mother's Day, it's not exactly a happy occasion for me. Not a day I feel like celebrating."

She felt hot. Of course. "Right. I'm sorry. That was—foolish of me."

Cheryl put her bowl in the sink. "Maybe so."

"I wasn't thinking."

Cheryl turned around. "You know. For a long time, it was just me and my mother. When I was a kid. Homemade cards, brunch at Denny's. It's stupid, but it meant something. It still does."

"It's not stupid. I shouldn't have—I wasn't thinking."

Cheryl corrected her. "No, you weren't thinking of *me*. You don't, do you."

Rebecca was quiet. "Why would you say that? That's not how you feel." It was meant as a question but sounded like an argument.

"Rebecca, please. Please don't tell me how I feel." Cheryl was calm.

"I've upset you." Rebecca put the spoon down. From upstairs—a heavy sound, the children leaping from the bed to the floor, maybe.

"You just don't see me, Rebecca. Sometimes. Most times. You just don't—"

"I do—"

"No, please." Cheryl held up a hand. "Don't interrupt. Don't deny, not right now. Just listen. For once, let me explain myself."

"For once?" Rebecca fiddled with her coffee. She looked at Cheryl, her face serious, her clothes ridiculous, spandex and sports logos.

"It's ten years I've known you. Longer, actually, but ten years we've been—whatever we are. There's no word for it. And in that time, I don't think you've ever seen me. I don't think your impression of who I am has changed, even one bit."

Rebecca did not want to break the silence that Cheryl seemed now to need. She did see Cheryl. She saw a woman the brown we term black, beautiful with kindness, soft with maternity, not unbreakable (no human was) but unbroken. Rebecca saw the woman she'd known for what felt an entire lifetime, in her ridiculous exercise clothes, skin dewy from having sweat. Her hair was pulled back revealing a face that felt familiar, like one glimpsed after many years and surprised because it had not changed as much as it ought to have. But this was not the recognition of something once-seen; she saw Cheryl all the time.

"You think I'm an extension of you. A character in your world, a supporting role. It's not fair. I'm not that, I'm a person, your son's sister. Your friend, sort of."

"Hm." Rebecca still did not know whether she should speak. Her friend, of course, Cheryl was more than that, she was so dear to her. Did she not know this?

"A person who might, maybe, have a reason to not feel all that celebratory on Mother's Day. Which you should know. Because, as you were just telling me, at your party, just a couple of weeks ago, you *adored* her."

Rebecca stirred the coffee, though now she didn't want any. "I did. Adore your mother. And I adore you. It's not true, that I think of you as a supporting character in my life. You're very important to me, to our family. You're wonderful. I couldn't imagine—"

"I'm not wonderful. I'm not a saint. This is what I mean. My mother's dead, I get it, it's hard to see her as a real person. But she was, a real person. A stubborn teenager who had a baby, and refused to talk to the rest of her family, and, I don't know, liked to eat out and had a lot of credit card debt and felt embarrassed about not finishing school so she made me be this perfect student."

"I thought so highly of her. Even when she was alive. It's not just because she's gone, it's not just because of Andrew, it's because she helped me—"

Cheryl laughed. "That was her job! She was your nanny. No, first, she was the lady who had a five-dollar-an-hour job at the hospital because her daughter stuck her neck out and got her a five-dollar-an-hour job at the hospital. The hospital where her daughter worked! Where the HR manager was— less than thrilled when the job her daughter had arranged went unfilled three months later. Because she had a patient— sorry, a mother—who wouldn't take no for an answer. But that's fine, let's forget that. That HR lady, she wasn't so mad. And I was like—fine. Mom needs real work, she needs real money. It'll be good for her, so what if it's a little uncomfortable for me."

Rebecca could barely remember what happened in December of 1985. The millennium was about to arrive. "But she—she helped me, I trusted her. She was so wonderful with Jacob. She knew how to do everything. She freed me, to do my work, to be a wife, to be a better mother. I adored her."

"She used to call you Lady Di. You know? Pretty. Sophisticated. Well-meaning."

Rebecca did not know that. Was it apt? Or was it just irony?

"She was a good mother. She wasn't a saint. And I'm not a saint. You don't even—how many times, in the past ten years, have you come to this house, to my house?"

"I'm here now."

"That's not my question. You know it's not."

It was rare, to be at Cheryl and Ian's house. But they had so much more space, on Wisconsin Drive. Cable television. A basement full of toys. A trampoline in the yard. "Maybe I could. Bring Andrew, more often."

"You didn't even believe me when I told you that my husband and I have fights. That we disagree, that I might understand a troubled marriage because I have a marriage, too, and they've all got some trouble in them."

"I did."

"I saw your face. Like you couldn't believe it. That Ian and I were real people who continued to exist when you weren't around and went home and had fights just like everyone else. That we weren't just—cardboard cutouts."

"I don't see you as—as not a real person."

"It was the gas guy."

"What was the gas guy—"

Cheryl sat on the stool beside Rebecca. "Andrew's father was the gas guy."

Rebecca put her hands on the island. "You know. You know who Andrew's father is?" It was a whisper.

Cheryl sighed. "His name was Charles. He came, you know, every month. To read the meter. I figured it out. Parents don't have any secrets from their kids. Or my mother didn't. It was just the two of us, you know, in that house, my whole life. I knew what she was doing."

"You're sure. You know this." She studied Cheryl. She seemed, suddenly, more beautiful. There was a ripple in her brow, her lips were drawn tight, her expression was dour—yet there it was. Beneath the fury or whatever this was, there was a layer of beauty. It made no sense.

"He looks like him, Rebecca. He looks just like him."

This pained her more. She didn't think she could feel worse, but she did. "You lied. Cheryl, you lied to me. You lied to the judge, the court. It's perjury." Every shade, every ghost, every version of her baby's father, departed, vanished, drifted away like smoke. She'd loved them all, every imagined father, loved and hated them all, and now she was alone with this.

Cheryl shrugged. "What does that matter?" She stood and walked away. She turned back. "I told you, I'm not a saint. I'm a real person."

"Why would you lie, about this?"

"He wouldn't have wanted the baby, Rebecca. It doesn't matter. It's—a victimless crime."

"What about your brother? Doesn't he have the right to know?"

"What about me? Don't I have the right to decide? He's my brother."

"He's my son."

"Because I said he could be." This was not anger. This was pride.

Rebecca was exasperated but this was true. "Well, why did you then?"

"Because it was obvious. Because it was easier. Because my mother was dead, and I didn't know what else to do. Because I was going to have a baby. Because I was overwhelmed. And because you wanted him. You *wanted* him. I couldn't take him. It was simple."

"But we lied."

"But it worked out. I thought it would—you would give him a good life. And you had money, and education, and you're nice, and my mother liked you, and Christopher, and Jacob, and she *knew* you. It was a fitting end."

"My God, Cheryl." Rebecca wanted to do something: take off her shoes, take off her jacket, have a drink, go outside, run around the house, scream, go upstairs, grab Andrew, drive home, pretend this had never happened. "I don't know what to say."

Cheryl was quiet. "I shouldn't have told you like this."

Rebecca was still whispering because now it seemed important the children not overhear, though the children mostly ignored them. "Does Ian know?"

"He's my husband, Rebecca. He knows."

This was further betrayal, which she'd not thought possible—Ian, she was so certain that they were close.

"Ian had his reservations, if you want the truth."

"About lying. About perjury." This was a relief.

"And about—a black boy, a white family. He had his concerns. You know, he grew up with six big brothers and sisters. Uncles, aunts, cousins, great aunts, neighbors, the whole thing. It was just me and my mom, in it together. I went to the good high school and there were no black girls there. Three or four. And mom wouldn't let me talk to them, be friends with them. I couldn't get *distracted*. So—it wasn't that big a worry, for me, not the way it was for Ian."

Rebecca knew; Ian had tried to tell her about this, before. "Right."

"He says it's different, for boys, than for girls."

"OK." Rebecca still didn't know what to do with her body. She was pacing around between the island and the sink. "You shouldn't have done this."

"What should I have done?" Cheryl was no longer scolding, was sincerely asking. "I made a choice; maybe it was a mistake, but that goes back to my point. I'm just a person, just another fucked-up person, just like you, making mistakes, trying to be."

"It does something to it, to know that we lied."

"It just shows you what you don't always remember, Rebecca. That I'm a real person, and not only that, I'm a person who—your entire life, now, it's because of me. I'm not just someone you visit once a month. Someone whose kid plays with your kid."

"You hate me." Rebecca braced her hands against the countertop.

Cheryl laughed. "Don't you realize—you're more than forty years old, how can you not realize? How can you not understand that I'm as capable of hate and love, annoyance and happiness, at the same time, as you are?"

Rebecca looked around the room, the bent wire dish rack, the ceramic saltshaker, the bent metal spoon rest on top of the stove. "Maybe. I'm sorry." She was close to tears, maddeningly.

"What do you think family is, anyway, Rebecca?"

Rebecca floated above the anger, the confusion, the heat of her own embarrassment and shame. She thought of Andrew, upstairs, a father, somewhere in the world, the life they had made for him and whether or not it was an honest one, a good one. She'd have said that it was, said it with confidence, a reflex without reflection. Cheryl was her family and Cheryl was her friend and Rebecca did know her and she wanted to say that all, but she knew that Cheryl wasn't waiting, she knew it was the sort of question with no particular answer.

35

JIM WILLIS SENT A BOY NAMED TYLER TO FETCH HER. THAT'S WHO would inherit the world next: boys named Tyler. This one was a poet—Jim's pet student would of course be a poet—who had the sort of handsomeness that was simply a lack of ugliness, and was, too, utterly without character: symmetry, nice proportion, no offense, all framed by thick brown hair shaped in a generic way, like a Ken doll. He could have been an extra in a film, about to be shipped off to Normandy, where he'd be certain to die. He was like a glass of milk or a bar of soap come to life as a person.

But Tyler was pleasant, even nervous. She *made him* nervous. It was not his usual way: What would a boy like Tyler have to fear in this world? He had polished manners and a late-model luxury car. He smelled of suburban comfort, of Grosse Pointe, Oak Park, Westchester County. Rebecca wondered what his parents made of their son, whose swim meets they'd dutifully attended, going off to write sestinas in Ohio, spending a hundred grand of their hard-earned (a doctor? a lawyer? an ad executive?) dollars.

"We read your books." Tyler was attempting nonchalance, failing. The fact of it, the fact of the books, was astonishing to him. But he was twenty-one, twenty-two; the world was astonishing.

"Thank you." This was not, strictly speaking, a compliment, but Rebecca understood what it concealed. "Tell me about your work."

This was a defensive position disguised as kindness. Talking about her books usually laid bare the fact that most people were quite dumb. She liked seeing people holding their copies, cradling close both *Galatea* and *Diana,* loved the idea of Jim's seminar room, eleven urgent undergraduates poking and prodding at her books. Just leave her out of it.

Jim was known as a great teacher. But you couldn't teach the deployment of the skills you were honing. The kids were skilled chefs who could only cook hot dogs, *petit* Picassos unable to complete a connect-the-dots. Their poems were finely built but *about* the stupidest things possible. What did Tyler, what did any American boy, know? Parental love, cable television, organized sports, liberal politics, peacetime, prosperity? You had to get this out of your system. You had to reach the point where those things seemed the fallacy they were. You had to grow the fuck up. Rebecca wondered about Tyler's poetry the way you wondered about spoiled food, the same perverse pleasure in how awful it smells.

"I loved the Icarus part, most. If I can say so." Tyler shifted the car's gear smoothly and gave her a sideways glance.

The road looked like every road. Buildings with some mysterious purpose she'd never learn. "Thank you." Everyone loved the Icarus part, because they understood it the best.

"It's one of my favorite paintings, actually. The Bruegel."

"Poor fellow. An afterthought." Everyone loved the Bruegel; who alive did not love Bruegel?

"Right!" Tyler was excited. "Like. He was even more—he thought it was so big but it was so, so small."

"The incredible folly of believing in your significance." Rebecca turned and looked out of the window.

They said their good-byes with some lingering awkwardness. Maybe that was in her mind. She'd gone further with Tyler, telling him about the Air Florida flight that had crashed in Washington, and how she'd met her husband just days later, telling him that there was something in this even she didn't understand. Tyler made her smile. They're all quite beautiful when they're young. She thought that under that T-shirt and jeans Tyler would be a kouros, hairless, flawless, for the time being, anyway. The poets at Hopkins were all soft bodies and serious minds.

The hotel was the opposite of haunted. There were no memories there. The place had never seen an assignation, nor a declaration of love or hatred, nor a business deal, a night of martinis to cap off a weeklong binge. It was a way station, a void, horizontal lines and musty upholstery, staff with eyes that weren't even sad—sadness would be interesting—just blank. The man at the desk: his patter seemed rehearsed. She took the elevator though there were only three floors.

The room's curtains were brown; even an interior designer would hesitate to christen them *cocoa*, or *tobacco*, or *mocha*, or *loam*. The view had some promise, there was a park at the center of town, at best a charming public good, at worst the rubicon that divided the campus from the rest of the people who lived in this place: laid-off autoworkers, cleaning ladies, the hairnetted men and women who served the food in the institution's three cafeterias.

Rebecca herself had worked in the student mailroom, filling out little slips of paper that she'd slide into lucky students' mailboxes to let them know L.L.Bean had sent that cable-knit sweater, Eddie Bauer had sent those back-ordered boots, that the fat package of cassette tapes had finally arrived from Columbia House. She couldn't remember the wage, but she remembered she shopped at the thrift stores, though so did everyone else in that city overrun with people like her: a class that lived in poverty but were not condemned to it. They'd return to Boston, Ohio, New Hampshire, years later, as the parents of incoming students, in expensive cars fitted with racks to hold skis, and feel nostalgic about the Salvation Army's particular funk: sweat, dusty cloth, desperation, and cigarette smoke. That's who she would be, in four years' time, when Jacob went off to school. She had made it.

She sent away Tyler with the assurance that they'd see each other the next day, when she was scheduled to visit the classroom and field questions. She left the hotel with a deferential uptick of the eyebrows to the man behind the desk. She did not want to be anywhere near that man and that lobby, which reminded her of those phantom, windowless rooms on the upper floors of department stores, displaying rugs, mattresses, furniture designed and sold in coordinating sets.

She found a coffee shop, and Rebecca opened her book on the table but didn't read. She ate her chicken salad sandwich and wished she were the sort of woman who carried a toothbrush in her purse. She ought to think about what she was going to say that night, something valedictory, something grandiose, that would make those people in the audience unaware of her think: this was a woman deserving of platitudes.

She ordered a cup of tea to take away. It was nice enough outside to feel spring feverish. Rebecca had been at Hopkins for long enough to be accustomed to how young college students looked but this crop was different, more homogenous, wealthier, more coddled. These were *kids,* cigarette smoking,

boisterously laughing, hurriedly walking or luxuriously am-
bling kids. Jacob wouldn't have stuck out in this particular
crowd, that's how young they seemed. The country's future
leaders, or anyway, the ones who'd shoulder the taxes that al-
lowed society to continue on its merry way.

It helped, when speaking, when writing, to have your in-
tended audience, your fat woman on a porch. Rebecca sup-
posed Karen, sardonic, aimless Karen, was hers. Once, it
had been Priscilla, but maybe that was one more of Rebecca's
flights of fancy. She'd known the woman for three years; she'd
been dead for ten. Rebecca and Priscilla had shared salads
and laughter and a son but maybe nothing else. Maybe every
intimacy was just wishful thinking. There were days Rebecca
could barely remember what Priscilla looked like. She'd try to
conjure Priscilla but come up with only Cheryl.

Rebecca had reached the limit of the campus. There were
modern buildings from the 1970s alongside gracious edifices
from decades past; there was lovely landscaping and people on
bicycles. She took out her pencil, a notebook, because some-
times the performance of work proved productive, but noth-
ing came to mind. Maybe that was what she'd talk about that
night: stand at that podium, offer thanks to the college, to the
magazine, to Jim, to the Jameson Foundation, and remind ev-
eryone: this all passes. Hug your spouse; kiss your sleeping
kids' foreheads, even though you know they wouldn't want
you to. A plane flew high overhead and Rebecca thought
about Christopher. His work was as much an act of imagina-
tion as hers. He believed there was some moral debt owed.
Rebecca liked the smaller world in which she was a person
of consequence. She put the pencil away, went inside, found
Jim's office, the door standing open, the tall man in the monk-
ish cell on display like an animal at a zoo. She knocked on the
doorframe, tentative.

"Rebecca Stone." He drew his body up to its full height. The desk was messy in an unembarrassed way. The room smelled of yellowing paper.

What was intended, a hug or a handshake? Rebecca split the difference with an outstretched arm and a forward lean. Jim took her hand and pulled her close. He was thin and bony, strong and capable. Rebecca wished he were fatter, that his body didn't so closely recall Christopher's.

"It's so wonderful to meet you at last. Of course, I feel like we're old friends."

"Aren't we?" Rebecca had mostly lost her power to charm. This was not flirtation but honesty.

"Well, we published you for the first time five years ago. So it's been at least that long that we've known each other."

Rebecca couldn't tell him that, years before, she'd left Jacob with Priscilla one Saturday and taken the train to Philadelphia to hear Jim speak at a conference. It had to have been twelve years now. Jim was not much changed. More white in the hair, more tautness to the face. Rebecca knew that she would be unrecognizable to anyone who only knew her from that one day, but fortunately no one had known her, that day. "Well, I trust you with my work, so you know me better than most."

"You had a good flight? Sit, sit." Jim jabbed at the general disarray on the desk. There were postcards taped to the wall and two plants on the sill, basking in the afternoon sun. "Tyler met you without a problem? You're OK at the hotel?"

"It's lovely. Tyler was very sweet."

"A promising writer." Jim dropped his voice. "They're rare. You teach. You understand. But Tyler might actually have something there. Only time will tell. You know that, too."

"My students come in so eager to become something that I never have the heart to tell them how long it actually takes."

"There's nothing worse than being fully formed at that age. But they confuse success with the rest of it."

"Mine think of publishing as some sort of transcendent act. A blessing from God. A miracle. Water into wine."

Jim chuckled. "What's the point of youth without ambition? Anyway, you're still young."

"I throw *The New Yorker* away every month. At least I read most of the poems. But it goes into the garbage. And I don't feel young, though thank you for it. The word, I believe, is midcareer. That's a nice euphemism."

"You were a kid when you got started! I looked it up. I've been boning up on Rebecca Stone."

"I was almost thirty. I just had a student come to my office hours and complain about *Best American Poetry*. He thought they weren't reading the right journals. He felt overlooked. Imagine feeling overlooked at twenty-two! Twenty-two-year-olds are the only people anyone cares about."

"Let's walk. I've got office hours at three, but we should get some fresh air."

They left the office, the dignified enough basement that was nevertheless a basement. The day was cool. "The walls here have ears."

Rebecca fell into step beside him. The place had the quiet purpose of many people engaged in a single endeavor: thought. There was another plane overhead and some gathering clouds.

"I can't tell you, what an honor it is."

"You should get used to it. You know I think the world of your work, but that secret is out. The National Book Award! We want to publish as much of it as possible, I hope you won't forget about us. The kids don't know, they think it's so competitive out there, but there are so few of us who make it this far. People give it up. It's a vice. They get married and have kids and they become interested in more interesting things, more remunerative things, or they realize that there's nothing left to say."

"I got married, I had kids. It was like an infection. I can tell the serious writers from the less serious writers because for the one it's a compulsion. An illness. Or unhealthy, almost, anyway."

"Did you ever stop? I went to the Peace Corps. Benin. I don't know what I thought I would get there but I wanted so badly to get away from myself. I was twenty-three, myself was all I had."

"I didn't know that. Have you written about it?"

"It seems pointless. It wasn't a teaching experience. It wasn't something to write about. It was a hiatus. A reset. A hibernation."

"It's like having a child, actually."

"But you wrote about that, didn't you?"

"I guess. My husband says my poetry isn't about anything but poetry itself. Ex-husband, I mean." She felt that need to clarify. Because, part of her wondered. That night, there would be table wine, one red, one yellow. There would be subpar chicken and there would be her speech. There would be handshakes for the people at the Jameson Foundation and there would be the silent, judgmental congratulations of the assembled undergraduates, the faculty emeriti who had nowhere better to be, the locals from the prosperous suburbs who were interested in literature. Perhaps Jim would see her back to the hotel. It was a hike, from the reception, if any distance in a college town could be considered a hike, and the beacons of blue-lit telephones were testament to the fact that even here, in the groves of academe, dangers lurked. A woman was better off escorted by a man. Perhaps he'd suggest a drink at the bar. Perhaps one scotch would become a second and a third, perhaps the defenses would draw down enough that he could admit to her that he had hoped for this, and his hand would be on her knee, or her waist, and his breath would be hot as he confessed it. Perhaps, Rebecca, drunk also on the power of her own accomplishment, would lead him by the hand—what was to be ashamed? they were unmarried!—to the third floor of the hotel and show him that vantage on the small town where he would while away the remaining days of his small life.

Perhaps his kiss would remind her what a kiss even was, and perhaps his hands would be rougher than she'd expect a poet's to be. Jim looked capable, the kind of man who could fix a broken car. Perhaps she'd let him lift her to the edge of the bed, perhaps he'd get down on his knees and stare at her appreciatively. Perhaps he'd push her dress up around her waist, impatient, and tug at her underclothes, and fix his attention on her, and perhaps she'd feel self-conscious at the level of this particular exposure or perhaps she'd be delirious and not care. The simple trace of her own finger could move her; what would Jim be able to do? Perhaps she'd find out. Perhaps he'd bite her thighs. Perhaps his stubble would burn her skin. Perhaps they would slip into a collaborative rhythm like two sticks trying to make a flame. Perhaps they would laugh or cough or revise the scene, in the moment, removing errant hairs, excess flesh, unflattering angles. Perhaps they'd find something, something it took two people to find, and perhaps that would be enough for some kind of temporary relief.

"Well, what does he know, your ex-husband? Your work is—well, you don't need me to tell you what it is."

Her work was important. Midcareer meant more to go. She was forty-two years younger than Virginia Hamilton Adair. Many things could fit into forty-two years; Priscilla's entire life had lasted that long. Rebecca was no longer the Younger Poet, but she was the better for it. "How is your own work going?"

Jim talked about a project, something to do with birds. Rebecca barely listened; though this was the sort of conversation she often craved, given it, she realized that her fantasy left her wanting, that it belonged as fantasy. What she wanted was not to hear someone else talk, but to talk herself, of ideas, of the beginnings of things, of what she might make, when she found time. She thought herself lonely, sometimes, as did Karen, as did her sisters, but maybe what Rebecca lacked was not connection but an audience. Maybe she was just selfish.

"You should be so very proud, Rebecca. The stars are aligning around you. It's an honor for us to have you here."

"Please."

"I mean it. I know Hopkins will want to hold on to you even more, after this, but . . . Well, if you would ever think about relocating, we should talk."

"My boys are so young, still. Their father is there."

"They're ten and thirteen, I thought you said? The big one will be applying to colleges before you know it."

It happened, just like everyone said, the leaps, the changes. Jacob thought like a child but looked, roughly, like a man. Andrew had grown fatter, and Rebecca knew what it was: the body building its reserves. Soon, he'd follow his brother, and his voice would deepen, his legs grow lean, and he'd want to sleep all the time, and not hug her. Andrew was the only person in the world who was still willing to touch her body, and soon even he would not. It was said the babies in orphanages in Bucharest went mad from not being touched. "I suppose. It's hard to see into the future."

"It's impossible!" Jim chuckled. "But you prepare. You try. You have a sense of what the future might hold, you organize your life to allow it."

"Maybe." She had foretold this, once, one of those heady candlelit dinners when Christopher was still her boyfriend, or before, one of those illicit evenings in Isaiah's marriage bed, or before, to herself, in the shower; but Rebecca had been wrong about what the future held, or hadn't bargained on what she was capable of doing in between that present and the future that was still somewhere far off. Rebecca didn't know that she was the kind of person who would take on mothering someone else's child, make that child her own, change his life and her own and the lives of everyone around them. "We'll see what comes next." She wasn't sure if she was the kind of person who said this sort of thing. "I'm doing my best work. I've never felt more energized. I want to get to it. I don't feel midcareer, but if this is midcareer, it's great. It's bracing." The boys would fly out of the nest and she would be truly alone and she would do something remarkable.

"There's no rushing it. My students all want to rush it."

Rebecca felt for Jim's students. Handsome Tyler: she should have told him to go to law school. A bit of Christopher's well-worn patter; *With a law degree, all things are possible*. "That's what it is to be young."

"But I'm in a rush now, myself." Jim was confessional. "For the first time. It seems like time. You teach, and you realize that the world is filling up with people younger than you, and that sooner or later you've got to make room for them all."

"I'm in a rush, too." It felt good to admit. She welcomed what would come: Jacob and Andrew in high school, then college, then both men who would return to her, handsome and strong and happy and amazed at the things she'd done.

Jim had to go. There would be, she knew, poets eager to discuss something with him at his office hours, poets supplicant, jealous.

There was a museum near the hotel, Rebecca knew, because there was a brochure celebrating the place in the hotel lobby. There was an Oldenburg on the lawn, and a klatch of smokers, presumably art students, stained jeans and bandannas holding hair in place, in the relief of the April sunshine. It was one of life's rarest gifts, to be in a strange place with no particular demands on your time. Rebecca went inside.

The place had a Mediterranean affect: pleasant, instantly transporting. Rebecca admired, as you were meant to do in a museum. She waited for that deeper, transcendent feeling to arrive, like a teenager who's just tried drugs for the first time, nervously running mental diagnostics, am I *feeling* yet? She wandered, taking in the Cindy Sherman, the Beuys felt suit, hanging ghostly and unseeing over the proceedings. Rebecca barely looked and certainly didn't see. Her footfalls echoed off the high ceilings. She was alone in the place, alone with art so valuable its worth couldn't even be calculated. It was the nearest she'd ever get to church. Jim Dine had never meant anything to her.

In a little gallery at the back of the building, there was a small exhibition composed of relics from the earliest era of photography. Such pictures often seemed the same to Rebecca, whose eye lacked imagination. She needed color, not these sober impressions in silver, though it was a thrill to look at people so long dead and realize they looked much as people now living did.

She read the explanatory text on the wall: these were Hidden Mother photographs. An unfamiliar but not opaque term, a studio portrait of a child in which the child's mother was hidden inside the frame. Junior would weep left alone before the camera's eye, and needed to be stilled for the primitive camera's long exposure, so he was perched on Mama's lap, and Mama was draped in black, like a shroud. It was a photograph of two people that looked like a photograph of one. It was the baby because he was the only thing that mattered. It was the most literal erasure of women whom history had already wholly erased. The pictures were a game. Spot the woman! The contours of a body gone plush from childbearing, a slipped cloth laying bare a hand, an outline, an impression, an errant hair. There she was! Too easy a metaphor but learning something new was interesting.

Rebecca had never intended it, she admitted to herself, only barely. She'd thought: two weeks, a month, maybe two. But she'd been naive, or impulsive. She'd loved Priscilla because she'd taught her something magical or something useful: Priscilla had taught her as much as or more than Princess Diana.

If she'd lived, Priscilla, would they be friends? More likely that Priscilla would simply offer Rebecca's name and telephone number to prospective employers, and Rebecca would have brief but excited conversations with nervous mothers. *Hire her!* she'd tell them.

Oh, sure, the nature of motherhood was invisible. This was a C-minus as an idea, like Icarus. We all have one, a mother, in some fashion. It was something to talk about, the having of a mother, in a way that the act of being one was not. Her sons were her suns, her life hostage to their orbit. Let it be thus. Drape her with bolts of scratchy black wool and place Andrew or Jacob on her lap. The baby was always the same. Cave painting, Christ on Mary's lap, Cindy Sherman in the next room over, all babies, all the same. The baby was the only thing that mattered because the future was the only thing that mattered.

She'd talked to Andrew about Priscilla. That was her responsibility. When he was smaller, and she'd insisted that he and Jacob called Cheryl *Auntie*, she'd simply plunged into it. "Cheryl isn't your auntie, in the way that Auntie Judith is, or in the way that Auntie Christine is. Cheryl is your sister."

"But she doesn't live in our house. And you're not her mommy."

"That's right. She's a grown-up sister. She lives in her own house. And I'm not her mommy. But I am your mommy. You have two mommies." She had improvised this one, then had the good fortune to remember to append: "You're so lucky. Two mommies!"

"Who is my other mommy?"

This unanswerable question. Your other mommy, she'd told him, sidestepping what she knew people said and thought—your *real* mommy—is dead. But she loved you so much. You grew inside of her and she loved you just as much as Daddy and I love you and we are so lucky that we got to make a new family that includes all of us together, you and Jacob and me and Daddy and Auntie Cheryl and Uncle Ian and Ivy.

"Why are we a family?"

What was the answer? An impetuous impulse? Terrible happenstance? Pure chance, like bad Fluxus art? She couldn't remember what she'd said, in answer to this, but the question echoed over the intervening decade, lingered in her ears even now. Impossible to explain to a child—impossible to explain to an adult—that we're all just making it up as we go along.

Rebecca had learned from Christopher that getting on a plane might mean never finishing your business. But she had got on that plane to Ohio without finishing hers, without saying to Cheryl, as she had to her sons, that she loved her. Every day brought a leap of faith: the plane to Ohio would not crash, the plane home would not crash. She would have years to finish that business.

She went back to the hotel. Rebecca took a hot shower. She massaged the shampoo into her hair, she soaped her skin. She dried herself with a towel, used another towel to wrap up her hair. She was so callous with hotel towels, but that was one of the perks of a hotel stay, that brief interlude of pretending abundance. She wished there were music. She felt like a song, something big and silly and unembarrassed.

Rebecca had packed something inoffensively chic for the evening's dinner. Black trousers, the kind of simple you knew was expensive, and a black top, which telegraphed a certain coastal sophistication. They would want a celebrity more than a poet, and she would want not to disappoint. She'd packed heels, and she'd packed jewelry, some of the real stuff that her mother-in-law had given her. An emerald like the emerald used in metaphors, set in a sterling bracelet. She faced herself in the mirror, barely able to see herself because of the room's poor light. She hoped that it would not rain, but knew it always rained in April.

She still had no words. She was receiving the Ruth Jameson Award in Contemporary Poetry because she was good at words. She ran the wand over her lips, trying to will herself to see them, as though light were something that could be willed.

"Thank you so much, to the Ruth Jameson Foundation, to the college, to the Department of Creative Writing, to my friend and editor Jim Willis. This is an astonishing honor." No, that was an overstatement. This was her due. "This is a great honor. I am truly honored. I am deeply honored."

She frowned into the mirror and her nostrils flared.

"I am so grateful to Ruth Jameson. I am so grateful her grandfather was a huckster who sold soap powder and cocaine as a headache remedy and prophylactics and whatever other crazy things he did. I'm so sorry they poisoned the people in that town in India.

"Ruth Jameson was born in 1909 in Saint Louis. It's ninety years later and I'm standing in Ohio and accepting a check from her.

"My thanks to the Ruth Jameson Foundation, to the college, to my friend and editor Jim Willis for his tireless support of my work. I am glad that people have liked my poems. I have tried, in some small way, to say something. That I get to be allowed to do so, it feels like pure luck, but I am a woman who has had good luck, dumb luck, great good luck, all my life.

"Ruth Jameson was born in 1909. It is 1999. The millennium approaches, you all know. We will turn the page of history.

"The future has arrived. And tonight, I feel good about that future. The world, it is getting better. Because how can we let it get anything but better?

"Ruth Jameson was born before the start of the First World War, which was called the Great War because they didn't know there would be another. We live in a time of no war. We have forgotten about war, and if we had one now, we wouldn't know what to call it. We are lucky. We are blessed, that war is forgotten. When Ruth Jameson was born, William Howard Taft was the president. I don't know anything about him. For the women in this room who are pregnant, or whose daughters are, when their children are born, Al Gore will be the president. I look forward to that, personally. I trust him to do something about the hole they say is opening in the sky.

"The planet is in disarray, but the right people will do something about it. I'll stay at my desk and write poetry about it, and other things, or about poetry. It doesn't matter.

"Poets are not oracles. But I know the world is improving. You can see it all around us. Good men will do good things. We'll never have a war good enough to be called great. My black son will be judged the equal of my white son." She fitted the silver bracelet around her wrist with a snap. The stone was so beautiful it was ridiculous. She studied her face and tried to see the whole. She liked the emerald, because it made her think of Diana. Rebecca looked nothing like Diana, and Diana was dead now, anyway. "It's 1999." She lost her train of thought.

"The millennium is looming. But history always is. I believe we will do history proud. I believe we will heal the hole in the sky. I believe we'll create a world in which my black son and my white son will be judged equals. I believe in a world that will be better even than the one we now share, which is quite wonderful." She thought, fleetingly, of Christopher, of her sons. She would call them, before leaving, make sure they'd been to the allergist, that their homework was being seen to, that they knew she loved them, even from the distance of Ohio. "It's 1999," she said again, unembarrassed, aloud, in her clearest, most oratorical voice. "It's 1999 and I believe a better world is coming."

ACKNOWLEDGMENTS

I am grateful to everyone at Ecco; Megan Lynch and Sonya Cheuse deserve special thanks. Thanks to Julie Barer and her colleagues at the Book Group, and to Julie Barer and Colson Whitehead for their generosity. Thank you to Rebecca Cross, Lynda Dougherty, Samantha Turner, and others who have educated me on motherhood. Thanks to Laura Larson for her beautiful book *Hidden Mother,* and to Lindsay Hatton, Karen Good Marable, Celeste Ng, Meaghan O'Connell, Danzy Senna, Rufi Thorpe, Robin Wasserman, and especially Lynn Steger Strong. And profound thanks to superb husband/ father/person David Land.